Anne Allen lives [...] her [...] daughter and [...] has [...] meant a numb [...] in Guernsey for fourteen [...] and and the people. She co[...] ure a valid reason for fre [...] in London, ideal for her [...] ist, Anne has now publi[...] at www.anneallen.co.uk

C000098644

Praise for Dangerous Waters
'A wonderfully crafted story with a perfect balance of intrigue and romance.' *The Wishing Shelf Awards, 22 July 2013 – Dangerous Waters*
'The island of Guernsey is so vividly evoked one feels as if one is walking its byways. An atmospheric and tantalising read.' *Elizabeth Bailey, author of The Gilded Shroud*

Praise for Finding Mother
'A sensitive, heart-felt novel about family relationships, identity, adoption, second chances at love... With romance, weddings, boat trips, lovely gardens and more, Finding Mother is a dazzle of a book, a perfect holiday read.' *Lindsay Townsend, author of The Snow Bride*

Praise for Guernsey Retreat
'I enjoyed the descriptive tour while following the lives of strangers as their worlds collide, when the discovery of a body and the death of a relative draw them into links with the past. A most pleasurable, intriguing read.' *Glynis Smy, author of Maggie's Child.*

Praise for The Family Divided
'A poignant and heart-warming love story.' *Gilli Allan, author of Fly or Fall*

Praise for Echoes of Time
'Not only is the plot packed full of twists and turns, but the setting – and the characters – are lovingly described.' *Wishing Shelf Review*

Also by Anne Allen

Dangerous Waters

Finding Mother

Guernsey Retreat

The Family Divided

Anne Allen

Echoes of Time

The Guernsey Novels – Book 5

Sarnia Press
London

A CIP catalogue record for this book is available
From the British Library
ISBN 978 0 9927112 4 5

Typeset by Sarnia Press
This book is a work of fiction. Names, characters,
businesses, organisations, places and events are
either the product of the author's imagination
or are used fictitiously. Any resemblance to
actual persons, living or dead, events or
locales is entirely coincidental

To my mother, Janet Williams, with love

"I do believe in ghosts, or at least in some kind of persistent spiritual echoes of the past in certain places."

Jennifer McMahon

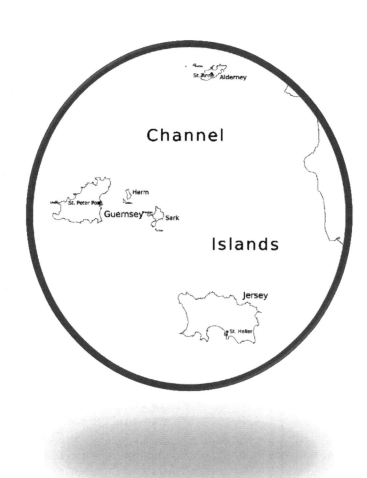

chapter one

Guernsey – 1987

Olive was cooking her usual meagre supper of scrambled eggs on toast when the sound of heavy footsteps outside made her jump. No-one ever visited and this was how she liked it. Always had. Her heart pounded as she moved the pan off the blackened range and turned to face the back door. Unlocked as was the custom in safe little Guernsey. Or was it safe? Grabbing a knife she watched, immobile, as the knob turned and the door began to open. The man stood silhouetted against the early evening sky and she stared hard at his shape, puzzled. There was something familiar about the slope of the shoulders and the angle of his head. Her mouth went dry in the moment before the door closed and he moved into the light.

It couldn't be! Not after all this time…She felt her legs tremble and leant back against the range.

'Hello, Olive. Bet you didn't expect to see me again, did you?' He chuckled, humourlessly.

She hid the knife up her sleeve and pulled the darned cardigan around her thin body. Old memories surfaced as she fought to stay calm.

'We…we heard you were dead. You didn't come back–'

'No, well, I found someone and something better, didn't I? But it doesn't look as if you have.' His gaze was contemptuous as he looked her up and down, and Olive was conscious of how unkempt she looked. Poverty does that to a person. Whereas he was immaculately dressed in what looked like a designer suit. A successful man. She watched, helpless, as his gaze wandered over the kitchen,

1

and she registered, for the first time in years, how dirty and shabby it looked. The kitchen which had once been kept spotless. Feelings of shame, mixed with overriding fear, flooded her mind. What did he want?

His eyes alighted on the only personal item in the room. And the last thing she wanted him to see. She moved forward, attempting to block his view, but he pushed her aside and picked up the photo in its cheap wooden frame.

'Who's this?' he demanded, his face flushed with anger.

A look she knew all too well.

Her stomach clenched. Could she lie? Pretend it was someone else? As her head whirled with possibilities he seized her arm, twisting it. She cried out in pain and the knife clattered onto the granite floor. Swiftly he grabbed it while still holding onto her arm. Olive's knees buckled.

He thrust the knife towards her chest and she screamed.

'Please...'

'Don't even think of lying,' he hissed.

'It's...it's my...our daughter–'

The world went black.

chapter two

2010

'And this is the kitchen, Miss Ogier. As you can see, it's been finished to the highest standard, with all built-in appliances.' The estate agent spread her hands in the dramatic gesture beloved by agents wanting to impress.

Natalie allowed herself to look, and feel, impressed. Although not a keen cook like her mother, she did appreciate a kitchen which looked as if it could produce an extravagant meal and complete the washing-up at the touch of a few buttons. The glossy cream fronted units, topped with solid granite worktops, encompassed built-in appliances even her mother would envy. The soft grey floor tiles complemented the worktop; all set off by warm yellow-gold walls. The effect was considerably more welcoming than the stark white and stainless steel kitchen she had left behind in London. A definite plus in its favour.

She sniffed. 'I can still smell the paint. When did you say it was completed, Jess?'

The other woman beamed.

'Only last week and you're the first person to view. But I have to warn you there's been some considerable interest. It's not often a brand new cottage in such a wonderful location comes up for sale. Shall we continue the tour? I'm sure you'll be as impressed with the other rooms.'

Natalie turned to follow Jess, but for a moment felt as if something was holding her back. The merest whisper. A soft sound which she couldn't place. She looked around, wondering if someone else had arrived unnoticed. The room was empty. With a shrug, she stepped into the hall and followed Jess into the sitting room at the back.

Although the cottage was new, it had been built to look like a traditional Guernsey cottage on the outside, granite walls and a slate roof, but brought into the twenty-first century with larger windows. One whole wall of the sitting room was taken up by floor to ceiling bi-folding doors opening onto the garden.

This mix of styles was what had attracted Natalie. She had been brought up in an old cottage and loved the feeling of cosiness, but also enjoyed the light and airiness of modern buildings. She could picture her sleek, modern furniture fitting in well with the style of the cottage and began to feel a slight thrum of excitement. Something she badly needed if she were to make a successful return to the island. Pushing down the unwelcome thought of why she was back, Natalie had to smile at the ultra-modern wood burner at the far end of the room. With the latest underfloor heating installed, it wasn't likely to see much use, but it did mean she could curl up on the sofa in front of a roaring fire if needed.

Jess continued to throw open doors and windows as they walked round, the smell of paint almost oppressive. Natalie liked everything she saw, silently complimenting the architect for his eye for detail and the happy combination of old and new. The tour ended in the garden. Or more accurately, what would be a garden. Natalie frowned as she saw the mounds of earth beyond the tiled terrace. The only saving grace was the uninterrupted view down towards Rocquaine Bay and the white tower of Fort Grey. The deep blue sea reflected light from the bright May sun.

'Beautiful, isn't it?' Jess sighed. 'A view to die for. I know it's a cliché, but it's true. It certainly beats the view from my town flat!'

'Mm, it's quite something. Just a pity there's no garden to sit in and enjoy it.'

'Ah, yes, I was coming to that. The seller thought it was more important to finish the house and let the buyer decide what they wanted to do with the garden. They've commissioned a landscape gardener who would work with you on the final design and then undertake the work.' Jess faced Natalie. 'So, what do you think? Are you interested?'

She nodded. 'Yes, I am. With three bedrooms it's a bit bigger than I really need right now, but it is lovely and the view...' she waved her arm towards the sea before looking back beyond the cottage to another property, looking newly renovated, a few hundred yards away. 'Who's the neighbour?'

'Oh, that's Stuart Cross, a teacher at the grammar school. He only moved in a few weeks ago and he seems a nice man. Related to the original owner of the farm, I understand. I'm sure he'd make a good neighbour,' Jess said brightly.

'Married?'

'I don't believe so, no.'

Natalie ran a hand through her short hair, wondering if it would be wise to move into such a secluded place with a single man as her neighbour. Considering what had happened in London...Telling herself not to be so paranoid, she managed a smile.

'What happened to the farmhouse? Surely it would have been better to reconstruct it rather than knock it down?'

'I don't know the whole story, but I understand it had been virtually destroyed by a fire years ago and it wasn't practicable to rebuild. This cottage has been built on the site of the original house, and the other cottage,' Jess said, pointing, 'was an old barn. Both have been built using as much of the original stone as possible, but the insides are completely new. It's taken years for the planners to agree on the idea of a new-build and the architect had to redraft his designs a few times. It does mean this cottage is unique, so you'd be buying something quite special,' Jess finished, with a wide smile

'I should hope so at this asking price!' Natalie chewed her lip as she considered. The price *was* steep, but the London flat had sold well and she wouldn't need a mortgage. It did seem a bit mad buying something so big when she was on her own but...she gazed once more down towards the sea and took a lungful of the clean, fresh air. Such a relief after the polluted air of the City. Trees set further down the hill formed a protective shield between the cottage and the houses below, without impinging on the view. Turning around she noticed for the first time that similar rows of trees surrounded what had once been the farm buildings, providing further privacy. It was blissfully quiet.

'Can I have another look around, please? On my own?'

'Sure. I'll wait here and you take as long as you want. My next viewing's not for another hour.'

Natalie wanted to see if the cottage would be overlooked by the one belonging to 'Stuart'. As she walked back towards the drive she noticed how the other property was set at an angle to the empty one, with its main windows looking down to the sea in a different direction. There was a decent expanse of land between them and trees provided extra privacy without sacrificing the views. Both properties had their personal drives for parking, approached by a shared private lane. Someone had put a lot of thought into the layout, she reasoned, before retracing her steps to the front door.

As Natalie walked round she imagined which pieces of her furniture would fit where. The sumptuous designer leather sofa would take pride of place in the sitting room and the circular maple dining table would set off the dining area next to the kitchen. In her mind's eye she was already in situ, boxes unpacked, and holding a house warming party. There was so much space for guests even if the weather meant they couldn't wander outside. A complete contrast to the elegant but tiny flat in Islington. She cast a last glance at the kitchen, head cocked on one side, but all was quiet. Smiling, she walked back out through the sitting room to rejoin the patient Jess, sitting on a large stone.

'I'll take it. Although it's more than I planned to spend, I'm sure it will be worth it.'

Jess jumped up and shook her hand.

'I'm so pleased. I think it's heavenly.' She consulted the notes on her clipboard. 'You've already sold your own property I see. Which is marvellous. Are you looking to move in quickly? I'm afraid the garden–'

'Oh, don't worry. I can live with it like this for a little while if necessary. I'd want to get some ideas together first. But I would want to complete as soon as possible as I'm living with my parents at the moment so...' She rolled her eyes. Jess laughed.

'Got the picture! Right, let's go back to the office and we can complete the paperwork. And I'll ring everyone else interested to tell them Beauregard House has been sold.'

'Even the name says it all – "nice view". Quite an understatement. What's the other cottage called?' Natalie asked as they headed to the agent's car.

'The Old Barn. Originally the properties and land formed Beauregard Farm and it was felt the name should be kept, hence Beauregard House. I believe Mr Cross chose the name for his cottage.'

Natalie nodded and slid in beside Jess. Once she had finished at the agent's office she'd go home to tell her parents the news. Then it was a question of shipping all her belongings over from England once a completion date was fixed. And she needed to buy more furniture to fill the extra space. It promised to be a busy few weeks. Briefly, she thought of the reason why she had finally returned to the island of her birth. She shuddered at the image of Liam's red, angry face as his fist connected with her jaw.

Thank God she was now safe.

chapter three

May 2010

'Please be careful with that mirror! It cost a fortune,' Natalie shouted at the two removal men attempting to squeeze past another man carrying a large chest. She drew a sharp breath as they missed each other by an inch. Natalie had forgotten how stressful moving was, particularly when the move involved a delay between moving out and moving in. If she hadn't made extensive lists she'd have forgotten what was in the various boxes now scattered around the house. Her parents were going to help her unpack once the removal men had disappeared. But for the moment chaos reigned and Natalie badly needed a coffee.

She slipped into the kitchen and filled the kettle. The men would be glad of a cuppa too, and she tipped out the teabags and pack of coffee from the supermarket bag. Moments later Natalie handed out mugs of tea to the men before pouring herself a fresh coffee. Although only ten in the morning, the summer heat was building up and everyone headed outside, those who smoked going to stand at the bottom of the garden. Natalie sank, with a sigh, onto one of the new garden chairs she had bought a few days before. They formed a solitary row on the terrace, still the only part of the garden which had been finished. As she sipped her coffee her gaze was drawn to the piles of earth and stones only slightly smaller than when she'd first viewed the cottage. The landscaper, Matt, had drawn up a proposed plan and Natalie had approved it, adding extra touches and planting for which she agreed to pay herself. So far all that had been achieved was the redistribution of soil from one area to another. She sighed. Her dream of having the garden finished before the end of summer seemed doomed. It could never compete with Jeanne's garden but she looked forward to having shrubs and flowers planted. And a small pond with fish. And a pergola over the terrace, smothered in scented climbers...

'Natalie! There you are. I wondered if you needed a hand,' called Jeanne as she stepped through the folded-back windows.

'Hi, I was just thinking about you. Or rather your garden. Where's the offspring?' Natalie asked, giving her friend a hug. She thought Jeanne looked trim and full of energy for someone with two children under three. Her dark hair swung behind her in a ponytail and her vivid blue eyes shone as she took in the view. One of the joys of moving back to the island had been re-establishing their relationship. Close friends during their childhood, they had lost touch after Jeanne had suddenly left Guernsey after her parents were killed.

'Harry's at nursery and Freya's at home with Nick. He's supposed to be supervising the work we're having done in the attic, but I suspect he'll be outside playing with Madam. She's got him wrapped round her little finger and she's not yet one!' Jeanne laughed.

Natalie smiled. 'Clever girl. If you'd really like to help, how about we tackle the boxes in the kitchen? I'll make you a coffee while we're at it.' They walked through to the kitchen, now stacked high with boxes bearing lists of contents. As Natalie opened the first one she thought she heard a voice hiss, 'Go away! Go!' Startled, she looked around but there was only Jeanne pulling out pans from the box.

'Did you hear that?'

Jeanne looked up. 'Hear what?'

'I thought I heard someone say "go away".'

'No, didn't hear anything. Apart from the noise of those men clattering up and down the hall. Perhaps you imagined it.'

'Perhaps. I've not entirely felt safe since I left London and...and Liam. I keep thinking he's going to follow me here.' Natalie felt foolish even as the words left her mouth.

Jeanne's brow puckered and she stroked Natalie's arm. 'Hey, it's natural to be a bit on edge after what you've gone through. But now you're surrounded by your family and friends and he wouldn't dare to cause trouble here. Apart from anything else, he doesn't even know you're back in Guernsey, does he?'

Natalie shook her head. 'No, he doesn't. You're right, I've been a bit stressed out with the move and starting a new job. I'm sure I'll be fine. And I'm looking forward to being in my own space again. Mum and Dad are lovely but...' she grinned.

'I enjoyed my stay with them when I first came back, too. They looked after me brilliantly, but I knew I had to be independent and move into my own cottage.' Jeanne laughed. 'You could say I was Mollycoddled!'

Natalie broke out into giggles, the joke releasing the earlier tension and neither of them could stop laughing for a few minutes. At least the mood was lighter as they continued the unpacking. Being a mere five feet three, Natalie had to stand on a stool to reach the top cupboards. She was called upon occasionally by the men to confirm the resting places for the furniture, but within the hour all the boxes in the kitchen were unpacked and the contents stored in drawers and cupboards.

'Fantastic! At least I'll have plates and cutlery for my takeaways,' Natalie said, pushing a hand through her hair. She had always enjoyed choosing beautiful items for her kitchen, even though some were hardly used. Like the pots and pans. A designer-styled toaster, kettle and coffee machine now graced the worktop. The kitchen was once more immaculate, all signs of the recent invasion of boxes obliterated.

Jeanne's eyebrows shot up.

'Takeaways? But surely you can cook? Molly would have taught you.'

Natalie perched on a stool. 'Oh, she did and I used to cook a bit. But working silly hours in the City meant I was always too tired to rustle up a meal when I crawled home. I'd either grab an Indian takeaway or pick up a ready meal from a 24-hour supermarket. I barely had time to shop let alone cook. But I guess I won't have that excuse now I'm working normal hours again.'

'I forgot to ask how the job's going,' Jeanne said, sitting beside her at the central island.

'Okay, thanks. Everyone's very friendly and although we have to work hard, at least I'm not burning the midnight oil. Being in charge of a team at an investment bank is much more civilised, time-wise. The salary's well down on my old one, but it's enough. If I start cooking again I'll save a fortune on takeaways.' Natalie smiled, eying the super-duper oven.

'You were lucky to beat the crash with that last big bonus of yours. I was so envious! Fancy being able to pay cash for your gorgeous flat!'

'Yes, I was lucky, but I'd worked like a dog for years as a hedge fund manager and the pressure was unbelievable.' She shook her head. 'Looking back, I don't know how I managed to stick it out so long. In a way the crash did me a good turn and made me re-evaluate my priorities, including relationships. You know, I'd hardly been out with a guy since I'd moved back to London. How crazy is that?' She frowned.

They were interrupted by one of the men asking where she wanted her bed positioned and Natalie went upstairs with him. The main bedroom was light and airy, with views over the bay and she wanted the bed on the wall opposite so she could wake up and gaze at the sea. The floor was almost obliterated by cardboard wardrobe boxes and Natalie decided they were the priority once the bed was assembled. She left them to it and went downstairs to find Jeanne.

'Are you happy to stay for a bit longer? I thought we could tackle the bedroom unless you need to go home.'

Jeanne glanced at her watch. 'I'm okay for a bit longer.'

An hour later the bedroom was looking habitable and the bed made up. Natalie flopped onto it and groaned. 'I could quite cheerfully fall asleep, but there's so much to do.'

'And I have to get off and relieve Nick; so come on, up you get and make yourself some lunch. Assuming you have some food in that posh kitchen of yours.' Jeanne laughed.

'I bought a few things, enough to make a sandwich. I'll see how the men are doing; they said they'd be finished by lunchtime.'

Downstairs they arrived in time to see the last of the empty boxes being thrown into the van.

The foreman asked her to sign the ticked-off list. After pocketing the generous tip, he and the other three took their places in the van and drove off. As Jeanne gave Natalie a hug, she reminded her to keep in touch.

Suddenly all was quiet and she would be alone for the first time in her new home. A rumbling in her stomach reminded Natalie she needed to eat and she headed for the kitchen, somewhat reluctant to enter the house alone. Telling herself not to be an idiot, she grabbed ham, cheese and butter from the fridge and opened the pack of sliced bread. A few minutes later she went out into the garden with her sandwich and a fresh mug of coffee, glad to sit in the sun and relax. The move, although exhausting, had been smooth and Natalie found herself thinking back to that awful day she had moved out of her flat. And Liam had turned up.

chapter four

March 2010

It was a miserable, blustery wet day in March and the weather matched her mood as Natalie sought to finish the final packing. The removal men loaded up the lift for the umpteenth time. The lengthy process of loading, unloading, then loading up the van before returning to the fifth floor was, for her, made worse because she had loved her flat, despite the fact she was hardly ever there. The adrenalin rush of London had coursed through her veins for the past five years and the flat represented her success in the predominantly male world of high finance. If it hadn't been for that bastard Liam she wouldn't be leaving. She cursed herself for not seeing through the outward charm and good looks to the real, damaged man that lay beneath. Wearily, she taped the final box and sat back on her heels, gazing around at the open plan living area which looked larger now it was devoid of her designer furniture. The floor to ceiling windows looked out at nearby rooftops, some covered in miniature jungles.

Natalie stood up as Steve, the foreman, returned for the last couple of boxes and to get her signature – and the tip. Then he was gone and she was alone. She was about to pick up her bag and suitcase when the bell rang. What do they want now? Annoyed, she went to open the door.

'What the hell are you doing here? You know there's a restraining order–' Cold fear struck through her as Liam stood inches away.

'You bitch! Thought you'd slink away without my knowing, did you? Too bad I saw the van outside and your stuff going into it,' he snarled, moving towards her. As her mind raced with thoughts of escape, salvation arrived in the form of Steve, striding from the lift. He seemed to size up the situation in a glance.

'Is this man bothering you, Miss Ogier?'

Her legs went weak with relief and she flashed him a smile.

'Yes, he is. And he's not allowed to be anywhere near me. Can you call the police, please?'

Liam's rugged face darkened. 'There's no need for that. I'll leave. But I'll find you. Wherever you go,' he said, stabbing a finger at her.

'Hey, mate, leave her alone or I'll throw you out,' Steve said, grabbing his arm. Tall and muscular, he was quite capable of doing it, she thought, even though Liam was equally tall. But she knew his muscles were turning to fat, no longer the fit ex-soldier she had met eighteen months ago.

Liam shrugged off the restraining hand and headed for the lift. She watched, holding her breath until the lift opened and swallowed him up. Suddenly, it was as if all the air had been squeezed out of her body and she sagged. Steve caught her, saying, 'Hold on.' He steered her towards her case, and eased her down on top. Fortunately it was a hard shell and made a secure seat.

'You okay?' He knelt down to eye level.

Natalie drew a deep, ragged breath. 'I am now. Thank God you turned up! But why did you? I thought we'd finished.'

'My fault, I forgot to ask you to fill in your forwarding address. Lucky I did, eh?' He grinned.

She suppressed a shiver at what might have happened if Steve hadn't arrived when he did.

He handed her the form and she filled in her parents' address in Guernsey. At the moment she still had to find a new home. And if she didn't know where she was going to live then neither could Liam.

Steve insisted on carrying her case and bag, waiting while she locked up before calling the lift. Natalie was secretly pleased he was with her; she couldn't get rid of the feeling that Liam was hanging around, waiting for her. But if he was, he kept himself out of sight when they arrived in the basement parking. Steve didn't leave her side until she was safely locked in the car. With a quick wave he was gone and she drove out through the security gates for the last time, the in-built satnav guiding her towards Poole and the ferry to Guernsey. Although she had visited her family a number of times over the years, she hadn't lived there since going off to university. It was to be a completely fresh start, and with the image of Liam's angry eyes still in her mind, she was glad for the stretch of water which would soon separate them.

chapter five

Spring 1940

Olive was both nervous and excited. Today was her wedding day and that night...well, she would become a real woman. She knew what to expect, of course she did. A farmer's daughter like her had seen the animals doing 'it' enough. Her mother had never bothered to explain the finer details, like love and how good it made you feel to have a man share your bed. Olive was left to imagine that bit after talking to married girlfriends. And her soon-to-be husband wasn't exactly the romantic type who bestowed copious kisses and waxed lyrical about her beauty. No, Bill was the down-to-earth type who had chosen her more for her experience of farming than her looks. Even though other men had given her the wink as they admired her long curly brown hair, wide hazel eyes and youthful curves.

As she picked up her wedding dress and held it in front of her, Olive wondered, not the first time, why she had agreed to marry Bill. She knew it wasn't for love. Oh, he was attractive all right, tall with dark hair and eyes and as well-muscled as any farmer would be. But she had never felt a lurch in her stomach when he bothered to give her a kiss, like it said in the romance novels she read. She trembled at the thought of their first night together. Would he be gentle with her? Olive had to admit the signs were not good, Bill wasn't known for his gentleness. He had a terrible temper on him and liked to get his own way. She had seen the way he treated the lads on his farm and shivered, this time with fear. So why had she said yes to his brief and most unromantic proposal?

'Look here, Olive, I need a wife to help me run the farm. What do you say?'

She had been speechless. He had given no clue as to his intentions when he turned up at her parents' farm that day six weeks before. Olive had noticed previously how his eyes had that funny look men had when they fancied a woman. But he'd not said anything. Until now. What was she to say? Her mind raced. No-one else had shown serious interest and with most of the young men off to join the forces, the choice was limited to the infirm or old. She cursed the war for the lack of suitors. With her looks she could have taken her pick. Even though people said the war would be over soon, it would be foolhardy to bank on it if she didn't want to end up an old maid. She was already eighteen and people married young on the island.

If she said yes to Bill she would have her own house and be someone of account, he having inherited his father's flourishing farm near Rocquaine. Much bigger than her parents' farm, it even possessed a bathroom. She'd be secure for life.

Mentally crossing her fingers she said, 'Yes, Bill, I'll marry you.'

He nodded, grabbed her and pushed his tongue between her lips. The smell of beer and sweat nearly made her gag.

Looking back now to that proposal, Olive was inclined to run and tell her father she'd changed her mind. But before she could move, her mother came into the bedroom carrying a small posy of wild flowers for her bouquet.

'Why are you not dressed, girl?' she cried, throwing the flowers on the bed before tugging at Olive's work clothes. 'Let's get you ready. I know brides are supposed to keep their grooms waiting, but I don't somehow think your Bill would be too pleased.'

Olive shivered. No, she didn't think he would be.

The next morning Olive woke feeling sore and dispirited. Bill had been pretty drunk when he came into their bedroom at the farm and seemed keen to get it over with so he could sleep. She, on the other hand, had made an effort to look enticing, wearing a pretty silk nightdress her mother had made for her bottom drawer. Olive had taken a bath and dabbed some of her precious perfume on her neck and between her breasts. Bill smelt of beer, whisky and sweat and he lunged at her, almost ripping the silk in his eagerness to pull the nightdress over her head.

'You won't be needing this, girl. I like to see what I'm getting, not have it covered up. Now lay still and I'll make you a proper wife.'

He plunged into her and as pain shot through her body, she gritted her teeth to hold back a cry. It was over in moments, possibly seconds, and with a grunt, Bill rolled off her and promptly fell asleep, his snores taking the place of the sweet nothings Olive had hoped for. Brushing away the tears, she turned on her side, a sticky wetness clinging to her thighs. It wasn't until daylight she realised some of the wetness was blood. Her only consolation was that she might now be pregnant. Something to make being married to Bill more bearable, if not entirely worthwhile.

Olive hadn't conceived that night, her period arriving the same day as the Germans at the end of June. Both occurrences were a disaster as far as she was concerned. If she hadn't been married she could have evacuated with other women and children earlier that month. As it was, she was stuck. Stuck with Bill and stuck with the bloody Germans, she thought, as she dressed ready to go into St Peter Port. It wasn't fair! They'd been assured by Britain the Germans wouldn't bother with the Channel Islands and all military personnel had been withdrawn. Bill had moaned about them being thrown to the wolves, and for once she agreed with him. Being only a dozen miles from the Normandy coast, they were an easy target for that blighter Hitler, Bill had said.

Olive wasn't surprised Bill refused to go into St Peter Port to see the soldiers marching down High Street, but she needed to see it with her own eyes. To see if the soldiers were the devils they'd been described. She caught a lift with neighbours in their car. As she stood waiting in the High Street it chilled her to the bone to hear the sound of jackboots on the cobbled street of Le Pollet. Then they came. Hundreds of marching soldiers bearing rifles, helmets glinting in the sun. She felt sick. The memory remained with her for days.

When Olive went into Town a few days later she found Nazi flags flying everywhere and islanders had been forbidden to fly either the Union Jack or the Guernsey flag. As she cycled along the narrow lanes German lorries and jeeps sped past, causing her to take refuge in the hedges. Bile filled her mouth at the arrogance of the invaders literally driving locals off the roads with the shortage of petrol and ban on civilian vehicles. Bill only had a horse and cart, and as a farmer was allowed to keep it, but he never allowed Olive to use it.

By Christmas Olive's spirits were at a particularly low ebb. Olive had been too busy to see much of her parents and was shocked one day in December to get a message from her mother saying her father was ill with pneumonia and not likely to live more than a few days. She wrapped up in as many layers as she could, the wind bitter along the coast, and cycled up towards Perelle and their farm. By the time she arrived, her ears burned and her face was frozen. Throwing the bike down on the frozen ground she rushed into the kitchen.

Her mother was stirring a pot of soup on the range and turned at her entrance. Her face was etched with lines and she looked years older than her forty years.

'How…how's Dad?' Her breath came in short gasps and her chest hurt.

'Still with us, but not for much longer, the doctor said. You'd best go up. Tell him I'll bring the soup up shortly.' Her mother gave a brief smile. 'He'll be pleased to see you, for sure.'

Olive shot up the granite steps of the *tourelle*, a circular stone staircase common in old Guernsey farmhouses. She pushed open her parents' bedroom door and gagged at the smell of illness, of decay. Her father, a big, strong man in his heyday, lay white and shrunken under the bedcover. He smiled as he saw her, saying, 'There you are, my girl. A sight for sore eyes. Come and give your old dad a kiss.'

Her eyes pricked at the sight of her beloved father reduced to little more than skin and bones, and not yet forty-five. She kissed him gently on his bristled cheek, seeing a flicker of light in the dulled eyes.

'I'd have come sooner if I'd known, Dad. Why did no-one tell me?' A surge of anger rose in her gullet.

'I told your mother not to bother you, thought I'd get over it soon enough. But it took hold of me and wouldn't let go and the doc's told me he can't do no more for me. They've run out of penicillin, he says. Only the Germans have medicines and they're waiting on more supplies.' He broke into a spasm of coughing and Olive supported his head until it stopped.

'This bloody war! We'd have medicines if it weren't for the Germans. It's all their fault!' Hot tears dripped onto her cheek and she hastily brushed them away. The past few months had been the worst of her life. She'd had to take on the workload of the lads who'd worked for Bill when they had evacuated to enlist and now had to look after the cows and chickens, take care of the house and grow the vegetables needed by the islanders. Then in the summer she'd watched, petrified, as the ranks of German and British planes flew overhead, ready to do battle with each other, praying that no stray bombs would fall. And now Dad was ill…

Her father lay back, exhausted.

'Don't waste what time we've got being angry, Olive. I want you to tell me what you've been up to. And how's that husband of yours? Treating you alright is he?' His eyes searched her face and Olive dropped her eyes. She'd have to lie, but it was hard.

'We're busy on the farm as you'd expect, Dad. And Bill…he's well enough and we rub along together just fine.' She caught his hand and kissed it.

'That's good. I had my doubts about him, but if you're happy, that's all that counts. I can die happy if I know you're looked after.'

She forced a smile.

'Don't worry, Dad, I'll be alright. Oh, Mum said she's coming up with the soup–'

She stopped as a deep rattling sound came from his throat. She ran to the door, shouting, 'Mum! Come quick!' She heard her mother clatter on the stairs, but as she turned back to her father, she saw it was too late.

He was dead.

chapter six

2010

Natalie was exhausted. It had been a long, but productive, day. Her parents, Molly and Peter, had arrived after lunch to help with the unpacking and between them all they'd unpacked every box. Looking around the sitting room, Natalie was amazed at what had been achieved. Books were stacked on shelves, along with photos and ornaments she had collected over the years. A Buddha from Thailand, a figure of a Maasai woman from Kenya, and small pieces of sculpture from London galleries. All that remained was to hang up her pictures, now stacked against one wall. The same was true of the downstairs study, furnished with new bookshelves and a sleek, glass topped desk. Her top of the range iMac gleamed, ready for business.

'I think we deserve a drink, don't you?' her father said, coming up and putting his arm around her shoulder.

She turned and smiled. 'You bet! You and Mum have been amazing; I couldn't have got anything like as much done on my own. Sit down and I'll get a bottle from the fridge.' She collected three glasses and the bottle of champagne, chilling since early morning.

With a practised movement, she eased the cork out and laughed as the wine bubbled over the top. She filled up the glasses and joined them on the enormous sofa. Peter cried, 'Welcome back and good luck in your new home,' as they clinked glasses.

Natalie took a sip and grinned. 'Thanks, it's good to be back. And in such an amazing house.'

Molly gave her a kiss. 'You don't know how happy we are you're back for good. I don't think either of us realised quite how much we missed you until you came home.' Natalie noticed the tear in her mother's eye and felt a pang of remorse. She had only done what so many of her generation had: made their lives on the mainland after graduating. Her brother Phil was settled in London, married and with a toddler. Another high-flyer as she had once been.

Her father coughed. 'Well, the girl's home now,' he said, patting Molly's arm. He smiled at Natalie. 'And although it was lovely to have you staying with us the past few months, I'm glad you're now in your own house. I was feeling a bit out-numbered with two women around all the time.'

Natalie laughed. 'Liar! You loved every minute of it. I don't think you made yourself a cup of tea or coffee the whole time I was there!'

Peter chuckled. 'Okay, there were some advantages. But seriously, I think you've found yourself one hell of a house and I hope we get invited round fairly regularly so we can admire the view.'

'Sure. Although it's going to be a bit chaotic and noisy while the garden's being sorted. Can't say I'm looking forward to that,' she said, sighing.

'Nonsense. I think you'll find it exciting seeing a proper garden emerge from the mess it is now. You'll be at work during the day so you'll come home to peace and quiet. And the design looks wonderful, doesn't it, Peter?'

Her mother was right, as usual. She just didn't like the idea of anything disturbing the tranquillity of this beautiful cottage. It was one of the attractions of the place. She stifled a yawn.

'You're tired. We'd better leave and let you get an early night. Don't forget to eat that casserole I brought round. It won't take long to heat up in the microwave.' Molly rose and Peter joined her.

'Thanks, Mum. Don't worry, I'll eat it. I'm famished.'

They kissed goodbye and left, her father saying he'd be round the next day to help hang the pictures. Natalie collected the glasses and the bottle of champagne and walked into the kitchen. Pouring another glass of the golden liquid, she took a sip before putting the casserole in the microwave. She took a plate and cutlery and set them on the breakfast bar, too tired to contemplate taking a tray outside. She would eat then go straight to bed. Glancing at her watch she saw it was almost nine o'clock. The light evenings were deceptive; she had thought it much earlier. The ping of the microwave announced the bringing to life of her meal and she scooped the coq au vin onto the plate, the wonderful aroma sending her gastric juices into overdrive.

The first mouthful told her it was one of her mother's best offerings and she chewed slowly, savouring the taste of wine and herbs in the sauce. After Natalie finished the last of the casserole, she stayed to drink the rest of the champagne and it was as she raised her glass for a final sip that she heard it. A voice hissing in her ear, 'Go away! Go.' Terrified, she clutched the glass so hard the stem broke, cutting her hand. Slowly, her heart pounding, she turned round. There was no-one there.

chapter seven

2010

The doorbell rang and Natalie jumped. Clutching a tissue to her cut hand she looked around for an innocuous looking defensive weapon. Grabbing the empty bottle of champagne she went into the hall and switched on the light. It had grown darker while she was eating. The solid oak door hid the caller from view and, taking a deep breath, she called out, 'Who is it?'

'Stuart Cross, your neighbour. I know it's a bit late but…'

She sighed with relief and opened the door. On the step stood a man she guessed to be in his late thirties, with curly blond hair and a tentative smile. In his hand was a bottle of wine.

'Sorry to be round so late, but I had a parents' evening at school and wanted to welcome you properly. I saw the light on so risked calling. Here,' he said, thrusting the bottle towards her, 'I believe it's traditional for the seller to leave a bottle for the new owner.'

'Oh, right. Thanks.' She took the bottle, adding it to the empty one under her arm. 'I'm Natalie Ogier, though you probably know that already. Please, won't you come in?' She was being polite and hoped he'd refuse but, to her dismay, he accepted and walked into the hall.

'I was in the kitchen, if you'd like to join me.'

She led the way, still feeling disturbed by the voice she had heard only moments before. Could it have been Stuart? But he wasn't around when she heard it that morning so…

'You've hurt your hand. What happened?' he said as she put the bottles on the worktop. His voice was deep with concern. She looked at her hand and saw the blood seeping through the tissue.

'It was an accident, I...gripped the glass too hard and it broke. Only a small cut, I'll run it under the tap.' Natalie turned her back to him as she stood at the sink and let the cold water flow over her hand, the sting making her wince. Stuart came up behind her, saying, 'That looks deep. Do you have a first aid kit handy? I could help bind it up for you.'

He was right, it was deep and she prayed it didn't need stitches. 'Yes, there's one in that drawer over there. Thought it was a good idea to put it somewhere near the knives,' she said, nodding towards the knife rack. Stuart fetched the green box and studied the contents. Looking up he smiled, and for the first time she noticed his eyes. They reminded her of blue opals, edged with a darker outer ring; an eye colour she had never seen before.

Stuart placed a sterile dressing over the cut and then wound a fine bandage around her hand, finishing with a neat knot.

'That should do for now, but if it seeps through you may need to go to A & E for stitches. Does it hurt?' He released her hand and she felt it throbbing.

'A bit, but I'll be fine, thanks.' Natalie remembered something he'd said. 'I don't recall your name being on the sale contract and yet you mentioned being the seller.' Overcome with tiredness, she fought to stifle a yawn, but failed.

'Technically my mother was the owner, but I'm her next of kin and as she's living abroad I acted on her behalf.' He stood up. 'I can see you're tired, so I'll go. Just give me a shout if you need anything. Living so close, I'd like us to be good neighbours.'

'Thanks, but my parents only live along the coast, so I hope not to have to call on you.' She walked with him to the front door. 'Thanks again for the wine.' She managed a tired smile as she opened the door.

Stuart nodded. 'You're welcome. See you around.' He strode off towards his own cottage, visible only by a porch light glimmering in the late evening darkness. Natalie shut and locked the door and returned to the kitchen to switch off the lights. As her hand went to the switch she remembered the voice which had startled her earlier. With a shiver she plunged the room into darkness and went upstairs, exhaustion dragging her feet. She didn't bother cleaning her teeth or removing her make-up, but crawled naked under the duvet, after checking blood hadn't stained the bandage. It hadn't. Moments later she was asleep.

A bright light burned through her eyelids and Natalie slowly opened her eyes, disorientated. Sunshine streamed through the un-curtained window and realisation dawned. As she began to push herself up into a sitting position the pain in her hand made her look down. A small patch of brown stood out against the white bandage. Easing herself up carefully, she drew up her knees and gazed out of the window. The sea sparkled against the blue sky, dotted with a few soft clouds on the horizon, and she could make out boats bobbing up and down near Fort Grey. She sighed. It was idyllic. But she felt exhausted not exhilarated. Her sleep had been infiltrated by weird dreams which had left her drained, as if she had spent the night under attack. Vague memories of angry voices and raised fists percolated into her mind. What on earth was it all about? Of course, she had had bad dreams before, everyone did. But the last one had been months ago, when she was still in London and after Liam had hit her. So why now? She was safe from him and lived in a beautiful cottage with a stunning view. Shaking her head Natalie swung her legs out of bed and padded across to the en suite.

Glancing at the mirror she saw the tell-tale shadows around her blue eyes, dulled by exhaustion. Her short fair hair was tousled and her narrow face looked pinched. God, she looked a mess! She needed rest and sun to bring back her normal sparkle. Once showered and dressed in shorts and T-shirt, she felt revived and, after exchanging the bandage for a plaster, went downstairs to the kitchen. Light flooded the room and it felt warm and welcoming, but the outside beckoned. Natalie filled a tray with juice, coffee and toast and went out to the terrace. Only the occasional cry of a wheeling gull disturbed the peace and her spirits lifted. She told herself moving into a new home was a stressful, tiring experience, and it was no wonder she'd had bad dreams. It was Saturday and she wanted to make the most of her free time. With a bit of luck she and her father would get the pictures hung that day and she could relax on Sunday. On the way back inside she heard a car pull up and guessed he'd arrived. Time to get going.

A couple of hours later the sitting room walls were adorned with bright splashes of colour: original water-colours and acrylics that had caught her eye in London galleries. The predominant colours of blue, green, gold and red gave the room warmth, she thought.

'You have a good eye,' her father said, standing back to admire the effect.

'Thanks, they're by up-and-coming artists and didn't cost the earth, but I do love their use of colour. And at least you can tell what they've painted instead of having to guess like some of those paintings by so-called top artists. I particularly love these,' she said, pointing to a group of smaller paintings of almost photographic quality, 'they're by a Spanish artist of Andalusian towns, but with a twist. See? The way he's placed his figures? Reminds me of Dali.'

They stood for a few moments amiably discussing the paintings before Natalie made a pot of coffee and they sat outside for a break.

Peter sipped his coffee, looking thoughtful. 'You know how worried we were about you after that man landed you in hospital.' His voice held an edge to it Natalie hadn't heard before and she gripped his hand. He went on,

'You…you are okay now, aren't you? He hasn't been in touch?'

She felt guilty about lying but didn't want to worry him. 'No, not since I obtained the restraining order. It's in the past, Dad, I've moved on and I'm glad to be back.' A twinge in her hand reminded her of the events of the previous day and for a moment she wasn't quite as certain. Had she been so traumatised by Liam's behaviour she now heard imaginary voices? When her father had asked about her hand she had shrugged it off as a minor cut. She could hardly have told him the truth!

His voice broke into her thoughts. 'Good. You may be all grown up now, Natalie, but you'll always be my little girl.'

Natalie couldn't help laughing. 'Not surprising, Dad, seeing as how you're over six feet tall and I'm a nudge over five!'

He grinned and suggested they get back to the job in hand. With a last glance at the mesmerising view, Natalie picked up the mugs and they went inside to finish hanging pictures in the other rooms. In the London flat her 'Art Collection', as she called it jokingly, had filled the open-plan living area and the only bedroom. Friends had remarked it was like walking into an art gallery. Here, there were so many walls the paintings could be spread out and hung to suit the rooms and furnishings.

Natalie enjoyed walking round the cottage with her father as they debated what should go where and the time passed quickly. By three o'clock all the pictures were in place and they took a final tour to double-check Natalie was happy. She was. In fact she loved the difference it made to all the rooms: affirming her personal touch and individual style. Bold, colourful and unusual. Proud of her new home, she reached up to kiss her father.

'Thanks, Dad; you and Mum have been brilliant. It looks as if I've been here for months.'

'You're welcome, sweetheart. Now, I must be off as I think your mother has another job lined up for me. No rest for the retired, eh?' He moved towards the door and then stopped. 'Nearly forgot, we'd like you to join us for dinner tomorrow, about one, if you've no other plans?'

'Lovely, thanks. Give my love to Mum.' Natalie closed the door and sauntered outside. Much as she loved the cottage, it was sitting in the garden and drinking in the view which drew her. That and the feel of the sun on her body. Natalie unfolded a lounger and stretched out. The warmth from the sun made her drowsy and it was hard to keep her eyes open. Perhaps a short nap wouldn't hurt...

Natalie must have fallen asleep and she became aware of a distant voice filtering into her consciousness. It became closer and closer and she woke with a start.

'Where are you?' The voice was louder now, coming from behind her, and she froze in terror. Was she imagining voices again?

chapter eight

2010

'Hello, Natalie? Are you there?'

She sagged with relief. Matt! The gardener. She had completely forgotten he planned to pop in. Getting out of the chair, she called, 'I'm in the garden.' A minute later he appeared round the side of the cottage.

Natalie must have looked dazed as he said, 'Sorry if I startled you, but I kept calling out. Guess you were enjoying a nap?' He grinned at her.

She pushed her hand through her hair, scratching her scalp in an effort to focus. Blood still pounded in her ears from her earlier fear. God, she must be losing it! And in front of a hunk like Matt, too. He looked so in control, standing with his hands in the pockets of his cargo shorts, head tilted to one side as he gave her an appraising look.

'Yeah, well, it is hot today. And I forgot you were coming,' she said coolly, thrusting her hands in her pockets. Two can play at that game, she thought.

Matt laughed. 'Fair enough. I've written out a timetable for the work to be done next week, if you'd like to take a look.' He pulled out a folded sheet and handed it over.

Natalie read the scrawl with difficulty. Glancing up she said, 'I see the carpenter's arriving on Monday to start building the pergola. Is that right?'

'Yes, I know it's sooner than planned but it works for him and he won't be in my way as I'll be down there.' He pointed to the far boundary. 'As it's also one of the noisier jobs I thought you'd be glad to get it out of the way.'

'No, it's fine. I'm back at work anyway. As long as I can still use the terrace in the evenings, I don't want to lose the only bit of the garden that's finished,' she said, frowning.

'Don't worry, I've told him he has to keep the area tidy. I don't blame you wanting to sit out when you can. I'd be the same if I lived here.' He stared down towards the sea before bringing his attention back to her, his eyes locking onto hers.

Natalie shifted under his gaze. She was sure he fancied her, you could always tell with men. But although she found him attractive, the last thing she wanted right now was a relationship.

'Okay, so you'll be planting the shrubs and the small palm trees we chose? Anything else?'

They walked round the garden and Matt explained the order of the planting. Some things would be left to autumn but the main body of the garden would be planted over the next few weeks. Natalie wanted a water feature and a spot had been chosen near the right-hand side, close enough to be seen and heard from the terrace. Matt was to dig out two ponds, one below the other, with a continuous waterfall between them, powered by a hidden pump. Evergreen shrubs would be planted around the ponds with a small seating area to offer shade and privacy. Natalie loved the sound of running water and was excited about the design Matt had produced. They had agreed there should be a small lawn but most of the garden would be planted with shrubs, flowers and small trees. Low-lying hedging would form the boundary without distracting from the view. In fact the planting was designed in a way to lead the eye down towards the furthest hedge and on towards the sea. The fields between her property and the coast road were at a lower level and did not intrude on the perspective.

By the time Matt had outlined the projected time frame Natalie thrummed with excitement. It would be so good to have a garden to complement the house.

'Well, as long as you're happy with everything, I'll leave you in peace. Be back around eight on Monday morning with Trev the chippy. Enjoy the rest of your weekend,' Matt said, shaking her hand.

'And you, Matt. See you Monday.'

Alone again, Natalie headed into the kitchen for a drink. The sun must be over the yard-arm, she told herself, pouring a glass of chilled white. Grabbing a bowl of olives she returned to the terrace and settled down to admire the view. Bliss!

Natalie woke on Sunday morning refreshed after a solid night's sleep. If she had had any dreams she didn't remember them and was in a light-hearted mood as she showered and dressed. The clear blue sky signalled another shorts day and Natalie skipped downstairs humming to herself. After breakfast on the terrace, spent day-dreaming of the promised delights of the proposed garden, she forced herself to catch up with overdue paperwork and spent an hour in the study. Later, as she was drinking a late-morning coffee outside, Natalie heard the doorbell. Scrambling to her feet and readjusting the straps of her vest top, she walked through to the front door.

'Hi Stuart. I've just made some coffee, would you like a cup?' Aware she can't have made a great impression on Friday evening, Natalie wanted to be neighbourly. And he seemed a decent bloke, offering wine and first aid.

'Love some, thanks. I was wondering how your hand was doing, but I can see it's better,' he said, nodding at the small plaster. Again she was struck by his eyes. Leading the way to the kitchen Natalie picked up the cafetière and filled a mug for Stuart and topped up her own. After offering him milk and sugar – no to sugar, yes to milk – she said, 'I hope you don't mind my saying this, but I've never seen eyes that colour before. Do they run in your family?'

He shrugged. 'I guess so. My mother's eyes are the same colour so I obviously inherited them from her. Dad's were grey. As I never knew my maternal grandparents, the ones who owned the original farm, I assume one of them must have had the same shade. Someone once told me it's a rare shade of blue, not often seen in Britain. He grinned. 'It's nice to feel a bit different, but I did get called "spooky eyes" at school.'

Natalie gestured for him to follow her outside, saying, 'They're not spooky at all. I think they're lovely.' The words were out before she could stop them and she felt herself flush. She hadn't meant to pay him such a compliment when they hardly knew each other. Averting her face Natalie settled into the chair she had vacated earlier. Stuart, perhaps feeling her discomfort, continued to stand and gazed seawards. A silence hung in the air as they sipped their coffee.

Stuart, half-turning, said, 'I saw Matt was here yesterday. Have you finalised the plans for the garden?'

For a moment Natalie wondered how he knew Matt. Then the penny dropped.

'Of course, you're the one who employed him. I'd forgotten. Yes, he's starting on Monday and...' she went on to tell him about the design and they were soon deep in conversation about what had been decided. Natalie found him easy to talk to though he didn't know much about gardens. Neither did she. Her parents were experts, but when she was still living at home she hadn't been interested in more than a space to sunbathe or have a barbecue. Talking to Stuart made Natalie realise she must, at thirty-six, have finally matured, valuing the form of a garden as well as its function. The conversation about the garden dried up and Natalie, intrigued about Stuart's background asked, 'How come we haven't run across each other before? Guernsey's so small.' She laughed. 'Which school did you go to?'

Stuart grinned. 'I'm not local. I was born and raised in England and only came here for the first time a few months ago. But my mother was born here, in this farm,' he said, nodding at her cottage.

'I see. It's a bit of a coincidence, isn't it, us arriving here more or less at the same time? Although I grew up here, I haven't lived in Guernsey since I graduated.' She pursed her lips. 'Seems like we're both having a fresh start.'

Stuart regarded her, his look thoughtful.

'I don't wish to pry, but could a man be involved in your fresh start?'

'It usually is, isn't it?' she said more sharply than she'd intended. Seeing Stuart draw back, Natalie muttered, 'Sorry, didn't mean to sound like a man-hater. And it's not a case of a broken heart but of wanting to get away from a...a stalker.' She was too ashamed to admit the truth.

His eyebrows rose.

'I'm sorry to hear that. It's a horrible thing to happen. A female teacher at my last school was stalked for months, becoming a nervous wreck until the man was finally stopped. Turned out he'd been diagnosed with mental health issues but had stopped taking his medication. Once he was readmitted for treatment, she returned to work, but it took a while for her to feel safe again.' He rubbed his chin. 'Would you have come back to Guernsey if not for the stalker?'

'Good question! Not really sure. Though I was beginning to feel a bit burnt out, I still loved the buzz of London.' Natalie turned to face the sea, smiling. 'But it's beautiful here and I do feel safe. Which is a plus,' she added.

'I'm finding the island one helluva contrast to where I lived in Coventry. The city centre's a concrete jungle and although it has some decent countryside, it can't compete with this.' Stuart waved his arm, taking in the surrounding woods at the back of them and the fields leading down to the sea.

Natalie found it hard to imagine him in a concrete city: he looked as if he belonged in the outdoors, dressed in faded khaki shorts, a washed-out T-shirt and trainers. She wanted to know what had prompted his move to Guernsey, but a quick glance at her watch told her there wasn't time.

'Sorry, Stuart, I have to rush or I'll be late for lunch with my parents. I need to change.' She went to collect the coffee mugs but he stopped her.

'Allow me. I'll clear away while you go and get ready. See you around,' he said, picking up the mugs. He flashed her a smile and Natalie shot upstairs to change into a skirt and apply a quick slick of make-up. She heard the front door close behind Stuart and, as she put on some lipstick, recalled his smile and those brilliant blue eyes. Wondering how he came to be single, she toyed with the idea of asking him around for a drink sometime. She did owe him one after the gift of the wine but...the memory of what had happened with Liam caused her to hesitate. The last thing she needed was a stalker next door. Frowning, Natalie ran downstairs and was about to leave when something made her stop in her tracks. The door to the sitting room was open, and she could have sworn it had been closed. Going in, her eye was drawn to the shelves holding books and ornaments. She remembered placing a photo of her parents next to the bronze Buddha. The photo was no longer there. Blinking in disbelief, she searched the shelves for any sign of it but it wasn't there. Natalie rushed into the study but again drew a blank.

Convinced she was going mad, she walked into the kitchen to get a glass of water and spotted the photo on the breakfast bar. As she moved to pick it up she felt the temperature in the room drop to that of a winter's day and shivered. And what was that awful smell?

chapter nine

February 1941

Olive threw the spade down in disgust. The frosty ground was proving too hard to penetrate and the more she tried the more the blisters on her hands hurt. She pushed her sore hands under her armpits in an effort to soothe and warm them. The freezing February air conspired against her and Olive stomped off towards the barn for a much needed respite. She needed to check on the chickens anyway, she reminded herself.

The barn was only marginally warmer, numerous holes in the roof and gaps around the doors let in piercing cold draughts, but at least it offered protection from the worst of the wind. Olive continued to stamp her feet and swung her arms in a good imitation of a windmill, trying to get the circulation pumping through her frozen body. A mass of feathers half-buried in the straw parted to reveal the hens woken from their slumber by Olive's stamping. A lone cock perched in haughty isolation on a roof beam.

'Morning, girls. I hope you've laid plenty of eggs today as they're needed by our customers, they are. Let me take a look, now. Give me some space.' Olive waved her arms at them and began searching the usual places. Each hen had a favourite spot to lay their eggs and it could take a while to check them all. Olive carried a basket in one hand and smiled as she spotted the first egg. By the time she had finished the final count was a round two dozen, not bad for her modest flock.

'Thank you, girls. I'll leave you to rest now.' She knew it was odd to talk to them, but somehow it was a comfort to talk to something. Bill never talked to her, except to issue orders or complain about his dinner or something she hadn't done. The hens gathered round when she talked to them and cackled away as if in reply. Olive left the barn and strode towards the farmhouse, anticipating with pleasure the warmth of the kitchen. She pushed open the door to be met with the glowering face of her husband.

'What are you doing back here? You're supposed to be digging up the parsnips.' He was ensconced in his chair by the range, warming his hands over a hotplate.

Olive's heart sank. So much for enjoying a peaceful cup of tea on her own.

'I couldn't get the spade in the ground, Bill. It's too hard. Thought I might try later if it warms up a bit. Or perhaps you could make a start for me? You're so much stronger than I am.' She had learnt early on to try flattery. Olive placed the eggs carefully on the table and picked up the kettle. 'Fancy a cup?'

Bill nodded and leant back in his chair, a comfortable padded affair with arms. Hers was a wooden ladder-back with a seat cushion. He wanted her to know her place.

'You carry on with the digging; I've got to go out for a while. You're probably not trying hard enough, woman. Getting lazy, you are.' He scowled at her and she bit back a reply. It was Bill who was getting lazy and she was sure he was meeting up with his pals to share a jar or two of some black-market liquor.

Once he had gone Olive allowed herself a few more minutes by the range, sitting in his chair, before wrapping up her hands in old cloths to protect them. She dragged herself back into the cold to attack the digging, knowing it would be the worse for her if she didn't. Money and food was scarce and what they earned from their vegetables, milk and eggs kept them from starvation. Life had continued to offer more challenges since the Occupation. As Olive forced the spade into the resistant earth, her mouth twisted in a bitter smile. If she had known what was to happen, she would have chosen to stay at home with her parents and not marry Bill. Her vision of freedom, her own farmhouse and a comfortable life had disappeared even before the jackboots marched into St Peter Port and the German flag raised at the Royal Hotel.

As the Occupation dragged on the need for home-grown food grew stronger and Olive had to plant on a bigger scale to help feed the hungry islanders. Bill ploughed the field next to the farmhouse but left it to Olive to plant, only giving her a hand when it suited him.

Leaning on the spade she let her eyes focus on the landscape spread out before her. Heavy, dark clouds loomed over the sea looking as grey as the sky. Even the fields and trees had been leached of colour and the effect made Olive more depressed. She had never liked winter and this past one under German rule had been worse, thanks to the shortage of food, clothing and fuel. She had been so desperate for warm clothes she'd raided the attic where Bill's late parents' stuff had been stored. Sorting through his mother's old clothes she had found heavy-weight skirts, jumpers and jackets which she'd altered to fit her much slimmer figure. The muddy colours didn't suit her and the old wool scratched her skin, but at least the clothes offered warmth. Olive's vision of being able to shop in town for new clothes when she wanted was soon scotched, firstly by Bill's meanness and then, since the Occupation, by the lack of stock in the shops.

As she painfully dug up the reluctant parsnips, Olive's eyes glistened with threatening tears. She missed her father. He was the one she ran to as a child when upset or hurt. He'd sit her on his lap and cuddle her, while she poured out her woes. Her mother, on the other hand, had idolised her brother, Ross. He was definitely the blue-eyed boy. Olive had long given up trying to win her mother's love but was happy her father made such a fuss of her. He and Ross didn't see eye to eye as Ross grew into manhood and Olive was secretly pleased. She resented the fact her mother always took Ross's side in any quarrel between them. Ross was the adored first-born and couldn't possibly have done anything as nasty as aiming his catapult at the cat, causing it to jump in terror and rush up a tree where it stayed for hours until her father had managed to coax it down.

Olive had been only too happy to encourage Ross to sign-up when war was declared, but their mother was devastated.

'No, you can't go, Ross. We need you here on the farm, your father can't manage without you, can you, Larry? Tell him he has to stay.' Her mother stood in the kitchen, twisting a tea cloth in her hands, despair painted on her face. Olive watched her father fidget uncomfortably in his chair and crossed her fingers.

'Well, now m'dear, I'm sure I could manage if I have to. I wouldn't want no-one thinking my son was a coward and afraid to go off and do his duty for king and country, like. I did my bit in the last war and came back, didn't I? So who's to say our Ross won't return when it's all over? And they do say it won't last long, anyways.' Larry didn't meet her eyes, but nodded at his son, pacing around the kitchen floor in his impatience.

'Thanks, Dad, I knew you'd understand. Although I'm old enough not to need your permission, I'd like your blessing.'

Olive, smiling inwardly, watched her mother's face crumple. Perhaps now she'll love *me*, she thought. But there had been little more warmth from her mother after Ross left to join the army, only showing more interest in her after Bill proposed. Before then, Olive's workload on her parents' farm had increased and she began to regret being eager for Ross to go. And when Bill seemed to offer salvation in the form of her own home and lads working on the farm, it had not been a difficult decision.

Her bitterness at the unfairness of it all – the awful, awful marriage and the Occupation by the Germans – caused Olive to attack the soil with increased vehemence. Each time she forced the spade into the soil, she imagined she was battering either Bill or anonymous Germans. If only this war would end! The trouble was they had little news coming in. They'd had to hand in their wirelesses on pain of imprisonment and the Germans issued news bulletins full of their own victories. Some brave souls had either secretly hidden their wirelesses or made crystal sets and some news filtered through that way. Unfortunately, this wasn't enough to raise their spirits as the Germans seemed to be winning on all fronts.

Olive could have coped with all the hardships if only she had been blessed with a child. It was the continuing hope that she would fall pregnant which sustained her while Bill had his way with her. You couldn't call it love-making, she thought bitterly. His rough approach made her feel like a brood mare, not a wife, leaving her sore in mind and body. Self-pity engulfed her and the tears flowed down her numb cheeks as she continued to dig.

chapter ten

2010

Natalie ran out of the house and locked the door. Within seconds she had started her car and hurtled down the lane. Was she really losing it? She certainly hoped not but...As she passed the entrance to Stuart's cottage she was struck by a possible explanation. Could Stuart have played a trick on her? He had been downstairs when she went up to change and had the chance to move the photo, for sure. But why? Taking deep, gulping breaths Natalie forced herself to be rational. Stuart had come across as a decent bloke, acting the part of the friendly neighbour. He had nothing to gain from scaring her like that. Quite the opposite. What good would it do him to have a frightened woman next door?

Once Natalie gained the coast road she had to slow her speed to match the traffic going north. It seemed no-one else was in a hurry for their Sunday lunch, driving at the speed limit of 35mph and no more. Sunday drivers! She braked as the car in front made an unannounced right turn. Coming up on the left, Natalie spotted a display of flowers in a parking area and pulled in. She chose a bunch of freesias and dropped the money in the box provided. She was about to get back in the car when she hesitated. Might as well buy some for her own place and bought the last bunch.

Natalie eased the car carefully through the stone arch to her parents' cottage and switched off the engine. It was only a few days since she had left but it seemed like weeks. Grabbing the flowers she pushed open the front door, calling, 'Only me!'

She found her mother in the kitchen and gave her a hug and the flowers.

Molly beamed. 'Thank you, darling. Could you put them in water while I finish off here? Your father's outside laying the table. There's a bottle of wine chilling on the worktop if you'd like to pour yourself a glass.'

Natalie took a vase from a cupboard and filled it with water before dropping in the flowers. Her mother would probably arrange them properly later. Helping herself to a glass of wine, she asked if there was anything else Molly needed.

'No, all under control. You go and talk to your father. I'll bring the food out in about ten minutes.'

Natalie gave an appreciative sniff. Roast chicken and all the trimmings. Delicious. She went through the back door to find her father sitting at the wooden terrace table, his long legs stretched out in front of him and a glass of wine in his hand. A pile of Sunday papers lay on the floor.

'Hi, Dad. I see you're working up an appetite by reading the papers,' she said, laughing as she kissed his cheek.

He smiled. 'I'll have you know your mother had me peeling veg for what seemed like most of the morning. Does she need a hand?' He went to stand up, but Natalie told him to sit still, she'd help if needed.

'So, what have you been up to? Enjoying that lovely home of yours?'

She whirled the wine in her glass, avoiding his eyes. 'Oh, this and that. The gardener, Matt, came round yesterday and...' she told him what had been discussed and had got to the part about the placement of the pond when her mother came out bearing a laden tray. As Peter relieved her of it, Natalie went inside and filled another tray. Within moments the table was covered in dishes and they began helping themselves.

Natalie was glad of the focus on the food, not yet wanting to say what was uppermost in her mind. That she might be going mad. Not something easy to say when your mother was a psychotherapist. The conversation drifted onto local issues, with the usual grumbling about the latest edicts from the States, the local government. Then Peter once more brought it back to Natalie and her cottage.

'Natalie was telling me the gardener's starting work in earnest this week so it won't be long before everything's shipshape. And the cottage looks even better since we put the pictures up, right, Natalie?' Her father smiled at her and she nodded.

'I think it's beautiful and you were so lucky to get it, darling. You–' Molly stopped as Natalie brushed away a tear. 'Whatever's the matter? Has something happened?' She reached over to give her a hug.

Natalie fought to calm herself and blew her nose on a paper napkin.

'I...I don't know what's happening, Mum, but somehow the photo of you and Dad, which was in the sitting room, ended up in the kitchen. And it definitely wasn't me who moved it.' She sniffed.

Peter and Molly looked at each other and Natalie saw the faint lift of their eyebrows. So, they thought she was mad too.

'Are you absolutely sure you didn't move it, without noticing? When you were thinking of something else, for example?' Peter said, calmly. 'I do it all the time.'

She shook her head. 'I had no need to move it and certainly wouldn't have left it on the worktop.' Natalie chewed her lip. 'It...it's not the only thing that's happened. I've heard a voice twice, both times in the kitchen, when there's no-one there.'

This time she saw her mother's forehead crease and wondered if the men in white coats would soon be on their way.

'What did the voice say? And was it a man or a woman?'

'I couldn't tell whether it was male or female. It was a hiss – "Go away. Go!" A bit threatening.' She could still hear the voice in her head.

'Darling, do you think the place might be haunted? I know it sounds a bit far-fetched, but I've always had an open mind about these things. Ghosts have been seen on the island. And the farm did have the reputation of being haunted after the fire,' Molly said, stroking her arm.

Natalie was shocked. Ghosts! She'd never thought of that, but…

'I don't know, Mum. I've never had any truck with such stuff. To be honest, I was wondering if it was Stuart. He had the chance to move the photo, though God knows why, and he might have been able to stand outside and hiss.' Natalie looked from one parent to another. Saying it all out loud somehow made her feel stupid. What would be worse – going mad or having an in-house ghost? Tough call.

Peter cleared his throat.

'I never used to believe in ghosts or spirits either, but since that business with Jeanne's cottage, I've learnt not everything has a rational explanation.' He gripped Natalie's hand, adding, 'As you say, Stuart has no obvious reason to distress you. But if you're feeling frightened, you can come back any time, you know.'

She smiled half-heartedly.

'I'm not frightened exactly, just scared I'm losing my mind. At least if the place is haunted, we could have it exorcised or whatever it is they do nowadays. Couldn't we?' She looked expectantly at her parents, who nodded in unison.

'The lovely vicar who helped Jeanne, Reverend Ayres, would, I'm sure, be only too happy to help if it came to it. But it's only been a couple of days, so perhaps we should see if anything happens again before talking to him. I believe he retires shortly as the vicar of St Saviours, and you're in St Peters. Not sure if that makes a difference,' Molly said, frowning.

Natalie played with her cutlery. In a way it *was* a relief to think she wasn't mad. But the thought of a restless spirit on the prowl wasn't exactly comforting. It could still be Stuart playing silly-devils, but that was equally depressing. It could indicate *he* was a bit unbalanced and he'd seemed so normal. Sighing, she glanced up at her parents, concern etched in their faces.

'Yes, let's wait. After all, I'm not in any danger. And I do love the house.'

'Right, I'll fetch the pudding, shall I? You need feeding up, sweetheart. Fill out those pretty cheeks of yours,' Peter said, pushing back his chair. Natalie smiled. Her thinness was a family joke, compared to her more cuddly parents, she looked thinner than she was, a healthy size ten. She helped clear the plates and dishes and within minutes they were tucking into a fresh strawberry pavlova. Molly steered the conversation towards the holiday she and Peter were planning for September and the atmosphere lightened. When Natalie left an hour later, she was feeling much better about what had happened in the cottage. Just a blip.

The next morning Matt and the carpenter arrived bright and early as Natalie was wolfing down her breakfast of coffee and toast. Part of her would have liked to stay at home and watch the men working in the garden but having taken time off last week she knew her in-tray would be full of letters from clients needing her attention. She had time for a quick word with them and admired the weathered oak to be used for the pergola. Next to her car Matt's pickup truck overflowed with shrubs, plants and more oak. Natalie smiled at the thought of a soon-to-be completed garden. As she jumped in the car Stuart came out of his cottage and waved. She waved back automatically, even though she was not entirely convinced he was innocent of the odd happenings in her cottage. Since the previous morning nothing had happened and Natalie hoped sincerely it would stay that way. The idea of ghosts was too weird. She drove off down the lane as Stuart followed, both heading into St Peter Port. It was only as they reached the grammar school in Footes Lane that Stuart turned left, giving a quick toot on the horn, and Natalie continued towards Les Banques and the swish offices of the investment bank where she had worked since her return. One of the benefits of her senior position was a dedicated parking space in the basement and she drove in to be met by smiles from colleagues heading for the lift. Not a bad start to a Monday morning, she thought, catching up with them.

Natalie arrived home feeling tired. It had been a long, busy day dealing with letters and making phone calls to her most important clients: the ones who expected instant responses as befitted their wealth. All she wanted was to curl up in a chair with a glass of something cold and alcoholic. But first she wanted to see the progress in the garden and walked straight through to the sitting room. Folding back the windows, Natalie smiled at the sight of the new planting. Stepping outside she admired the posts and beams of the pergola overhead, the beautiful oak gleaming in the evening sun. By the following year it would be a mass of vines and honeysuckle, offering dappled shade from the sun. It was part of Matt's remit to plant around the bases of the posts once the rest of the garden was finished. She stroked the solid wood before crossing to the nearest patch of planting. Evergreen shrubs formed a backdrop to what would be herbaceous borders. Only a few of the flowers she'd chosen were now in place. Natalie continued her inspection, reaching out to touch the oleanders bringing a much-needed splash of colour amongst the green. The piles of earth were no more and the shape of the garden was now visible.

Releasing a contented sigh, Natalie made her way back inside to change. Time for that drink on the terrace.

Much later, after an easy meal of omelette and salad, Natalie settled down in the sitting room for a spot of television. Within an hour she was yawning, and realised she had completely lost the plot of the complex drama advertised as 'unmissable'. Uncurling herself from the sofa, she picked up her empty wine glass and went to the kitchen. Standing in the doorway she froze. Her state of the art kitchen was no longer there. Instead she saw, as if through a mist, a room that would not have looked out of place in the local folk museum. An old-fashioned kitchen with free standing cupboards and a black iron range by a butler's sink. A big wooden table. And was that a door? Natalie tried to take it in, shocked to her core. She blinked and the image disappeared, replaced with that of her own kitchen. She walked in, reaching out to touch the nearest cupboard. It was solid. Leaving the glass on the worktop, she fled upstairs, convinced she was, after all, going mad.

chapter eleven

2010

Weird dreams filled Natalie's sleep that night. She appeared to be a farmer's wife, living in an old bleak farmhouse and at odds with her husband. At one time they were having a blazing row in the kitchen and he struck her around the head. At that point she woke up, instinctively putting her hand to her head where she had been 'hit'. But there was no pain and Natalie, covered in sweat, realised she was in her own bed and it must have been a bad dream. Or was it? As she staggered to the bathroom, part of her still seemed to be in that kitchen, cowering from the big, angry man. With a shock, she realised the kitchen in the dream was the one she had imagined the previous night. The range was the same. Shaking, she stood under the shower until she felt calmer. It must have been her overactive imagination, she told herself as she dried her hair. Or a touch of the sun – or both. Either way, she was in dire need of strong coffee and threw her clothes on before running downstairs.

Natalie hesitated outside the kitchen door. Taking a deep breath she turned the handle and pushed. Relief flooded her body as she saw her own kitchen looking undisturbed. She took her coffee and toast into the garden. An early morning mist hovered over the fields and obscured the sea, but she caught a glimpse of the sun burning through in the east. She took a swallow of coffee and immediately felt better. More in control. Bad dreams had started after Liam turned violent, and she wondered if this latest dream was actually a rehash of what had happened between them. Not entirely sure why the dreams would have followed her here, where she was free of him, nevertheless the thought helped. But that didn't explain the kitchen...As Natalie nibbled her toast the mist slowly lifted and she once more drank in the view which had seduced her into buying the cottage. Perhaps she'd made a mistake...

A glance at her watch told her Matt would be arriving any minute. Brushing the crumbs off her skirt she took her plate and mug to the kitchen. Through the window she watched him pull into the drive and went out to say how pleased she was with the progress so far.

'Glad to hear it. We both worked like crazy yesterday to get the pergola finished and the shrubs planted so you could have something nice to look at instead of heaps of earth,' Matt said, grinning.

Natalie smiled. Was he trying to impress her or genuinely wanting to get the job done as soon as possible? She again detected a glimmer of interest in his gaze but that didn't mean anything. It was okay men finding her attractive, but she didn't want them coming on to her. When she was ready to hook up with someone, it would be on her own terms.

'Thanks, please tell Trev I'm grateful. What's on the agenda today?'

Matt pointed to the back of the pickup, full of plants and pots which he said would be in place by the end of the day and Natalie left him to unload while she returned inside to collect her bag and keys. Work beckoned.

Natalie returned home later than usual that evening having shopped for groceries. Once the food – mainly ready-prepared meals – was safely stored, she poured a glass of wine and went into the garden. Matt had definitely been busy again. She was excited to see the miniature palms, so beloved in Guernsey, waving gently in the soft breeze. What had once been grassy mounds and heaps of soil now looked an inviting place to walk around and unwind. A colourful mix of blue, green and terracotta pots, brim-full of herbs, stood dotted around the terrace. The scents of lavender, thyme and rosemary clung to her fingers as she gently brushed through them. Natalie had also chosen other culinary herbs, including basil and coriander, in case she felt inspired to cook properly. The combination of the herbs and the cook's delight of a kitchen gave the illusion of her being a competent chef, she thought, grinning.

Lost in thought, Natalie drifted down to the end of the garden in order to look back towards the cottage. The soft grey tones of the old granite shone in the reflection of the sun and, together with the emerging garden, gave the cottage an appearance of establishment, as if it had been there for years. Which in a way it had. Sipping her wine, Natalie allowed the utter silence to embrace her. It really was the most fantastic spot. As she took her time walking back to the terrace, Natalie wondered what it was like for Stuart living in a place once owned by his forefathers. She was intrigued to see the inside of his home. Could she find an excuse to pop round? His car wasn't in the drive so it would need to be another time, but that was okay. There was no rush.

The next few days passed without any unusual disturbances or dreams and each day Natalie arrived home keen to see what was new in her garden. Matt had lain a small turf lawn in the middle and it transformed the whole area. Pleased with the progress she invited Jeanne, Nick and the children to come round for lunch on Saturday. Natalie not only wished to show off her home and garden but wanted to talk to Jeanne about the odd 'happenings'. Still unsure about Stuart's possible part in events, she had put off popping round to the barn. He was hardly ever at home, anyway. Her mother phoned to see how she was and Natalie assured her all was well. Time to say what was really happening later…

On Saturday morning Natalie rushed around making sure the house was immaculate, not that it was ever in a mess.

But she wanted to impress even though two small children were about to invade her space. Anything breakable was moved out of harm's way before she concentrated on preparing lunch. Natalie did not possess a barbecue and would not have been keen to be in charge of one, and had bought a selection of ready-prepared meats which she popped in the oven with jacket potatoes, and then prepared accompanying salads. June was continuing to be hot and dry, perfect for al fresco dining.

A crunch of tyres on the gravel announced the arrival of the Maugers and Natalie went to greet them.

'Hi! Good to see you all.' Natalie hugged Jeanne and Nick before picking up Harry and giving him a kiss. He looked at her solemnly, his dark blue eyes the image of Nick's. Seemingly satisfied he did know this woman who had kissed him, Harry's face split into a grin and he planted a wet kiss on her lips.

''Ello, Aunty 'Atalie. We've come to see your new house and Mummy says I'm not to touch anything. And I have to make sure Freya doesn't. She's only little but I'm big. I'm three!' He wriggled in her arms and Natalie let him go.

She smiled and ruffled his curly dark hair before turning to Jeanne, now holding Freya in her arms. At ten months, Freya was at the crawling stage but showing signs of wanting to walk. She reached out her arms to Natalie who lifted her up and kissed her. She favoured Jeanne, with her straight, dark hair and sparkling blue eyes. Natalie reckoned she would be a stunner one day.

Nick stood holding Harry's hand, taking in the front of the cottage. 'I'm impressed, Natalie. From the outside it looks so old. I think Andy's done a great job, don't you, Jeanne?'

Her friend agreed, saying to Natalie, 'Andy's a good friend of ours, and Nick told me on the way over that he was the architect of the project. I hadn't realised when I came round before. Andy told Nick what a problem he had with the planning department.'

'That's interesting to know. I might want to speak to Andy sometime.' She waved a hand towards the front door. 'Let's go in and you can have a good look round before lunch.' Still carrying Freya she led the way. They started downstairs, progressing upstairs and back down again before going through the sitting room and onto the terrace.

'Well, what do you think?' Natalie handed a restless Freya back to Jeanne.

'It's even better now you've unpacked everything and hung the pictures. And you have a garden!' Jeanne nodded towards the new greenery.

'It's fantastic, Natalie. Not only has Andy surpassed himself with the design, but you've furnished it beautifully.' Nick grinned, struggling to hold onto Harry's hand. 'Is this it now? Your final move?'

'I guess. I have no desire to return to London, for sure. Let me show you round the garden and I can tell you what the plans are for the rest of it. And it's okay to let Harry loose, it's quite safe.'

Harry beamed his delight and set off ahead of them, peering behind bushes and stroking leaves. Once Natalie had shown them round Nick strapped Freya into the chair he had brought along and the women fetched the food.

Natalie asked them to help themselves and poured white wine for Jeanne and herself. Nick settled for lager. The meal was messy, noisy and fun. Natalie warmed to the role of hostess and being able to spend time with her friends, in spite of the lack of uninterrupted adult conversation. When Freya began to nod off Jeanne took her inside and settled her in the buggy and Natalie cleared away the dregs of the meal. Once again sat outside, the women watched as Nick played with Harry on the grass.

Natalie cradled her glass of wine, summoning up the right words.

'I...I think this place may be haunted. I've had odd dreams and seen things–'

Jeanne's head spun round, her eyes wide with shock.

'No! Tell me more.'

Natalie explained what had been happening and Jeanne listened intently, her brows creased.

'You don't think I'm going crazy do you? I told Mum and Dad about the voice and it was Mum who said perhaps there's a ghost, but they don't know about the other things that have occurred since.' She bit her lip as she recalled the shock of seeing the old kitchen.

Her friend shook her head.

'No, I don't think you're crazy. Andy told us there were strange rumours about the farm after the old lady, Stuart's grandmother, went missing after a fire. No-one would go near it.' Jeanne looked thoughtful for a moment, adding, 'You remember what happened in Gran's cottage?'

Natalie nodded.

'Well, for years I had sensed there was something odd about the small bedroom. It always felt freezing to me, but no-one else. After...what was found I realised I'd picked up the vibes, if you like, of what had happened. Perhaps because I had suffered a tragedy, like Gran had.' She leant forward and touched Natalie's arm. 'You've experienced an abusive relationship so maybe you're sensitive to what happened here. The couple fighting.'

'Suppose I could be. But I wish I wasn't! I'm not keen on the idea of sharing my home with a ghost and having such vivid dreams.' Involuntarily, she touched her head.

'No, of course not. We need to find out what really happened here and enlist the appropriate help.' Jeanne smiled brightly. 'Reverend Ayres was very understanding.'

For a moment they were both diverted by the sight of Nick running up and down with Harry on his back screaming his delight at playing 'horsey'. It looked a world away from ghosts and all-too-real dreams. Natalie took a sip of wine, willing herself to stay anchored in the present moment and not relive the horrible dream.

'Try not to let it bother you. Remember, if there is a ghost, it can't hurt you and you're perfectly safe here. What about Stuart? Have you told him anything about this?'

'God, no! He'd think he had a looney next door! And, to be honest, I've wondered if he was behind the voices and the moving of the photo.'

Jeanne frowned.

'But why would he do that? It's not like you're a nuisance tenant he wants rid of. You paid a small fortune for this place.'

She sighed. 'I know; it's daft to even think about it. Guess I'd like to think someone was playing tricks on me rather than it was real. If you can call ghostly voices and teleporting objects real!'

'Hey, you two! What's making you look so serious on such a lovely day?' Nick panted as he trotted up with a laughing Harry on his shoulders. Helping his son down, he flopped in a chair and grabbed his lager.

'Oh, nothing much, darling. Just girl talk.' Jeanne lifted Harry onto her lap and offered him his beaker of juice.

Natalie turned the conversation towards the work her friends were undertaking on their house and allowed herself to be carried away with their enthusiasm for the latest project. Leaning back in her chair she observed the way Jeanne and Nick smiled at each other, clearly still in love after five years together. Inwardly she felt a spark of envy and was immediately annoyed with herself. Her friends deserved all the happiness they could get, particularly Jeanne. She would never forget the sight of her unconscious friend lying in that hospital bed, wired up to machines, after the terrible boating accident. At the time it wasn't clear if Jeanne would pull through...By the time her guests had departed, carrying a fractious Harry and a newly awake Freya, Natalie was ready to reclaim the peace of her home. All she wanted to do was clear away the mess, pour a glass of wine and settle in front of the television for some escapism. She had got as far as pouring the wine when the doorbell rang. Swearing under her breath she went to the front door.

'Stuart! Hi, how are you? I've been meaning to call round, but you're never in.' She forced a smile.

He stood on the step, a half-smile on his lips.

'It's been manic at work, what with the GCSEs and A levels in full swing and a couple of teachers are off sick, so...' he shrugged. 'I wondered if you'd like to come round for a drink this evening? If you haven't got anything better planned, that is.' He pushed his hands in the pockets of his chinos, shifting from foot to foot.

Then it hit her. Stuart was shy! Or possibly nervous around women. So used was she to the alpha male, always taking the lead and acting full-on macho, that it hadn't occurred to her he might be different. She relaxed. Even though she was tired, it was a great chance to see inside Stuart's place and perhaps learn a bit more about his family.

'I'd love to. What time?'

'Say about eight?' His incredible blue eyes lit up.

'Perfect, I'll see you later.' Natalie watched him retrace his steps back towards The Old Barn, all her tiredness washed away. The evening promised to be somewhat livelier than the planned slump in front of the television.

Stuart stood in the kitchen area of the open-plan living space, setting out glasses and crisps. He had opened a bottle of white wine and filled his glass. A tiny tic under his left eye hinted at his state of mind. Much as he was looking forward to spending time with Natalie, he was also nervous. A bit in awe of her. A woman who, he'd heard, had been a successful hedge fund manager before the financial crash. And was now reclaiming her roots in Guernsey. Add to this the fact he found her incredibly sexy and his nerves went into overdrive. It's not as if it's a date, he reminded himself, taking a sip of wine. He only wanted to be a good neighbour, as he had shown by taking round a bottle of wine the previous week. If he had known beforehand what a stunner Natalie was – elfin face with huge blue eyes, short fair hair and a petite curvy figure – he might have chickened out. Another slurp of Dutch courage. Out of the corner of an eye, he saw Natalie walking towards the front door. He could hardly miss her; the end gable of the barn was now a wall of glass the size of the original barn doors, with a hinged glass panel acting as the front door.

Stuart saw Natalie's eyes widen as she took in the mass of glass and enjoyed her surprise; the gable wasn't visible from her own cottage. The softly tinted glass allowed him to see out but she couldn't see in. As he strode to open the door, Natalie stood with her back to him facing Rocquaine Bay.

'Hi and welcome to The Old Barn.'

She swung round, smiling.

'This wall is brilliant! I had no idea your place was so, so futuristic. You can't tell from the other sides.'

He stood back to let her in, saying, 'That was the idea. It's why the architect had one hell of a fight with the planners, but he wanted to make the most of the view. And he was right.'

Stuart led the way past the living area containing enormous sofas towards the kitchen, sited American-style between the living and dining area.

'What can I get you to drink? Red, white or a G & T?'

'White would be lovely, please.'

He topped up his own glass and filled a new one for her.

'Cheers!'

Holding her glass, Natalie stood and gazed at the barn.

'This is some fantastic place you have here, Stuart. Did you have a say in the design?'

'No, it was all but finished by the time I arrived on the island, although I did choose the kitchen and bathroom fittings and the décor. I hadn't even considered moving here when Mum had the cottages built. Her aim had been to sell them for profit. Then my circumstances changed and Mum suggested I move here.' He felt the usual pang at the memory of what had changed.

'May I look around?'

'Of course.' He showed her the dining area the other side of the central kitchen and led the way towards the back door and the adjoining utility cum store room. Adjacent to this he pointed out the two bedrooms and a shower-room.

'Andy told me he wanted to keep the focus mainly on the living space and the master suite, upstairs on the mezzanine, making the most of the great views through the front window-wall.' He pointed to the cantilevered floor floating above their heads.

'It's beautiful! I love that it still has the look of a barn, with all the exposed beams and granite,' Natalie remarked, waving her arm around. 'And there's so much light. You wouldn't expect that from an old barn.'

'True. Andy compensated for the lack of windows along the other sides by fitting Velux windows in the roof.'

'It's absolutely stunning, Stuart. And for such a big open space, it feels so cosy.' She looked around. 'Does it have underfloor heating like mine?'

'Yes and the wood burner feeds extra heat up to the master bedroom above,' he said, pointing to the stove under the mezzanine. 'Obviously, I've yet to see what it's like in the winter, but Andy assured me it's well insulated and more than adequately heated.'

Natalie nodded, seeming transfixed by what she saw. Stuart, who'd been slouched against a wall, pulled himself up straight, buoyed by her admiration of his home. It was good to be proud of something, even if the kudos belonged to someone else.

'Shall we sit down? I've got some nibbles to go with the wine.'

She sat in a corner of one of the sofas. Stuart placed bowls of crisps and nuts on the coffee table nearby before joining her, leaving a respectable space between them. The sofa was placed to catch the best of the view and Natalie's gaze focused on the seascape laid out before them. He caught the faint whiff of her perfume, a hint of musk and exotic flowers, and took a gulp of wine, unsure what to say. It had been so long since he had indulged in much more than small talk with a woman and he wanted to make a good impression. Natalie had been somewhat cool when they first met, but he'd sensed a thaw since. Stuart forced himself to relax. Before he could say anything, however, Natalie asked how he liked living in Guernsey.

'I'm adjusting to the slower pace of life. Apart from when everyone's in a hurry driving to work, people seem to take their time. Which is quite refreshing unless you're waiting for a tradesman to turn up.' He grinned.

Natalie pushed her fingers through her hair and smiled.

'Oh, you can't rush anyone here, but that's part of the island's charm, don't you think? When I was younger I didn't see that as a positive thing, I wanted excitement and the buzz of a city. That's why I stayed in England after graduating. Guernsey was much too sleepy for my taste then.' She frowned, looking down at her glass, and then looked at him with a hint of what Stuart thought was pain in her eyes.

For a moment there was an uncomfortable silence. Stuart didn't want to intrude, knowing what it was like to have come out of a long-term relationship.

Natalie sipped her wine and said, 'Why did you never visit Guernsey as a child? You had grandparents here, surely?'

'Ah, my family's a bit odd. My paternal grandparents died before the war and my mother had a falling out with my maternal grandmother and stayed in England after leaving for uni. It's where she met my father and they married a few years later, settled in the south-east and started a property development business together. I think Mum did write to my grandmother occasionally, but rarely spoke about her. As for my grandfather, he died in a Nazi prison during the war.'

'That's awful! How did that happen?' Natalie's eyes widened.

'I only know what Mum was told as she wasn't born until after my grandfather, Bill, was sent away. He was arrested for hitting a German officer and sent to a prison, along with a number of other local men, in France. He never returned, having apparently died in a prison fire.' It felt strange telling someone else the story. His mother had made it clear she did not want to discuss her parents, and Stuart had always wondered why. It wasn't as if his grandfather had done anything bad, in fact the opposite. Anyone living under the German rule would have wanted to punch a soldier, given the chance.

'How sad for your mother not to have met her father. But you would have thought she would have been even closer to her mother to compensate. Do you know why they fell out?'

He shook his head.

'No, Mum never said and if I mentioned my grandmother she got cross with me. I'd have liked to meet her. I had this image of a wild-haired woman living in a remote farmhouse, surrounded by cows and chickens, and cut off from the world.' He smiled.

Natalie laughed.

'That's a bit extreme, isn't it? Is that how your mother described her?'

'Not exactly, I think I picked up odd bits from Mum and made up my own picture of Olive, my grandmother. I always did have a fertile imagination.' Stuart chuckled.

'I don't suppose you have any photos of your grandparents, then? It would have been interesting to see who used to run this place as a farm,' Natalie said, leaning forward, her big eyes shining.

Stuart cleared his throat. She really was so sexy…

'No, none. At least, if Mum had any photos, she never showed them to me. Like you, I'd like to know more about the people who lived here, especially as they were my family.'

'What happened to Olive? I heard there was a fire here.'

'Yes, in the late '80s, though we didn't find out until years later. Mum tried to contact Olive when my father died suddenly fifteen years ago. When she got no reply she came over and found the farm had been virtually destroyed by fire and Olive was missing. But no-one had seen her for weeks before the fire and as there was no sign of her body, it was assumed she'd left and gone to England to visit my mother.'

'Oh! So what did happen to Olive?'

Stuart shrugged.

'No idea. But after all this time with no sight of her, it was assumed she was dead and Mum was declared her heir. And now I'm here,' he said, arms outstretched. 'And the fate of my grandmother remains an unsolved mystery.'

chapter twelve

Summer 1941

Olive didn't know whether to be happy or not. One of her old school friends, Nell, was to be married at St Peters Church and she and Bill were invited. Of course she was happy for Nell, a sweet girl if a bit on the drippy side, and Olive looked forward to the celebrations, muted as they would be with so little food and beverages available. Not to mention the lack of any decent dresses for the women. The problem for Olive, and she knew it was mean of her, was Nell had fallen in love with her beau, Stan, and he with her. They were the proverbial besotted couple and Olive didn't know if she could cope with seeing them so happy. If her own marriage to Bill had been a love-match, it would have been different, she admitted to herself as she scrubbed cooking pans in the sink. Not that Olive fancied Stan, she didn't. He looked all right, she supposed, a bit on the skinny side, but that was true of most men these days, except her Bill who managed to eat more than his fair share of food. Stan was another dreamer, like Nell, and made a living, if you could call it that, by doing odd jobs for anyone who asked. He'd given Bill a hand on occasion, like when Bill needed another pair of hands to refit a gate which had blown off in a gale.

Leaving the pans to drain, Olive wiped her hands and put the kettle on. It would have to be bramble tea as she hadn't been able to buy any acorn coffee recently. Nursing the chipped enamel mug, she thought about the wedding. The miracle was Bill had agreed to go. Mind you, it had taken a lot of persuasion on her part; in spite of her own reservations, she wouldn't miss it for the world. She knew Bill had only said yes because he knew there'd be not only more choice of food than he got at home, but also a supply of spirits, stashed away for this kind of event. Every guest had to contribute something to the wedding feast and Olive planned to bake a carrot cake and take along a few punnets of strawberries and a tub of their own cream. Bill had reluctantly offered to take a few bottles of beer.

Having made her decision about the food, Olive's next, and more difficult decision, was what she could wear. She'd had no new clothes since her wedding and her two summer dresses were looking decidedly shabby. Perhaps her mother could help? Edith had been a seamstress before her marriage and made all Olive's clothes before she got married, including the wedding dress. She decided to visit her and see if she could alter one of her own dresses to fit Olive. Edith had barely gone out over the years and her dresses were likely to be in better condition than Olive's. With two weeks to the wedding there was no time to waste.

'Hello, Mum, how are you doing?' Olive tried to hide her shock at Edith's appearance. It had only been a few weeks since she'd last visited, but her mother had changed almost beyond recognition. Her hair was now completely white and her face etched with deep lines. Never fat, she looked little more than skin and bones, as if she hadn't let a morsel of food pass her lips in weeks.

'Not so bad. Glad summer's finally arrived, for sure. The winter, it was so long and I couldn't get warm. Even now, I find it hard.' She wore a thick skirt and stockings, matched with a Guernsey jumper, and sat hunched by the range. Olive, in contrast, wore a thin cotton dress and her legs were bare. She worried her mother had taken ill, she hadn't seemed well since her father died.

'You don't look that clever, Mum. Have you seen the doctor? Could be a tonic you could take.'

Edith grunted. 'Don't need no tonic! I'll be fine once this war's over and Ross comes back to me. It's been hard, losing him to the army and then your dad going...' Her dull eyes seeped tears and Olive felt a pang of pity for her. She seemed to have given up and that wasn't like her mother.

'Tell you what, I'll make you some nourishing soup, shall I? Vegetable with a bit of ham to give you strength. Doesn't look to me like you're eating properly.'

'Don't have much appetite these days and there's not much to eat, anyways. But if you bring me some soup, I'll try to eat it.' She stared at Olive. 'It's not like you to offer to do something for me, girl. Did you want something in return?'

Her cheeks burned. Her mother could read her like a book!

She told her about the wedding and the need for a dress. Edith nodded, a small smile lifting her lips.

'There should be something in my wardrobe that'll do. I made a blue shantung dress for your cousin's wedding a few years back, might not need much altering. Go and fetch it and we'll take a look.'

As Olive opened the bedroom door, a wave of sadness washed over her. She hadn't been in the room since her father's death and all she could see was him lying in the bed. Shutting her eyes and then opening them again, the image had gone, but the feeling of loss was still there. She pulled open the heavy mahogany wardrobe and was dismayed to see her father's meagre supply of clothes still hanging on the rails, alongside her mother's dresses and skirts. She stroked a sleeve of his best suit and sniffed the heavy wool. It smelt of his pipe tobacco and stale sweat. Olive brushed away a tear and quickly looked at the dresses, instantly spotting the shantung. She pulled it out and the iridescent colour gleamed. It was beautiful and she would love to wear it. She held it against herself and looked in the blemished mirror. The colour suited her dark hair and the sheath style would make her look elegant. Glancing at the bottom of the wardrobe Olive saw, amongst others, a pair of deep blue shoes which she remembered her mother wearing at the wedding. Slipping them on, she found them a bit tight, but not enough to not wear them. She scooped them up with the dress and returned downstairs.

Edith noticed the shoes.

'I'd forgotten about them, but they're a perfect match. Put the dress on so I can see what needs altering.'

Olive slipped the silk over her head and it slithered, with a soft whisper, over her body. Her mother did up the zip at the back and stood back.

'It needs shortening, I know you young girls like your dresses on your knees,' she said, tutting. 'Apart from a little tucking in here and here,' she pointed, 'it'll do.' She cocked her head. 'You look very nice, girl. Bill will be proud to have you on his arm.'

Olive's pleasure at her mother's rare compliment evaporated at the mention of her husband. He wouldn't give a damn what she looked like. Oh, if only she had a man she truly loved and who loved her!

The wedding celebrations were lovely, Olive thought, sipping a glass of refreshing home-brewed gooseberry wine, bottled when sugar was still available. Wine of any kind was a luxury and she savoured every mouthful, enjoying the sensation of light-headedness. Nell's parents had done her proud. A collection of odd sized and shaped tables filled the farmyard and in the kitchen all the surfaces were covered with food and bottles of drinks. The rare sight of ham joints, roasted chickens and fresh fish made her mouth water. The family and guests must have paid dear to provide such a spread. You wouldn't know there was a war on to look around the tables and the laughing faces of the guests. Nell looked a treat in her wedding dress, her flushed cheeks making her look almost beautiful. Olive's mind skipped back to her own wedding, a poor reflection of Nell's. Bill hadn't wanted a fuss and truth be told, hadn't wanted to spend much money, so few guests had been invited. Olive bit her lip, trying not to feel sorry for herself, but failing. She looked around for Bill and saw him smoking with his mates, glasses of beer in their hands. He wouldn't miss her company and when it came to sit and eat, she joined some friends with a spare seat at their table. If they were surprised she didn't sit with her husband, they made no comment. It wasn't long before they were talking about the good times they'd had before the Occupation and laughed at the fun they'd shared.

After the toast and the cutting of the cake, the tables were moved back for dancing, with music provided by an accordionist and a fiddler. Olive clapped her hands to the beat, itching to dance but knowing it was no point asking Bill. He didn't dance. A friend of the groom came up and asked if she'd like to dance and she accepted without a second thought. They stayed on their feet for several dances before, laughing, Olive said she needed to rest her feet. The shoes pinched and she eased them off with a grateful groan. She had barely sat down when a hand grabbed her roughly, jerking her to her bare feet.

'What d'yer think you're doing, making a fool of me in front of everyone? Not enough for you to sit on another table, but you have to go and dance with that man as if you're a couple.' Bill's eyes flashed at her and she trembled. 'Get your things, we're off.' Olive winced as she pushed her feet back into the shoes and grabbed her bag from her chair. She just managed to say goodbye to her friends and the bride and groom before Bill marched her off. They had walked to the church and then down to Nell's parents' farm and had a half-mile walk back home. Bill's rage flowed from him and he continued gripping her arm while not saying a word. Olive was too scared to say anything, convinced she'd only make matters worse.

By the time they arrived home her feet were throbbing and she could feel the blisters oozing blood. Once in the house she tried to shake off Bill's hand but he dragged her upstairs into the bedroom and flung her onto the bed. Horror filled her when he took off his belt.

'Bill, no! I didn't mean any harm. I'm sorry–'

'Oh, you'll be sorry all right by the time I've finished with you, my girl. You're going to get the hiding you deserve.' He turned her onto her stomach and she closed her eyes as the blows fell, pain ripping across her back, until she blacked out.

chapter thirteen

2010

Natalie returned home, her mind buzzing with what she had learnt about Stuart's family. To say she was intrigued was putting it mildly. She couldn't help wondering if the mystery of Olive's disappearance had anything to do with her dreams and the odd happenings in the house. It was strange Olive had vanished without a trace. As she switched on the lights Natalie looked around to make sure all was as she had left it. To her relief everything looked normal and she put the kettle on for a cup of tea. Perched on a kitchen stool she allowed herself to dwell on Stuart, the man, rather than his family mystery.

She could tell he'd been nervous. A muscle twitched under his left eye when he handed her the glass of wine. It was quite sweet, she thought, even though she couldn't imagine why anyone should be nervous of her. Except for those who had been her underlings in the London office. She was not one to suffer fools gladly. But Stuart was a schoolteacher in charge of hormonal teenagers and thus, in her opinion, not likely to have survived this far if he'd been of a nervous disposition. Perhaps he'd had a bad experience with a woman – or women – and been scarred for life. Natalie grinned at the thought. A bit melodramatic for this day and age. No, it must be her. After all, she had been a tad cool towards him at first and he was only being a good neighbour. She yawned. It had been a busy day, what with Jeanne's family round for lunch and then drinks with Stuart, no wonder she was tired. Thank God it was Sunday the next day. She could enjoy a lazy lie-in before Sunday lunch with her parents. Bliss.

The blows rain down thick on my back and the pain's so bad I can't stop myself crying out. He's so mad – and drunk – I'm not sure he knows what he's doing. I can't stand it much more...think I'm going to pass out.

Natalie woke with a start, her heart racing, convinced she was being beaten with a belt. But the terrible, burning pain had gone. It took a moment to realise it had been a dream. What on earth? It had been so real, as if she was the woman, in *her* head, not her own, experiencing the agony of the beating.

Hugging her knees to her chest, Natalie tried to make sense of it. It was possible the dream had been triggered by Stuart's talk of his family and the mystery surrounding his grandmother, but Natalie sensed something deeper was happening. It was if the woman was taking over. Was it someone who'd lived there? Someone who had left a trace of themselves within the stones of the original farmhouse? Natalie sat up and gripped her head. She didn't want to believe in ghosts, even though her mother – and even her father – seemed to think they might exist. A pragmatist, she liked dealing with facts and figures, needing the security of believing what she saw was real. But surely someone who must be long-dead couldn't recreate a scene from the past? It was too much to accept and Natalie flung the duvet aside in despair. In spite of the early hour – the bedside clock proclaimed it to be seven – she wanted fresh air. A shower, breakfast and she would go for a long walk. That should sort her head out.

Half an hour later Natalie shut the door behind her and set off towards the lanes leading to the shores of Rocquaine Bay. An early morning mist swirled around the nearby fields, muffling the faint birdsong and creating an eeriness reflecting her own mood. Taking a deep breath, she strode along, determined to shake off the feeling of being out of control induced by the all-too-real dream. Minutes later Natalie arrived at the main road running along the coast and the mist cleared, enabling her to take in the reassuring sight of the beach and the white tower of Fort Grey to her left. There was little traffic so early on a Sunday morning but she noticed keen fishermen loading rods and nets into their boats ready for a day's fishing. Natalie watched as the men called greetings to each other before switching on their engines and heading out to sea. Seagulls formed a cavalcade behind them, swooping down in a synchronised routine.

Natalie clambered down over rocks to walk on the small spit of sand not swallowed by the high tide. The strong ozone smell mingled with the pungent scent of the seaweed glistening on the rocks and her head cleared. She smiled and exchanged greetings with a fellow walker, a woman attempting to power-walk on the limited strip of sand available. Natalie headed up towards L'Eree, keen to stretch her legs as she attempted to understand the meaning of the dream. Shaking her head, Natalie gave up. For now she wanted to breathe the invigorating air and walk off the effects of yesterday's long lunch. Before she enjoyed another one at her parents' today.

'How did it go yesterday? Did the children wear you out?' Peter asked as he gave Natalie a hug.

'It was great, and no, the children were fine. Jeanne and Nick had them pretty much under control.' She smiled at her father before giving Molly a kiss. Their kitchen was the usual hub of activity for a Sunday and Natalie lent a hand with the final touches to the meal of roast lamb and all the trimmings. The smell of the rosemary and garlic infused lamb filled the room and set her stomach rumbling. In deference to a cool northerly breeze they decided to eat in the adjoining dining room and shortly after her arrival they took their places around the table. Peter filled their glasses with Rioja.

Molly wanted to know how the garden was progressing and Natalie brought her up to date. The meal passed pleasantly enough and Natalie savoured her mother's cooking, wondering if she would ever be as good a cook. She had just eaten the last bite when her father interrupted her thoughts.

'Any more signs of your "ghost",' he asked, with a chuckle.

She choked on her wine and Peter had to pat her back.

'Sorry, did I touch on a sore subject?'

'Well, yes.' She went on to tell them about the vision of the old kitchen and her latest dream, feeling herself tensing as she recalled the vividness of it. By the time she had finished both her parents looked shocked.

'Oh dear! How horrible for you, darling. Do you feel threatened?' Her mother squeezed her hand.

'Nooo, but it's a bit unnerving. And I'm beginning to think it has something to do with Stuart's missing grandmother.' She told them what Stuart had said about his family and the mystery of his grandmother's whereabouts.

'I'd heard rumours to that effect, but hadn't thought too much about it until now. Guernsey has always had its fair share of eccentrics and recluses and old Mrs Falla was one of them, apparently. Some of the older members of the Societé Guernesiaise have mentioned her.' Peter frowned, apparently lost in thought.

'Mum, do you think it's possible for a…a ghost to get inside my head and make me think I'm her when I'm asleep?' Natalie felt sick suddenly. Saying it out loud had made it seem more real, not something she had imagined.

'I really don't know. It's outside my experience, darling. Although I occasionally had a client who'd had some kind of ghostly encounter, no-one had such vivid dreams.' Molly paused. 'You're sure you weren't having a bad dream based on what Stuart told you?'

Natalie sighed. 'It's what I hoped had happened but I'm beginning to doubt it. It felt so *real*. As if I was there, in her bed. I felt the blows of the belt on my back, heard the man shouting.' She paused. 'And I think it was her husband.'

'Dear God! Bill was violent? Poor Olive,' Molly said.

'Yes, poor Olive. But why is she getting into my head like this? Oh, it's too weird! I can't be reliving this woman's life, surely?' she cried, jumping up from the table.

Molly gave her a hug.

'I don't think that's what's happening. For some reason, you may be picking up the memories of what happened in the farmhouse and it seems real, even though it happened so long ago. It must be Stuart's grandmother, as she was the only woman living there during the Occupation. Are you going to tell him?'

'I don't know. It sounds so off the wall, doesn't it? He's bound to think I've lost my marbles and I'm still not convinced I haven't!' She slumped back down on the chair, her head in her hands. Her father patted her arm and her mother dropped a kiss on her head.

'You're not going mad, darling. But something strange is happening and it might be we should seek the right help. Perhaps Mr Ayres.'

Natalie lifted up her head and looked from one parent to another. She hated seeing them so worried about her. She was supposed to be the strong, independent woman who could cope with anything. It was her brother Phil who had always been the one to cause them anxiety. Making a determined effort, she smiled.

'It's a thought, Mum, but I don't feel the need to bring in the Church yet. It could settle down of its own accord and, as I said, I don't feel in danger. But I think I'll get in touch with Andy and see if he can tell me anything about the farmhouse before it was rebuilt. Particularly the kitchen. Assuming there was anything left of it.'

Once home Natalie phoned Jeanne and asked for Andy's telephone number, mentioning how she'd 'seen' the old kitchen. Jeanne expressed shock and again suggested she contact Mr Ayres. But although Natalie refused to believe whatever had triggered the events of the past few weeks couldn't be undone, she wasn't yet ready for an exorcism or whatever the Church decreed was appropriate.

Her home emanated peace, as if nothing had ruffled the serenity Natalie had experienced when she had first viewed it. In spite of this she felt happier outside and made herself comfortable on a lounger on the terrace, and the warmth of the sun lulled her into a dreamless sleep. A few hours later Natalie woke up and stretched. The sun hung low on the horizon and, glancing at her watch, she was shocked to find it was after eight o'clock. She went to the kitchen for a drink and debated whether or not she was hungry enough to make some supper. Deciding she could make do with cheese and biscuits, it wasn't long before she was loading a tray with the snack and a glass of chilled wine.

 Once settled in the sitting room she switched on the television to watch the latest Sunday night drama. The sky began to darken as she became absorbed in the action on the screen. A sound outside broke her concentration and, looking towards the sliding panel of glass she glimpsed a shadowy figure on the terrace. Her heart raced as panic gripped her. What to do? Ring the police? They would take too long. Stuart? She wasn't sure if he was in, his car was missing when she arrived home earlier. Natalie's mind skidded with the options as she looked around for a defensive weapon. The kitchen. Knives. She stood up and edged towards the hall, glancing at the window to see if the figure was still there. It wasn't. Natalie was about to enter the kitchen when the doorbell rang. She froze. Would someone who meant her harm ring the bell? Perhaps it was Stuart! It could have been him on the terrace, after all she only caught a glimpse of whoever it was.

Reassured she flung open the door and came face to face with Liam.

chapter fourteen

2010

'Hello, darling. Bet you're surprised to see me, eh?' Liam leered at her, his speech slurred.

She stared at him in horror. Fear knotted her stomach and her brain ceased to function. It must be a bad dream…

'Aren't you going to ask me in? And after all the trouble I've taken to find you. Tut tut. Where are your manners?' He pushed her backwards into the hall and, gripping her arm, kicked the door back behind him. Natalie saw it didn't quite close and briefly thought of making a run for it, but Liam's grip was too tight. Adrenaline began to flow through her veins and she decided not to fight, to pretend to accept his unexpected arrival.

'Would you like a drink? A coffee, perhaps? The kitchen's just here.' She edged her way along the wall and Liam, still gripping her arm, followed. He lent in close and the smell of alcohol on his breath made her feel sick but she kept her face a mask.

Once in the kitchen he released her and pulled open the fridge door, grabbing a can of lager.

'This is better than stupid coffee. Wanna join me?' He proffered a can but she shook her head. Best not to drink any more if she wanted to outwit him. If only she could reach the knives…

Liam slumped onto a stool and Natalie eased herself closer to the knife rack, all the time keeping her eyes on his.

'How did you find me, Liam? You know you're supposed to stay away from me.' She kept her voice neutral, but inside she raged. How dare he invade her private space! And there was a restraining order against him. Surely it was valid in Guernsey, too?

He glugged down the lager, wiping his mouth with the back of his hand, and belched.

'Wasn't that difficult. While the boss man was busy offering you his, er, support,' he grinned wickedly, 'I was bribing one of his men to tell me where you were going. He only knew your stuff was going into storage, and that you were moving to Guernsey. I came over a couple of days ago and it didn't take much detective work to find out you'd bought this place.' He opened his arms wide, spilling lager on the tiled floor in the process, and added, 'And very nice it looks too. Bit bigger than the cosy flat in London, eh?' He stood up, staggering slightly, and moved towards her. 'You remember those cosy nights we spent in that flat, don't you? Couldn't get enough of me then, could you? Begged me for more, right? So why don't you show me around this place? Shall we start upstairs?' Lust clouded his eyes and Natalie, her heart thumping, reached behind her and grabbed a knife.

Thrusting it at Liam, she shouted, 'Stay away from me! Come any nearer and I'll stick this in you!'

For a moment he wavered, balancing on the balls of his feet, a surprised look on his face. Then his face darkened and he lurched towards her. Natalie held the knife steady with both hands and was about to stab at him when Stuart appeared in the doorway, grabbed Liam around the neck and karate chopped him. He fell senseless to the ground.

'You okay? Got here just in time by the look of it.'

The knife dropped from her fingers and she fell into Stuart's arms. He stroked her hair while she sobbed, the horror of what might have happened overwhelming her. Gently he steered her to a chair in the dining area before going to check on Liam.

'He's out cold. Shall I call the police? I take it he's not a friend of yours?' He returned to her side.

She shuddered.

'He was...once. But he was violent and...I had to get a court order against...him. Please, phone the police. I don't want him waking up here.'

'No probs. I'll tie his hands and feet together once I've made the call.' Pulling out his phone Stuart dialled 999 and then, taking Natalie's instructions, found some extra-strong packing tape in a drawer and quickly taped the recumbent Liam's feet and hands together.

'Right, that should do until the police arrive. Now, have you got any brandy?'

She pointed to a cupboard and he poured a couple of glasses and handed her one.

'I think we both need this, don't we? I've never tackled a man like that before.' He grinned.

Natalie took a sip and allowed the fiery liquid to flow down her throat, bringing warmth to her shaking limbs. She wasn't cold. It was shock.

'How, how did you know I...I was in trouble?'

Stuart sat beside her and sipped his brandy.

'I came home a few minutes ago and noticed a hire car parked at the top of the lane. Which was odd as we're the only ones down here. I walked across here in case someone had broken down. The front door was ajar, which alerted me something might be wrong. I crept in and could hear voices in the kitchen. I was debating whether or not to come in when you shouted and the rest, as they say, is history.'

Natalie smiled wanly.

'I was never more glad to see anyone! I wasn't sure I'd actually manage to stab him at all, let alone in time. He's such a big bloke and...an ex-soldier. I can't believe you managed to overpower him so quickly!'

'I always knew karate would come in useful at some point! It was the element of surprise that carried the day and the fact he was pretty pissed by the smell of him.' He wrinkled his nose.

'Yes–'

The doorbell interrupted her and Stuart went to answer it, coming back with two police officers. Their eyebrows rose at the sight of the trussed man on the floor, still out cold. Natalie and Stuart explained what had happened and the sergeant made notes, giving Stuart an admiring glance when he explained how he had overpowered Liam.

'Right, that'll do for tonight, we'll get this fellow out of your way, Miss, and I'd be grateful if you'd both come in and sign statements tomorrow.' He gave Natalie a keen look. 'Are you sure you don't need a doctor, Miss? I can get one to call round and give you something to help you sleep.'

She shook her head.

'It's all right, thank you, Sergeant. Knowing that man,' she nodded towards Liam, being dragged upright by the constable, 'is safe in the cells, I'll be fine.' A thought struck her. 'He won't be allowed out on bail or anything, will he?' Her hands grew clammy at the thought.

'Oh no. We'll get him off the island into the hands of the English police asap. He'll be locked up for assault and breaking the restraining order. We don't want scum like that here, do we constable?'

'No, Sarge, we don't.' The policeman grinned as he dragged Liam across the floor.

The sergeant nodded at Natalie before lending a hand with the prisoner and Stuart followed them to the front door. She drank some more brandy, willing herself to stop shaking. Stuart came back and grabbed her hands.

'You can't stay here on your own tonight, Natalie. Why don't you ring your parents?'

'They'd only fuss and I don't want that. I'd rather tell them tomorrow when things are back to...normal.'

'Hmm. Look, don't take this the wrong way, but how about if I slept in your spare room tonight? I'd feel happier knowing I was around in case you needed something. Shock can do funny things to people, you know.' His forehead creased as if from a memory. 'And I have some herbal tablets which will help you sleep. I use them whenever I get stressed.'

'Well, thanks for the offer, but I don't want to put you out even more–'

'You're not putting me out. What are neighbours for, if not to help each other? I can bring my sleeping bag if it helps.'

'That won't be necessary, the spare bed's made up. I would appreciate you being here, Stuart. I do feel a bit wobbly and I'd like some of those tablets you mentioned.'

Stuart shifted his feet. 'Was he the man who stalked you in London?'

She drew a sharp breath. 'He was more than a stalker. We…we had a relationship for a few months and he seemed like a nice guy. We met online initially. Always polite and quite the gentleman, he'd been an officer in the army.' She remembered that first date, when Liam turned up with a bunch of flowers and insisted on paying for the meal. With his rugged good looks and easy charm Natalie thought she had struck lucky. But it hadn't lasted…'Then it was like a switch had been thrown. He became moody and aggressive and lost his temper.'

'Was he violent?' Stuart asked softly.

'Yes. Oh, only the odd slap to begin with and he made it seem like it had been my fault. I deserved it. But then, this particular time, he…he punched me hard on the jaw and I ended up in hospital.' Tears of self-pity and shame filled her eyes and Natalie reached for a tissue. Looking back she couldn't believe she had allowed herself to become a victim.

'God, that's awful. What happened to change him like that?'

Natalie blew her nose. 'After he was arrested for what he did to me, the doctors diagnosed Post Traumatic Stress Disorder, brought on by something that happened in Afghanistan. He saw his best friend blown up and couldn't save him.' She tore the tissue into shreds. 'The docs prescribed treatment but either he isn't following it or it's not working. He...started drinking heavily and lost his job.'

'Poor bugger. It must have been difficult for you, knowing he was ill but threatening to hurt you.' Stuart patted her arm. She was glad he didn't think her a wimp.

'It was. I truly want him to get the help he needs, not just be locked up in a cell. I'll try and explain that when I go to the station tomorrow.'

He nodded and left to fetch his things and Natalie leant back in the chair, suddenly drained of energy. What a day it had been! First having to admit to her parents things were far from fine at the cottage; either ghosts from the past were invading her home or she was losing her mind. And then Liam had arrived on her doorstep. Thank God for Stuart! The thought of what might have happened if he hadn't turned up made her stomach clench. All Natalie wanted to do now was crash into bed and sleep, undisturbed, for as long as possible. She might go into work a bit later than normal, give herself time to feel in control. And there was the matter of the statement for the police...Definitely a priority in the morning. Standing up she went over to the fridge and took out the milk. Pouring two mugs' full into a pan Natalie switched on the hob before grabbing a tin of hot chocolate.

The milk was close to the boil when Stuart returned, bearing a rucksack which he dropped on the floor.

'Fancy a hot chocolate? Almost ready.'

'Great, thanks.' He fumbled in his pocket and pulled out a small bottle. 'And here's the tablets.' He placed it on the worktop.

She nodded her thanks and carried on mixing the drinks. After handing him a mug Natalie pocketed the bottle and headed for the door. 'I'll show you to your room. I'm exhausted and going to bed, but please feel free to stay up if you want to watch telly.'

'No thanks, I'm off to bed. I've got my most challenging class first thing tomorrow and need my sleep or they'll walk all over me.'

'Perhaps you should demonstrate the odd karate chop on one of them. That would keep them under control!' She grinned at him.

Stuart laughed as he followed her upstairs.

The herbal pills worked as promised and Natalie slept heavily until she was woken by a knock on her bedroom door. For a moment panic kicked in. Liam! But then she remembered Stuart and called out for him to come in, pulling the duvet around her.

Stuart's face appeared round the door. 'Morning, sorry if I woke you, but wanted to check you were all right before I left for work.' He kept his gaze averted from her.

'I'm fine, thanks. Slept like a log.' She rubbed bleary eyes and yawned. 'Thanks again for last night, Stuart. You were the proverbial knight in shining armour and I'll be eternally grateful. Hope the guest bed was comfortable?' Natalie pulled herself up, hanging on to the duvet. She saw his face flush.

'It was and I slept well, thanks. Now I'm off to tackle the monsters of year eight. If you're going to the police station this morning, please tell them I'll be in at lunchtime.'

'Sure. Catch you later.'

'Bye.' His head disappeared and Natalie stretched her arms and legs. Turning her head she saw the clock registering eight o'clock. Normally she would be on the way herself but there was nothing urgent on her desk that couldn't wait a bit longer. Reaching for the phone she called in to say she would be late but didn't give any details. Lying in bed she ran through the events of the previous night, focussing on Stuart. He was proving to be a man of surprises and Natalie realised she had misjudged him. There was no way he would have played tricks on her, he was too honourable. But it meant the voices and moving of the photo must have been the work of her 'ghosts'. If only Stuart could rescue her from those, too. Her musings were interrupted by the sound of a vehicle pulling up in front of the house. She had forgotten about Matt.

Showered and dressed Natalie caught up with him in the garden and they discussed the aims of the coming week. According to Matt, he would be finished with everything except the pond by Friday and that was delayed thanks to a faulty liner. He would be back once a replacement arrived. Natalie, normally impatient about delays, was sanguine. The proposed pond was planned for the far right-hand side, near the kitchen, and the delay would not affect the rest of the garden.

After breakfast Natalie drove into Town, heading for the police station in Hospital Lane. The muscles in her neck tightened as she parked the car and she hoped she wouldn't have to face Liam. Much as she knew he needed help more than punishment, he did scare her.

The sergeant took her statement and she added her view about Liam's mental state.

'I've requested a doctor checks him out this morning. He'll provide an assessment for our colleagues in the UK. It'll be up to the courts to decide what happens after that, Miss Ogier.'

'Right. I'd better get off to work and Stuart – Mr Cross – will be in at lunchtime.' The sergeant accompanied her towards the front desk. Before they reached it a door opened and a uniformed police officer came out, handcuffed to a prisoner. He glanced her way and Natalie gasped. It was Liam. His eyes flashed and he looked as if he was about to say something when the constable pulled him away. She drew a deep breath. His eyes had held a mix of anger – and despair.

chapter fifteen

Summer – Winter 1941

W hen Olive came round long shadows played on the bedroom wall and the glimpse of sky through the curtains was a golden orange. The house was quiet and she could only hope Bill had either gone back to the celebrations, or more likely, to the local pub. As she eased herself onto her elbow, her stiffened muscles sent spasms of pain through her body and she let out a cry. Slowly swinging her legs over the side of the bed, she eased up onto her feet and felt dizzy. Holding onto the bedside table she tried again and managed to stay upright and stumble to the mirror inset in the wardrobe door. With difficulty Olive pulled down the zip, pain knifing through her all the while. She stepped out of the ruined dress and twisted round to see her back. Deep red welts criss-crossed her skin, covered in dried blood and the beginnings of deep purple bruises. She looked down at her legs and saw the marks from the belt across her thighs. Her blistered feet were oozing blood. Olive sobbed from pain and humiliation at what he'd done.

She crawled across the landing to the bathroom and washed herself as well as she could. Her one thought was to get out of the house before Bill returned. She would go to her mother's for the night. Once she had dried herself she walked to the bedroom and pulled on her work trousers and a cotton cardigan, pushing her tender feet into sandals. She collected the dress and her night clothes and, step by painful step, got downstairs. Looking at the clock she saw she had half an hour to curfew and forced herself out of the door. Her bike leant against the wall and after putting the bundle of clothes in the basket, Olive mounted and rode off down the lane, gritting her teeth against the pain.

'Mum, oh Mum!' she said, hobbling into the kitchen where her mother dozed in the old armchair. Edith opened her eyes, trembling. 'Olive! You did give me a shock! I thought it was the Germans! What are you doing here at this time of night?'

Olive knelt at her knee and poured out the whole story. Edith's eyes widened with shock and she gently undid the buttons of the cardigan and pulled it off before turning Olive round.

'Dear God! That man's a monster! Your dad and I had heard he was a bully, but we didn't know he'd be capable of something like this. We'd never have let you marry him.' Olive's tears flowed freely, overcome by her mother's tenderness.

'Here, you go up to your old room and I'll make up some of the ointment I used when you or Ross cut yourselves. It'll speed up the healing, it will. And I'll make you a cup of camomile tea to help you relax.'

Olive did as she was told and fell face down on her old bed. Never would she have dreamt one day she'd be so glad to be back here. Her mother came upstairs with the tea and the ointment and, as gentle as the touch of butterfly wings, spread it on Olives wounds. Once she'd finished she helped Olive with her nightdress.

'There, my dear, that should help. And I've put something in the tea to help with the pain. Drink up and try and sleep. I'll see you in the morning.' To Olive's astonishment, her mother kissed her on the mouth before standing up and leaving. As she sipped the barely palatable tea, Olive tried to remember the last time her mother had kissed her that way. At her wedding she had pecked her cheek, but there'd been no real warmth behind it. But now! Well, that was a kiss of love.

Olive stayed with her mother for two days and when not involved with chores, they talked. Initially, Edith suggested Olive move back with her, but she knew it wouldn't work.

'I'm his property, Mum, he'd drag me back to the farm and my life would be a bigger hell. It's better if I go back of my own accord, and I'll not give him the satisfaction of knowing how much he's hurt me. But I'll sleep in my own bed from now on and will decide when he can…you know. I still want a baby, Mum, so I can't refuse him altogether, can I?' She twisted the handkerchief in her hands. There was nothing she'd like better than to remain with her mother, but…with a bit of luck the war would be over soon and life would return to normal in Guernsey. She would apply for a divorce and move in with her mother.

'If you want a child, you have no choice. But you must promise to visit me regular so I can see you're all right. Tell him I need your help now your father's gone. Which would be the truth, as it's not been easy these past months.' A flash of pain crossed Edith's face and Olive felt guilty for not offering to help before. She'd try and make it up to her mother and Bill could hardly refuse. Word would soon get round if he kept his wife from seeing her widowed mother.

The next few weeks weren't easy; Olive hated being near Bill and stuck to her guns about sleeping in the spare room. He shouted and threatened, but then, suddenly, gave in. She had threatened to expose him as a wife-beater if he didn't agree and with the island overrun with German soldiers, it would have rebounded on him. This was a time to fight back at the invader not a wife. Around this time he began to stay out overnight and Olive didn't believe his excuses of missing the curfew and needing to stay at a mate's until the morning. She suspected he had a woman on the side and was glad. If it meant he didn't bother her, then so be it. But Olive did allow him into her bed occasionally in an effort to become pregnant. Sadly, without success. Bill had made it clear he wanted a son when they married and blamed her for being barren.

Autumn arrived in a glowing burst of richness and vibrant colours. Olive picked blackberries from the heavy hedgerows in the lanes and mixed them with apples she'd bartered for butter. Several neighbours had good-sized orchards, heavy now with plums, apples and pears and were glad to exchange the fruit not good enough to bottle over winter. Olive made crumble using flour made from crushed nuts and took some to her mother, who had put on some flesh over the past weeks. The women enjoyed each other's company, discovering their mutual interest in films and live theatre. Once Edith had regained her strength they would cycle into St Peter Port to watch a film or a live show put on by local entertainers. It was good to get out and have a laugh and leave the war behind for a few hours and Olive found she coped better with Bill after a night out. He could be more bad tempered after such trips, but she didn't rise to it, buoyed by the happy memories of her evenings out. At least he couldn't take those from her.

'Have you heard the latest news about those German buggers?' Bill stomped into the kitchen and threw himself down into his chair, set close to the fire. The November mists and rain brought a chill to the bones and it was hard to stay warm.

Olive, scrubbing parsnips at the sink, reached for the kettle. She'd managed to buy some acorn coffee and by the look on his face, Bill needed a cup.

'No, what's happened? Don't tell me they've won another battle somewheres.' Ever since the sinking of the mighty KMS *Bismarck* in May, they had encouraged themselves to believe the war was finally turning against the Germans. With scant news coming through thanks to the constant removal of their radios, it was hard to know who was winning.

Bill shook his head.

'Not that I know. But it's worse than that, they've orders to start building fortifications around the island to prevent the British trying to land and rescue us. There's a special organisation set up, called after some chap Todt, who'll be bringing in thousands of slave workers to build the blasted things. They're even going to build some kind of railway around the northern coast to transport materials and the workers.' He spat into the fire. 'Seems to me they're here for the long-term and it's only going to get worse from now on.'

Olive handed him his mug and sat down in her chair, feeling winded. So much for an early end of the Occupation and escape from Bill! She wanted to cry, but held back. Later, when she was alone...

'So there'll be even more pressure on supplies. We've not got enough food as it is! How did you hear about this?'

'Me mate Percy told me. Says this Todt bloke is on the island now, planning where the fortifications are to go. And the first lot of slave workers are here, and all. Told you, it's gonna get worse, for sure.'

Olive kept her eyes down, not wanting him to see the despair flowing through her very being. How on earth would she survive?

chapter sixteen

2010

Natalie found it hard to focus on her work. She operated on autopilot for the most part, only giving full concentration on vital documents. The image of the look on Liam's face appeared in front of her. Wherever she looked, he was there. Mid-way through the afternoon she gave up, said she had a migraine coming, and went home. It was close to the truth as her head was pounding.

At home Natalie took some painkillers and made a cup of tea before ringing her parents. As she expected they were horrified and upset she had not called them the previous night.

'It was okay, Mum. Stuart kindly offered to sleep in the spare room and it was no big deal. I didn't want to drag the pair of you out of bed as it was late by the time the police left.'

'Mm, it seems Stuart is showing himself to be a good neighbour. Our only concern about your house was its remoteness, but with Stuart next door...' Natalie assured her mother she felt quite safe knowing Stuart was yards away, acting as a human version of a guard dog. As she said this she realised it was true. She did see him as her protector, shielding her from harm. It gave her a warm feeling to know someone wanted to keep her safe. Her father came on the line and they talked for a few moments before he signed off, reminding her they were only a phone call away.

Natalie finished her tea and went into the garden to find Matt. He was struggling to plant a bushy – and spiky – cotoneaster. A line of the prickly, but pretty, shrubs had been chosen to provide secure border hedging.

Matt finally wrestled the shrub into place and wiped the sweat from his brow. The day was the hottest yet and Natalie didn't envy him his job. He looked at his watch. 'I thought the time must have passed more quickly than I thought, but it's you who's early. Your bank run out of money or something?' he grinned.

'No, nothing like that. I...I had a bad headache and called it a day.' She shielded her eyes from the sun and gazed across the garden. 'You're doing wonders, Matt. It's hard to remember this was once more like a field than a garden.'

'It was a field for years. I doubt it was ever a garden for the farmer. From what I can tell they had a kitchen garden over that side,' he said, pointing to the area nearest to the kitchen, 'and the rest was left for chickens and any other animals they had.' He leant on his spade and squinted at her. 'How's the head now?'

'Better, thanks. But I think I'll lie down for a while. Shall I see you in the morning?'

'For sure. Hope you feel better.'

Natalie smiled and returned indoors. The sun's glare had made her head throb again. She went upstairs and stripped to her underwear before slipping between the cool sheets. She fell asleep almost instantly.

It was still light when Natalie woke, feeling refreshed but hungry. As she swung her legs out of bed her stomach rumbled, making her laugh. It wasn't surprising, she thought, as she'd skipped lunch.

There was little in the fridge and Natalie rummaged in the freezer to find something she could microwave back to life. Telling herself she had to start cooking properly or she would put on pounds, she pricked the film on the container and placed it in the microwave. A few minutes later the ping announced its readiness. Not even bothering to serve it on a plate, Natalie placed the carton on a tray with a glass of wine and went outside. The sun had lost its heat and intensity making it pleasant to sit on the terrace. Her head had cleared and the aroma of chicken cooked in red wine, complete with mash potatoes and green beans, was enticing. It actually tasted quite good, too. Particularly when washed down with a glass of wine. The only problem was the portion was too small and she went inside for a plate of cheese and biscuits.

By now the sun was dipping towards the horizon and the sky was illuminated by huge streaks of gold, orange and purple. Natalie was transfixed, for a moment forgetting to eat. The beauty and magnificence of the sight touched her soul. In spite of all that had happened, she was glad to be back on this gem of an island. Her roots lay here, generations of her family had breathed the same air, walked by the same sea. Some had actually sailed on it as fishermen. Perhaps others had been farmers. It was possible, even likely, for there had been little other work for islanders until the growing industry, followed by the arrival of tourism and now the finance industry. She sighed, swirling the wine in her glass, feeling a measure of peace after the events of the previous day. The only problem remaining was her unwelcome 'ghost'. The doorbell interrupted her musings and she immediately tensed. As she neared the front door Stuart's voice called out, 'It's only me, Natalie,' and she breathed a sigh of relief.

'Hi, sorry to be so late calling round, but I wanted to check you were okay.' He proffered a bottle of wine.

Natalie laughed. 'This is becoming something of a habit! I do hope you don't think I'm an alcoholic.' She let him in and led the way to the kitchen. 'I've got a bottle open if you'd like a glass? Or there's lager.'

'Wine's fine, thanks. It's been a long day.' He pulled out a stool. 'So, have you recovered from your ordeal?' He looked serious as she poured the wine.

'I guess, but it's been a strange old day. I couldn't get Liam out of my head at work and left early and ended up sleeping for a couple of hours. Feeling better now. What about you?' She sat down.

'It was a struggle for me, too. I felt as if I'd had a really bad dream. It was only when I called in at the police station that it became real.' He sipped his wine. 'Even though I knew I'd done nothing wrong, I felt like a criminal reporting in.'

'They're not my favourite places, either. But that should be it now. And to thank you for the trouble I've caused you, I'd like to invite you to supper one evening. Whenever it suits.'

His eyes widened.

'That's kind of you, but it's not necessary. I was only too happy to be of use.'

'Be that as it may, I owe you. What night would suit you best?'

'Well, Friday would. I'm working late every other night this week.'

Natalie was surprised at how pleased she was.

'Great. Let's say seven thirty and we'll eat outside, weather permitting.'

Stuart drained his glass and stood. 'I look forward to it. I'll leave you in peace now, but do shout if you need anything. I've still got the shining armour ready burnished if needed.' His lips twitched, and she laughed as she escorted him to the door. He gave her a quick peck on the cheek and left.

Back in the kitchen she topped up her wine. As she raised it to her lips, a voice behind her hissed, 'Go away' and Stuart's empty glass fell off the worktop onto the floor and shattered. Holding her breath, she turned her head. No-one. But a cold draught on her shoulders made her shiver. And there was an odd smell. Of farm. Animals and manure.

'Go away yourself! Whoever you are, leave me alone. This is my home now, not yours.' She gulped her wine, wishing Stuart had been there as witness. Natalie was tempted to ring him but what would be the point? Something more concrete than a broken glass would be needed to show him something was amiss. As she swept up the broken pieces she realised she'd learnt something new about the 'ghost'. It had definitely been a man's voice.

Natalie woke reluctantly to the alarm the next morning after a restless night. Her dreams had been disturbing but not as 'real' as before. She had vague memories of angry voices and slamming doors. It was becoming clear to her the previous occupants had had a stormy relationship and assumed they must have been Stuart's grandparents. What a pity he had no way of knowing how they fared as a couple. Natalie dragged herself out of bed, determined not to give in to whoever didn't like her presence. With all the trauma of Liam's unexpected arrival, she had forgotten to phone Andy, and made a note to do so later.

Matt arrived as she was leaving and they exchanged brief greetings. Judging by the amount of shrubs in the pickup, he was in for another back-breaking day. Once in the office Natalie phoned Andy and he offered to call in after work on Wednesday. Switching off her phone, she concentrated on catching up with her work.

Later in the afternoon the sergeant phoned to say Liam was being escorted to England on the next flight to Gatwick with a recommendation from the medic he be subjected to a psychiatrist's evaluation before standing trial.

'I'm afraid you will need to attend the trial unless he pleads guilty, which he might do if there's a psychiatrist's report in his favour. But nothing's likely to happen for months. The wheels of justice grind much slower in the UK than here.'

Her heart sank at the thought, and prayed he'd plead guilty. After thanking the sergeant, she rushed off to a team meeting, giving her no time to dwell on it.

On Wednesday Andy arrived in a sporty little number as Natalie was unlocking the front door.

They shook hands and she led the way into the kitchen.

'Thanks for coming, Andy. Would you like a drink? Tea, coffee or something stronger?'

'Tea's fine, thanks.' He placed a folder on the dining table and gazed around. 'Are you happy with the design? Anything you'd have liked different?'

'Totally happy. I've told everyone what a brilliant job you've done and I'm equally impressed with Stuart's barn.' She smiled at him and switched on the kettle.

'Good, I was worried there was something wrong.' He pushed his hair back behind his ears and grinned.

'Not with the design, no. But I do have a...a problem and I'm hoping you can help.'

'If I can. Sounds a bit mysterious.'

Natalie joined him at the table, carrying two mugs of tea.

'It is a bit.' She motioned for him to sit down. 'I'd like to know what the old farmhouse looked like when you first saw it. I know it was badly damaged but could you make out the layout?'

'The first floor was missing but the outside walls were still standing together with the ground-floor internal walls. Plus part of the stone staircase.' He opened the folder. 'Here's the photos I took and the plan I drew of what I thought it must have looked like. I needed the information when I submitted my own plans for the rebuild.' He spread the photos on the table and opened out the plan.

Natalie picked up the photos one by one. It was both odd and fascinating to see how the house had looked. Or rather, what had been left of it after the ravages of fire. Blackened grey granite walls and burnt-out windows and missing doors. It looked much smaller than it was now. She looked at the plan.

'You've changed the configuration a bit, haven't you? The front door used to go straight into what's now my study. And the back door was,' she turned round to check, 'where my fridge-freezer is now.'

'That's right. The old house was placed at a slightly different angle and didn't get the most of either the view or the sun in the main rooms. Where your sitting room is now, was probably the best parlour which was little used and had only a small window. This area here,' he waved his arm to encompass the dining area, 'would have been a separate dining room but much smaller. As was the kitchen, which is still roughly in the same spot. Your back door,' he nodded to the stable-door behind her, 'didn't exist. The original staircase was in a different place, too.' Andy pointed to the photo showing the remains of the original stone staircase.

'Fascinating.' She picked up one of the photos. 'This was the kitchen? Was that the range?' She pointed to a blackened object.

'Yes, it had survived more or less intact. Apparently when the fire brigade arrived they found the flames strongest in the kitchen, suggesting it was where the fire had started.'

Natalie tapped her lips. The photo showed the range in the same position as in both her dream and the misty image of the old kitchen. Any cupboards had been destroyed but she did remember a door being where the opening was in the photo. It did look as if she had 'seen' the original kitchen. The thought gave her goosebumps.

'Everything okay?'

She looked up and saw Andy staring at her.

'I think so. This is going to sound completely daft, but I dreamt about the old kitchen, as it was when Mrs Falla lived here. Or rather, I wasn't sure it was the original one until you showed me the photos and your plan. A bit spooky, really.' She shivered.

His eyes widened but he answered calmly. 'I see now why you wanted us to meet. When I took on the project from Mrs Cross, Stuart's mum, people told me the place was haunted. Rumour had it bad things had happened here, but no-one knew what, apart from the fire and the disappearance of Mrs Falla. The farm had bad vibes.'

Natalie nodded.

'Obviously something awful did happen: the fire nearly destroyed the farm. But I thought it was considered an accident.'

'That's the official view, yes. But you know how superstitious Guerns are, and how they love creating mysteries out of anything.' He laughed. 'Some folk still believe fairies congregate at the Faerie Ring in Pleinmont!' Andy must have seen her pensive expression as he stopped laughing and said, 'Has something upset you?'

'Let's say I'm getting the impression all was not sweetness and light chez the Fallas. But I still love the house.' She smiled brightly at him, thinking she'd said too much already.

Andy's drawn brows showed he wasn't convinced but tactfully, he left it at that.

Standing, he asked if she would like to keep the photos and his drawings for a bit longer, saying he'd be happy for her to make copies.

'That's great, thanks. I'll get the originals back to you soon. Has Stuart seen them?' She started gathering the photos into a pile.

'Probably not, he wasn't here at the time. Well, I'll be on my way unless you've more questions?'

Natalie shook her head. 'You've been very helpful, Andy. Thanks again for sparing me the time.'

They walked towards the front door.

'Jeanne said you were married last December. Congratulations.' She opened the door and he slipped outside.

'Thank you, I've been very lucky.'

Natalie waved him off and returned to the kitchen. This time she poured herself a glass of wine before sitting at the table and sifting through the photos. She was unsure whether or not to be relieved the kitchen in her dream (most definitely not her dream kitchen!) was a real one. Or had been until the '80s. Could this mean, as her mother had suggested, the stones had retained the memory of the goings on in the original house? And, if so, would they be able to 'show' her what had really happened to old Mrs Falla? Or would she relive it in a dream? Either way, Natalie guessed it would be an experience she'd rather avoid.

chapter seventeen

2010

The next few days passed without anything unusual happening. Natalie wanted to believe she was now free of her 'ghost' but a nagging voice in her brain advised caution. She amused herself planning what to cook on Friday evening, acknowledging even the most exquisite ready-meals produced by Waitrose would be a no-no. On Wednesday she had visited her parents in order to borrow some of her mother's extensive recipe collection. Many had a French flavour and had featured in Jeanne's first book, *Recipes for Love*, a bestselling mix of local and French recipes, served up with her grandmother's ill-fated love story.

Her menu planned, she bought the ingredients on Thursday after work. The weather promised to continue hot and dry and this gave her the perfect excuse to cook something simple but elegant. Her mother had drummed into her that presentation was crucial. Natalie chose a confit of duck salad, followed by scallops in ginger and rounded off with cheese and biscuits and summer fruit pavlova. She saved time by preparing what she could that evening and then rustled up a chicken stir-fry for supper. The sense of achievement felt good. She couldn't remember how long it had been since she had cooked from scratch. When she'd had boyfriends they usually ate out. Much more relaxing than cooking.

She sat outside and admired her almost finished garden as she ate. Matt wouldn't be back after tomorrow until the replacement pond liner arrived. To her right was the area as yet undug for the pond, looking drab next to the shrubs and plants springing up around her. Once the garden was completely finished, Natalie planned to invite her family and friends around for a party. She might even cook the food herself. Although if there were a lot of guests, perhaps it would be better to buy ready-prepared party food. Mustn't get too ambitious, she told herself. Later that evening Natalie went to bed with a light heart, looking forward to supper with Stuart.

Stuart checked himself in the mirror for the umpteenth time. He wanted to look cool and debonair but it wasn't happening. His usual cropped chinos didn't equate to debonair or sophisticated, only casual. And slogan T-shirts – well! He rummaged around in his wardrobe and dug out a pair of cream linen slacks he'd bought for a special occasion now long-forgotten, and not worn since. Another rummage and he pulled out a deep blue cotton shirt which matched his eyes. Hmm. Not bad, fella! You can scrub up well when you want. He grinned at his reflection in the mirror. It had been years since he'd had an intimate dinner with a woman, except Pam…Stuart sighed. He needed to get out more, but at thirty-eight felt ancient compared to the young men he saw out on the pull in the pubs. Not that he was much of a pub man, but a couple of his younger colleagues had dragged him out to The Cock and Bull in St Peter Port for a live music night. He hadn't appreciated the music – too off the wall for his taste – and they hadn't repeated the invite.

He ran down the stairs and picked up a bottle of wine and a bunch of freesias from the kitchen. Two minutes later he rang Natalie's doorbell. When she opened the door his pulse quickened. Not a good thing for a not-a-date meal together. But Natalie looked stunning in a white gypsy blouse and short denim skirt, her skin glowing from the sun. Stuart gulped.

'Hi, I come bearing gifts.' He offered the flowers and wine.

'That's very sweet of you, Stuart, but you know you shouldn't have. You've been more than generous. Please,' she stepped back, 'come in and let me get you a drink. It's been so hot today, hasn't it?'

Natalie put the flowers in water and poured two glasses of Prosecco.

'I thought some bubbly was just the thing on a summer's evening. Hope you like it.'

He would have drunk anything she offered.

They clinked glasses and Natalie suggested they go through to the terrace. The table was already set and she added the vase of freesias, smiling.

'I love freesias, they're my favourite flowers. Both their colours and heady perfume epitomises Guernsey for me. On the few occasions I was homesick in England, I'd buy a bunch to cheer myself up.' She drew a deep breath from the flowers and let out an appreciative sigh.

'It was a lucky choice of mine, then. My mother always liked them, too, even though she had no fond memories of Guernsey. I always thought that odd.' He crossed his legs and leant back in the chair, allowing the wine to ease his nerves. 'How have you been this week? Recovered from Sunday's drama?'

Natalie bit her lip.

'I've been okay, thanks. The sergeant said I'd be needed at Liam's trial, which is a horrible thought. Did he say the same thing to you?'

'Yes, I'm considered a vital witness. At least if he doesn't plead guilty, I'll be there to give you moral support.'

She brightened.

'Well, that's good to know. But let's hope it doesn't come to it.' She stood, saying she would fetch the starters.

Stuart was left to his thoughts, solely centred on his hostess. He had come to realise under Natalie's outward display of self-confidence, was a vulnerable woman. He wanted to protect her. Stuart told himself not to be so stupid, Natalie was still a strong, intelligent woman, and why would she want a schoolteacher as a partner? He swallowed his wine too quickly and spluttered.

'You okay?' She put a plate in front of him and sat down.

He nodded, trying to catch his breath and pointed to his glass.

'Went down the wrong way? Happens to me, too.' She waited until he'd got his breath back and added, 'Please start when you're ready.'

'Looks delicious.' He meant it. If Natalie was a good cook he could at least enjoy the meal even if she showed no interest in him.

They concentrated on their food, making the odd comment about the weather and the garden. Natalie asked him to give her a hand bringing out the main course and they collected plates and covered dishes from the kitchen.

'Wonderful smell! Ginger, isn't it?' He lifted off the lids to serve. Plump, juicy scallops sprinkled with herbs lay in a light sauce. Another dish held rice and a third a colourful mix of stir-fried vegetables.

'Hope you like it, I haven't tried this recipe before, but Mum's cooked it for the family and I always loved it.'

The first mouthful made him smile.

'Absolutely delicious. You've gone to so much trouble–'

Natalie shook her head. 'Nonsense! If it hadn't been for you, I might not even be here, remember. And I thought it was about time I did some proper cooking. I've lived off ready-meals for too long.' She took her first bite.

'Not bad.' She looked up and grinned. 'Now, how about telling me a bit more about yourself? What happened to spur you on to move here?'

'Similar to you, I guess. I lived with Pam for some years and we bought a house together. We were both teachers at the same school and I thought we'd be a couple forever, marry and have kids.' He frowned as the memory caused the familiar nag of pain. 'There was a...problem and then, out of the blue, she told me she'd fallen for someone else and left. And never came back. I had to pack her stuff and have it sent to her new place. The one she shared with...him.' He ground his teeth. Why had he never gone round and punched the bloke on the nose? Too much of a wimp, that's why. And embarrassed at the reason Pam left...

Natalie's eyes narrowed.

'How awful for you. I've never been deeply in love with anyone, though I did *think* I was with Liam. Looking back I realise it was infatuation, like my other relationships. But it must be horrible to love someone who walks out like that. Have you moved on?'

'I'm getting there. It's been a year so...' he shrugged. 'Coming here has helped because it holds no memories. The ultimate fresh start.'

She nodded, chewing her food.

Neither seemed to know how to continue the conversation and they ate in silence. Stuart kicked himself for lowering the mood of the evening. He should have prevaricated, said it was personal. But he believed in honesty, no matter the consequences.

'I'm sorry, Stuart, I shouldn't have pried. And now you'll be miserable for the rest of the evening and it's my fault.' Natalie's mouth drooped.

'Hey, don't blame yourself. I'm fine, really I am. Just get a bit maudlin at times. How about we forget my past and talk about something more cheerful? Like, do you have a holiday planned this summer?'

She smiled and his heart flipped.

'As it happens, no. It doesn't seem much point spending a fortune travelling hours to somewhere hot and sunny when it's the same here.' She waved her arms, embracing the sea sparkling under the descending sun. 'I'll book something later, autumn or winter. What about you?'

'I'm stuck with the school holidays, which is a bit of a bummer. But like you, I don't see the point of going away in the summer. I thought I'd go to Italy at half-term, see the sights and enjoy decent weather.'

Natalie asked him about his favourite places to visit and the conversation perked up. Before long they had finished the main course and Stuart helped her clear the table ready for dessert. Another bottle of wine was opened. He was becoming mellow and he sensed Natalie was as well. He even managed a couple of jokes as they ate the pavlova, and she broke into giggles. It set him off and they both ended up in fits of laughter.

She wiped her eyes.

'That one about the pig's one of the best I've heard in a long while. You're a natural, Stuart. Do you tell jokes to your students?'

He glowed. 'Sometimes. History can be a bit dull at times and I need to keep the students engaged. I find the *Blackadder* series gives me loads of inspiration.'

'They're brilliant, aren't they? I've watched the DVDs loads of times.'

This set off a discussion about which series were their favourites, continued over cheese and biscuits. The sun had set and Natalie lit citronella candles in enormous storm lanterns, creating a soft-lit ambience. Stuart couldn't help comparing Natalie's terrace with his own – a boring small table with two chairs. No plants or lights. Nothing. He must do something about it.

'I love what you've achieved in your garden, and this terrace in particular. Would you be willing to give me some tips? Like where to buy pots and which plants would be best?'

Natalie, her face cast in the warm glow of the lamps, smiled.

'Sure. I've got no plans for tomorrow, so if you're free why don't we head to the garden centre at Le Friquet? They have a fantastic range.'

'Suits me fine. How about the afternoon?' The thought of spending more time with Natalie was heady. They were only looking at plants and things but still...

A time was agreed and Natalie suggested a nightcap. They cleared the remains of the food and returned with glasses of Calvados. The night air was balmy and the candles kept the insects at bay. The sound of the soft whoosh of the sea and the occasional screech of an owl were the only sounds. Stuart was in heaven. If only...

Natalie yawned.

'Sorry, it's been quite a week. Do you mind if we call it a night? I've had a lovely evening and even enjoyed my own cooking for once.' She laughed.

He stood. 'I've enjoyed it too and the food was great. Can I help with the washing-up?'

'No need, the dishwasher will swallow everything.'

They headed into the kitchen with their glasses and Natalie went with him to the front door. Stuart wanted to kiss her properly on the lips, but was it being presumptive? He settled for a double kiss on her cheeks, which she reciprocated. He did manage to hold her in his arms for a moment longer than was strictly necessary, but Natalie didn't object.

'Night then. I'll see you tomorrow.' He let go reluctantly.

'Goodnight. Sleep well.' Her eyes seemed enormous in the dim light of the porch and he took a deep breath. He'd definitely fallen for her. As he headed homewards Stuart wasn't sure if this was a good or bad thing.

Natalie loaded the dishwasher in pensive mood. The evening had been a great success: the food had turned out well and Stuart had proved to be fun. Not only fun, but he'd sparked a flicker of desire in her body, not experienced since she first met Liam. She could drown in those eyes! Natalie slammed the door shut and switched on the machine, telling herself she wasn't up for a relationship. She was beginning to get her life back on track and it felt good. Why mess it up with a man? Particularly the neighbour. If it went tits-up it would be mighty awkward. Shaking her head she went upstairs, overwhelmed by tiredness. She was bound to feel different in the morning, copious alcohol had probably played havoc with her hormones.

chapter eighteen

1941–1942

The year dragged painfully towards the end, the biting cold draining Olive's energy, together with her fellow islanders. Supplies struggled to get through from France leaving the shops virtually empty. It was set to be a miserable Christmas and Olive took the bold decision to spend it with her mother rather than Bill. She didn't expect to be missed and knew there'd be no exchange of presents, just like the last time. They'd given up any pretence of caring about each other; the farm and the animals were all that kept them under the same roof.

On Christmas Eve Olive told Bill she'd be leaving for her mother's after the morning milking the next day. He would need to take over the evening session.

'Don't worry, I'll be back early on Boxing Day for the milking and I'll leave you some fresh soup to heat up and there's cake in the larder.'

Bill looked up from his plate of vegetables and a thin slice of ham, his fork held out in front of him.

'Soup? Is that all you can offer me at Christmas? Where's the meat and veg?' His eyebrows were drawn together in a scowl.

'I'm sorry, Bill, but I couldn't get any in Town, the butcher had sold out before I reached the end of the queue. It's the same for everyone, you only have to ask around.'

He grunted and continued chewing the meagre supper, washed down with weak beer. As they went upstairs to their respective bedrooms, he said, grabbing her arm, 'Just you make sure you're back early for the milking. There'll be trouble for you if you're not.' Olive nodded and slipped into her room, thankful to be having a whole day and night away from him.

Olive cycled along the coast road towards her mother's farm, a freezing wind bringing tears to her eyes. Wearing her thickest clothes, she still felt the numbing cold. The time spent in the barn milking the cows hadn't helped and the heavy, threatening sky looming above matched her mood. At least it wasn't raining and her mum had promised to have the fire going for when she arrived. A kind neighbour had given Edith some logs from old trees they'd cut down and the house promised to be warmer than her own. Smoke curled from the chimney as she arrived in the yard and she smiled. Mum had been up early as promised. She stored her bike in the woodshed and went through the back door into the kitchen. The fire sparked and spat in the large inglenook and Edith, sitting in her chair, had set up a spit on irons. The smell of roasting chicken wafted towards her and her stomach rumbled as she moved towards the fire. Her mother looked more content than for a long time.

'Happy Christmas, Mum. My, what a treat! I never thought we'd have chicken.' She bent down to kiss her mother who tapped her nose, smiling.

'I managed to barter for it with some of the wood. It was an old bird so might be a bit tough, but better than nothing, eh? You've brought the veg and potatoes?' Olive nodded, holding up her sack, thankful as ever that she could grow them and not have to compete with other housewives for the little in the shops.

'We'll have a feast, Mum. I've made a version of carrot cake that doesn't taste too bad and I've brought some whipped cream to go with it.' She sighed, adding, 'Wish we could have a proper Christmas cake like you used to make, loaded with fruit and soaked in brandy. Going without makes you appreciate what you used to have, doesn't it?' Olive peeled off the layers and started preparing the vegetables while her mother made cups of bramble tea. The vegetables ready, she joined Edith by the fire and drank her tea, mesmerised by the revolving chicken crisping on the spit.

The dinner, poor by their old standards, tasted delicious and they chatted over old times, relaxed in the warmth of the kitchen. In the evening Edith produced some oat biscuits and a piece of ham, saying she had something special to wash it down. Olive was intrigued. Had her mother bought some black-market alcohol? Edith took two cut glass tumblers from the dresser and rooted around in the bottom cupboard, lifting out a bottle of the single malt Olive's father used to drink.

'I never used to be fond of whisky myself, but I tried a wee drop the other night and I've discovered a taste for it. It'll put a fire in our bellies, for sure.' She poured a small measure in each glass and passed one to Olive.

'Merry Christmas!'

They touched glasses. Olive had never tried whisky either, but as the smooth peaty liquid flowed down her throat, she enjoyed the sensation of warmth and ease it produced. The whisky, soon topped up, made them maudlin and Edith told Olive of how she and Larry had met and the days of their courtship. By the time she'd finished, they were both wiping tears from their eyes, before reaching again for the whisky. Finally, feeling tipsy, Olive roused herself to stand up, saying, 'I'd best be off to bed, Mum. I've to leave as soon as the curfew finishes at six, to milk the cows. You have a lie-in and I'll be back soon.'

The next morning Olive woke to find her mother shaking her.

'Wake up, girl! It's gone seven!'

Olive opened her eyes and groaned. Her head pounded and her mouth tasted horrible. Trying hard to focus on her mother's anxious face, realisation dawned. 'The cows! Oh my God! The cows!' She scrabbled around for her clothes and her mother left her to dress. Two minutes later she was downstairs and splashing her face in cold water at the kitchen sink.

'I've made some tea–'

'Thanks, Mum, but I'd better go. You take care of yourself, all right?' They kissed goodbye and Olive rushed outside and dragged her bike out of the shed. As she jumped on the saddle her heart thumped in her chest. Bill wouldn't be best pleased.

As soon as Olive opened the barn door she knew she was in trouble. The cows stood in their stalls, contentedly chewing on their feed. Bill must have finished the milking!

Her heart in her boots, she pushed open the kitchen door. Bill turned in his chair and stood up. His face was puce as he advanced towards her.

'Bill, I'm so sorry–'

He threw a vicious punch at her and she fell onto the granite floor, barely conscious. She tasted bile in her mouth and wanted to be sick.

'I told you to be back in time, didn't I? Don't say I didn't warn you. I'm off now and I expect a meal on the table when I come back tonight.' She felt his boot land hard on her hip and bit back a groan, trying to appear unconscious. A minute later she heard him pick up his coat and slam the door behind him. Olive lay still for a moment longer before she pulled herself up, staggered to the sink, and was promptly relieved of yesterday's meal. She drank a glass of water and refilled it. Her head felt as if it had been crushed between two unyielding forces and her legs were refusing to support her weight. Stumbling to Bill's chair, she held her head in her hands as the tears fell. She knew she only had herself to blame, but the message was clear. From now on she'd have to tread carefully with Bill – or else.

The winter dragged on and Olive kept away from her husband as much as possible. She went about her chores with a hardness in her heart, knowing she had no choice. In March she was round her mother's one day when Edith showed her the local paper.

'See that? What's the world come to when they arrest our policemen.'

Olive read of the arrest of eighteen Guernsey policemen accused of stealing from the stores of rations for both Germans and locals and selling the goods on the black market. She looked up, shocked. 'Surely this can't be true? Those men wouldn't steal from their own. Do you think this is some made-up charge by the Germans?'

Edith pursed her lips.

'It's what I've heard, except they *did* take the supplies, but only as revenge against the Germans. They hid all the goods they took and didn't sell them. Wonder who tipped off the Germans, eh?' She shook her head. 'Hunger and greed make bad bed-fellows in times like this. By the time this war is ended, a lot of bad apples will be found, you mark my words. We're all being tested and I'm not sure what will become of our islands when it's over. Not that I'm likely to be around to see it,' she added, quietly.

'Mum! Don't say that! You've seemed better lately and you're no age yet.'

Edith twisted her hands and Olive noticed how the veins stood out against the pale skin. Giving her a closer look she realised the clothes were hanging a bit looser than a few weeks ago. 'Mum, are you ill?'

'I...I don't feel like I should. I get tired more quickly and my appetite's not what it was. Not that anyone has much to eat, of course.' She smiled wanly.

A spasm of fear clutched at Olive's stomach. Having become such friends only recently, she realised how much she *needed* her mother. She was all she had.

'Have you seen the doctor?'

'You know I don't hold much truck with doctors and anyways, he'd be far too busy seeing people who are really ill. I'll pick up again in the spring, when it's warmer. I never was one for winters.'

Olive had to be content with that; her mother could be stubborn as she well knew. But she'd keep a watchful eye on her, all the same.

By May, the island was blooming; in the woods and hedgerows, nestled amongst primroses and wild garlic, bluebells waved their dainty heads in the breeze. Olive loved to see the wild flowers and would pick bunches to brighten up her kitchen. They never lasted long, though, and she was constantly replacing them. Sometimes when on her bike to collect the rations, she would head out extra early, making for the cliffs of Torteval to enjoy the sight of the yellow gorse, phlox and tiny violets nestling in the grass. One particular day, she arrived to find her usual lane blocked by what looked at first glance to be a ghostly mob of departed souls. Blinking, she realised, to her horror, they were living men, more skeletal than human, whose rags barely covered their bodies, exposing their grey flesh. A plump, officious-looking man wearing a brown uniform she'd never seen before, headed towards her, waving his arms. A badge bearing the letters 'OT' was sewn on his tunic and he was gripping a baton in his hand.

'This area it is *verboten*, we are to build here a *Geschützstellung*. You must leave.'

'But...but who are these poor men?'

'Slave workers, scum. You do not need to worry about them. *Bitte*, go.'

Throwing a last glance at the men, who looked at her with deadened eyes, she mounted her bike and rode along the Route de Pleinmont, heading for St Peter Port. Olive felt chilled suddenly, even though the day was warm. She had known the slave workers had been arriving in large numbers over the past months, but hadn't seen any, giving them little thought. Clearly they were ill-fed and probably beaten, by the look of them. Pity flowed through her. They shared something in common, but at least she still had hope for release one day, unlike the poor devils being worked to certain death.

One day in June Olive came back from Town and showed Bill the latest edition of *The Star*.

'It says there's to be a permanent ban on all radios from now, on pain of imprisonment or death. So it's going to be even harder to know what's happening in the war.'

'That new underground newsletter which started last month will keep going I reckon. There'll always be someone with a set. We'd better hand ours in, I don't want to end up in prison.'

Olive reluctantly agreed. They'd handed in their wireless at various times since the invasion, but had always had them handed back after a few months. She'd miss listening to the news and the music programmes, but it wasn't worth risking going to prison – or worse – for. She'd pop into her mother's and tell her. Edith wasn't going out much these days and Olive was worried about her.

Later that day, after the milking, Olive rode up to her mother's farm. Along the way she saw gangs of slave workers toiling on the new railway, sweat pouring from their emaciated bodies. Men in the now-hated brown uniforms watched with steely eyes, and beat anyone who appeared to be slacking. Olive felt sick. There was little she or anyone else could do. If an islander was caught feeding or sheltering the POWs, they faced imprisonment or death. The Germans saw such aid as treason, while the islanders viewed it as compassion for men on their own side. Olive knew she wasn't brave enough to take risks and the shame sat heavy with her. She was still heavy-hearted when she arrived at Edith's.

She found her mother in her usual place in the kitchen, dozing in her chair. Edith sat up, startled, when she called out, 'Hello, Mum. It's only me.'

'Oh, hello, love. I wasn't expecting you and was having a little nap. Everything all right?'

Olive searched her mother's face. She did look pale, but didn't seem to have lost any more weight. She gave her the copy of the paper and turned to put the kettle on. Once the tea was made she sat down by her side.

'How are you keeping, Mum? You're a bit pale, today.'

'I'm all right, there's no need to fuss. I just get tired, as I've told you before. All I need is to rest and I'll be fine.'

'Hmm. I've brought you a cake and a couple of spider crabs, should help to build up your strength. Wish we could get proper fish, but there's little in the shops now.' She sipped her tea, frowning. Her mother was not being truthful, she was sure. 'Do you want me to hand in your wireless, Mum? Save you a trip.'

Edith nodded.

'Thanks, love. I shall miss it, though.' She coughed into her hand. 'Them devils are really turning the screws on us, aren't they? Don't want us to know what's really happening out there and don't mind if we starve,' she said, shaking her head in despair.

Olive left an hour later with the wireless tucked into the basket and cycled home no more cheerful than when she left home. She had a bad feeling about her mother and couldn't shake it off.

Summer eased into autumn and still the islanders suffered. The latest upset happened in September when all English-born islanders were rounded up to be interned in German camps. Olive was particularly upset and shocked as Nell's father was one of them. Although he'd lived on the island since a boy, he'd been born in England to English parents who moved to Guernsey before the Great War. She went round to comfort Nell, who was devastated, worried she'd never see her father again. Olive left her weeping into a sodden handkerchief, unable to offer any meaningful words of comfort. How could she? The Nazis weren't renowned for treating prisoners properly, that she did know. The Germans on the islands weren't Nazis and on the whole behaved decently, but still people were being sent to prisons and camps and the convicted policemen were rumoured to have been tortured before being sent to prisons abroad. Olive's fears for her mother's health also continued to press heavily on her. The only ray of comfort was that Bill hadn't raised a hand to her since Christmas and spent more time away from home. Olive sent up a prayer of thanks to whoever was fulfilling his needs and calming his temper.

By November Olive knew Edith was dying. No longer able to leave her bed except for short periods, her mother looked more and more like the ghostly slave workers she'd seen. Edith had repeatedly refused to send for the doctor, but Olive took it upon herself to cycle to his house in Cobo and ask him to call. He arranged to visit the next morning and Olive would meet him there.

One of the few civilians allowed to keep his car, Doctor Le Cras drove into the yard soon after Olive arrived. She took him upstairs. Outside the bedroom door, she whispered, 'Mum doesn't know I fetched you, she keeps refusing to see you. So I'm sorry if she's not best pleased, but I've been so worried.'

He nodded as he squeezed her arm and they went in together. Her mother lay moaning in the bed and, to Olive's surprise, didn't make a fuss when the doctor sat down next to her and started talking. Olive moved into the shadows, trying to be invisible but wanting to hear what was being said. But her mother's voice was too soft to carry far and she only heard the doctor's questions. He asked to examine her and gently ran his hands over

Edith's thin body. After a few more words he stood up, and turned to face Olive, his face grave. Motioning her to the door, they walked onto the landing.

'I'm afraid it's cancer and it's so far advanced there's nothing I can do. I'm so sorry, Olive. I think your mother's given up since your father died and hasn't wanted to get better. She's known for more than a year it was serious.'

Olive's hand shot to her mouth.

'More than a year? Oh, my God! I should have done something, called you sooner–'

He took her arm, saying, 'Even if you had, it might not have made any difference. We have few appropriate medicines and even surgery may not have been the solution. All I can do now is give her some morphine for the pain. And as we only have a limited supply of that...' he shrugged, helpless.

Olive understood. Awful as it seemed, it would be better if her mother died before the morphine ran out. She brushed away the tears before going back into the bedroom with him. The doctor had a word with Edith, then took a syringe and a small bottle out of his bag. After giving her the injection, he stood, saying, 'I'll be back tomorrow and you should be able to sleep now.'

He said goodbye to Olive and left. She sat on the edge of the bed and took her mother's hand.

'Why didn't you tell me, Mum? Why?'

Edith gazed at her with sorrow-filled eyes.

'You know why, love. My only regret is leaving you on your own. It wouldn't have been so bad if you'd got a good husband to take care of you, but you've only that bully who's not fit to lick your boots.' She paused, taking a deep breath. 'And I wish I knew Ross was safe, but there'll be no news until this blasted war is over. This'll be his farm one day, but if he...doesn't come back, then rightfully it'll come to you.'

Olive hushed her. 'Mum, don't wear yourself out worrying about me and Ross. You rest now. Is the morphine working?'

'Yes, the pain's easing. You'd best be going back before the next milking.'

Olive thought quickly.

'I'll go home to fetch some things. Bill can look after the animals for a while. I'm not leaving you alone, Mum, not now. You have a sleep and I'll be back before you know it.' Her mother's eyes were closing as she spoke and she ran downstairs and jumped onto her bike. At home she found Bill repairing a section of wall which had collapsed in a gale and told him about her mother. He wasn't happy about her going back, but could hardly refuse and she wouldn't have taken any notice if he had. Olive threw some clothes and food into a bag and rode back as fast as she could. Her mother was fast asleep when she tiptoed into the bedroom, her expression peaceful, free of pain. Biting her lip, Olive returned downstairs and built up a fire. Her mother's bedroom, immediately above the kitchen, would be warmed by the heat travelling up the chimney.

After a restless night, disturbed by dreams full of grey-faced slave workers advancing towards her, arms outstretched and mouths wide in silent supplication, Olive woke in a panic. Her mother! Shivering with the cold, she pulled on a dressing gown and stepped across the landing to her mother's room. Pale morning light glimmered through the gaps in the curtains, casting eerie shadows across the bed. Hardly daring to breathe, Olive tiptoed across the room. Hearing the sound of soft breathing, she relaxed. The prone figure neatly tucked under the bedclothes looked as if she hadn't stirred all night. Thank heavens for the morphine!

Washed and dressed, Olive went down the stairs to the kitchen to find a glimmer of embers in the fireplace. Quickly adding more wood, she stoked up the fire before putting the kettle on. Fed up with bramble tea she made some parsnip coffee, not much of an improvement, but better than nothing. Breakfast was porridge, which Olive sprinkled with cinnamon for flavour. She made enough for Edith, too, but didn't want to disturb her so covered a bowl for later. Once she'd finished her coffee, Olive picked up an old copy of *The Star* left by the fire and went to sit by her mother. Edith was still asleep, and occasionally muttered something unintelligible, as if in a dream. Olive picked up her hand and kissed it. It promised to be a long day.

Doctor Le Cras called in later that morning and seemed satisfied that Edith was still sleeping. He told Olive he'd be back the next day but she was to call him if her mother woke in pain. The day limped onwards and Olive took a turn around the yard to get some fresh air, away from the smell of impending death. She recognised it from when her father had died and shuddered, pulling her coat tighter round her body. As she circumnavigated the yard, surrounded by now empty barns, Olive pondered on the future. If Ross came back, he'd have an uphill task getting the farm back on its feet and wondered if he'd bother. All the animals had been taken in by neighbouring farmers after Larry died, except for a few chickens. Once Edith had taken to her bed, Olive had taken them home with her. The eerie silence of the once bustling farm made her want to weep. It had been handed down over the generations and now...? Olive didn't allow herself to think about the possibility of her inheriting. She didn't want another death in the family, even her brother didn't deserve that. And in the short-term – or longer if they won the war – the Germans would commandeer it and fill her old home with soldiers. The hateful thought drove her back indoors for a quick warm by the fire before going upstairs.

Olive spent the night by her mother's side, curled up in a chair. She nodded off a couple of times but by early morning she was exhausted. About to go down and make a drink, she saw her mother's eyes open and settle on her face.

'Hello, Mum. You've had a wonderful long sleep. How are you feeling?' She gripped Edith's hand as she leant over the bed.

'Olive! You still here? Thought you'd gone home.'

'I said I'd be back as I wouldn't leave you on your own. Do you want anything to eat or drink? I've made some porridge I can heat up.'

Edith shook her head.

'Not hungry. Thirsty. Water, please.'

Olive had left a jug of water by the bed and now poured some into a glass, holding her mother's head to drink it. Edith took a few sips before falling back onto the pillows. Her breathing changed, a long sigh escaped her lips, and she lay still.

'Mum! Mum! Not yet, oh, please, not yet!'

But Edith's eyes remained wide open.

Olive fell across her mother's inert body and wept.

chapter nineteen

2010

As she enjoyed her breakfast on the terrace Natalie's mind replayed the previous evening and she was disturbed to find how prominent Stuart was in her thoughts. Surely she wasn't falling for him? And she'd agreed to spend the afternoon with him! Not a clever move under the circumstances. Wanting to clear her head she headed out for a walk. A dose of sea air was required.

Stuart called for her at three and was cheerfulness personified.

'A beautiful day again, isn't it? I can't wait to brighten up my terrace and I'm grateful for your help.' His smile was warm and her pulse quickened. It promised to be a tricky afternoon.

'No problem, I enjoy mooching around garden centres, I always see something I can't resist.' It crossed her mind she might find it hard to resist more than the plants...

Their tour of Le Friquet, the largest garden centre in the island, took a couple of hours. Stuart had never visited before and was overwhelmed by the choice.

'To be honest, I've never bothered much with gardens before, but seeing what you and Matt have achieved has set me off. As you probably noticed, my garden's quite basic, Mum not seeing the point of spending too much on it. I'm tempted to ask Matt to come up with a more interesting design, but in the meantime if I can have an attractive terrace, it'd be a start.'

Natalie suggested large, colourful pots to create interest and Stuart picked out plants he particularly liked. He also bought the ubiquitous barbecue, saying it was one form of cooking he had mastered. After walking what seemed miles around the centre, inside and out, they took a breather in the café. It was pleasant to sit outside drinking tea and eating scrummy carrot cake, while watching children play nearby.

'I had a call from my mother this morning,' Stuart said, putting his cup down. 'She's coming over next weekend and bringing her boyfriend. We've not met so should be interesting. He's the first guy she's been with since Dad.' He frowned.

'Oh, that's a big deal. How do you feel about it?'

'Well, I'm pleased for her, naturally. She's been on her own long enough. Mum and Dad were joined at the hip, working together in the business as they did. She was devastated when he died so suddenly and became depressed for a while. She slowly came out of it and got on with life. But I knew she was lonely as she was always pestering me to move nearer to her. I didn't want to, I felt smothered, to be honest. And my girlfriend thought she was too clingy. A bit controlling.' He sighed. 'I felt bad about staying away, but I needed to live my own life. It was one hell of a relief when she met Alan a couple of years ago and moved to France. I'm wondering if their visit is to tell me they're getting married.'

'Would you mind?'

He shook his head.

'No, not at all. As long as he's not just after her money.' He must have noticed her raised eyebrows, adding, 'Mum was left well off when Dad died and attracted a number of admirers. Some were obvious gold-diggers but she soon saw them off. All I know about Alan is he's widowed and a retired businessman. So...' he shrugged.

'I hope I get the chance to meet your mother. It would be fascinating to talk to someone who'd actually lived in my house. Or rather the one it was.'

'Of course you'll meet her. She knows about you.'

'Oh! What have you told her?'

'That you're my neighbour and I think you're – very nice.' He took a sip of tea. 'Mum'll be able to tell us how your house looked before the fire.'

Natalie wondered what else Stuart had told his mother.

'This cake is scrumptious, isn't it?'

'Sure is.' He looked at his watch. 'Better check out soon. You about finished?'

She nodded and they collected the two trolley loads to take to the till. Stuart loaded it all into his estate. Once back at The Old Barn, Natalie helped him unload and position the pots on his terrace. She offered to help with planting but Stuart refused, saying he wouldn't dream of taking up more of her time.

'Thanks again for your help, Natalie, you made it more fun. I'll give you a shout when I've finished and you can give me your opinion, if you like.'

'Love to. Right, I'll be on my way.' She hesitated. Should she kiss him? Wait to see if he kissed her? Stuart placed the bag of compost he was holding on the ground and leant forward, kissing her cheeks. 'See you soon.' His smile lit his face, bringing crinkles to his eyes.

'Yes. See you soon.' With a quick wave she turned and walked home. Time for a glass of something cold on her terrace.

Her parents were out for lunch on Sunday and Natalie spent the day in quiet solitude. The weather had changed, a fierce wind from the north cooled the air and ominous clouds blocked the sun. She forced herself to take a walk in the afternoon and returned home feeling righteous. As she passed The Old Barn, Stuart shot out and waved her over.

'Come and see what you think before it rains.'

They walked round to his terrace and she was hit by a riot of colour. All the pots were filled to bursting: red and pink geraniums; deep purple petunias with their heavenly scent; orange nasturtiums; waxy red begonias and purple lavender.

'It looks wonderful, Stuart. Just in time for your mother's visit.'

He beamed.

'Hadn't thought of that. Mum always liked pottering in her garden, it was how she relaxed.'

A few drops of rain fell and Natalie said she should run. Stuart gave her a wave as she sped back home. She just made it before the heavens opened. Time to curl up with the Sunday papers and a cup of tea.

The next few days passed quietly. No bad dreams or ghostly presence. Natalie allowed herself to stop being fearful and enjoyed the early days of July, a mix of sunshine and showers which still allowed her to spend some time outside.

By Friday she was looking forward to meeting Tabby, Stuart's mother, due to arrive the following day about lunchtime. He had said perhaps they could all meet on Sunday for a drink or even lunch and would get back to her once Tabby and Alan had arrived. It would be strange to meet a woman who had been born and raised in what was now her home, although it was unlikely Tabby would recognise it. Judging by the photos Andy had shown her, the old farmhouse had looked pretty basic even before the fire. Natalie couldn't blame Tabby for not wanting to return.

That evening she arrived home from work in a good mood in anticipation of the forthcoming weekend. As she walked into the kitchen that mood evaporated. On the worktop was the same family photo which had been moved previously. This time the glass had been broken. Tears sprang into her eyes as she picked it up and picked out the pieces of glass. Upset turned to anger.

'Why don't you leave me alone? What have I got to do with your family? Just go away!' she cried, swinging round, as if to catch sight of a ghostly figure. At first there was nothing, then an icy draught filled the room. Natalie waited, frozen. Silence. Just that awful farmyard smell. Within seconds the cold air was gone, the kitchen warm once more. How much more of this could she take?

That night Natalie slept badly. She dreamt she was back with Liam in London and he was trying to get into her flat. Natalie kept locking the door but he would still push his way in. She was becoming more and more terrified and it was when Liam advanced on her with a knife in his hand that she awoke, shaking. In reality he had never attacked her with a knife, only his fists. Which was bad enough. As Natalie lay back, exhausted, she attempted to make sense of the dream. The sergeant had phoned during the week to say Liam was now safely held in a mental hospital, receiving the help he so badly needed, so she had nothing to fear from him. Deciding she was too tired to think about it, Natalie turned over and managed to sleep for another hour, waking not much more refreshed.

By the time Natalie was dressed and downstairs the details of the dream had receded, leaving a thin film of fear. Until she had met Liam, she had never been afraid of anything. Her life had been ordinary and without trauma and she had considered herself strong and independent. That had changed. And now, when she had thought she was safe and life would be calm and peaceful in her lovely new home, it wasn't. Thanks to something invisible invading her space Natalie was afraid again. Her hands shook as she made the coffee and put bread in the toaster. It was only after she took her breakfast outside into the bright warmth of the day that the anxiety lessened. Telling herself she would have to put on a brave face when she met Stuart's mother, she ate her toast.

Later that afternoon Stuart rang.

'Hi. Just letting you know Mum's arrived and Alan seems a good bloke. They're being a bit coy but I wouldn't be surprised if they tell me at dinner they're planning to get hitched.'

'That's good. I'm looking forward to meeting them, if that's still on?'

'Sure. I suggested we all went out for Sunday lunch and Mum's all for it, offering to pay and asked me to book somewhere nice. What do you reckon? I've not dined out much so haven't a clue.'

'I've been to the Bella Luce in St Martins and the food's divine. And the setting. Particularly if we can eat in the Courtyard. That's if you don't mind a drive?'

'Mum's said we'll take a taxi so no worries there.' He cleared his throat. 'Um, Mum wonders if she could have a quick look at your cottage? She's impressed with what Andy did here and I told her how lovely your place is. Look, I know it's a bit cheeky...'

'Not at all. I would have offered anyway as I guessed she'd be curious. When's best for you?'

'How about tomorrow morning before we go out for lunch? Say about twelve?'

'Perfect. I'll see you then. Oh, and enjoy your dinner tonight.'

Natalie threw aside the newspaper she had been reading and stood up, stretching. A quick whizz through the cottage with the vac and duster was called for. As she hauled the Henry out of the cupboard an unwelcome thought popped into her head. How would her 'ghost' feel about Tabby's presence? Would it make its feelings known? Shivering at the idea, Natalie consoled herself that if there were witnesses to anything odd, then it meant she wasn't going mad. Which was something.

'Natalie, may I introduce my mother, Tabby, and her partner, Alan.' Stuart stood on her doorstep, a wide grin on his face and flanked by his mother and Alan.

Natalie looked from Stuart to Tabby. The resemblance was uncanny. Same blond hair, though probably now dyed in Tabby's case, and unusual blue eyes. She smiled. 'Nice to meet you both.' She shook the proffered hands and ushered them inside.

Tabby's eyes widened.

'My, this looks so different! Mind, any change would be an improvement on the old place. Thanks for letting us invade your home, Natalie. Stuart's been telling us a lot about you and the cottage.' She turned to her son who shuffled his feet.

Natalie was amused. 'It's a pleasure. And I hope he's been telling you only good things. Shall we start with the kitchen? I've a bottle of Prosecco chilling–'

They had reached the kitchen door and Tabby was about to step forward when one of the glasses set out on the worktop appeared to be lifted by an unseen hand and thrown to the floor. As they all stood frozen in shock, Natalie heard the now familiar voice hiss, 'Go away! Now!'

chapter twenty

2010

'What the hell was that?' Stuart was horrified and looked from his mother to Natalie, both as white as a sheet. Alan looked dazed and put his arm around Tabby's shoulders.

'Did you hear it?' Natalie whispered, still rooted to the spot like Tabby.

'What? I didn't hear anything, did you?' Stuart looked from Alan to his mother. To his dismay she nodded.

'Yes. He said, "Go away! Now!".' Tabby put her hand on Natalie's arm. 'This has happened before?'

Natalie nodded, moving forward to pick up the glass, her hand shaking. Stuart brushed her hand away and asked where she kept the pan and brush. She nodded to the sink unit. Natalie sat on a stool and was joined by Tabby and Alan who watched in silence as Stuart swept up the shards of glass. Satisfied he had left none, he said, 'I think we could all do with that drink. Shall I?' He gestured to the fridge and Natalie agreed. 'There's more glasses over there,' indicating a wall cupboard.

Stuart opened the Prosecco and poured the wine into four glasses.

'Shall we go outside? Might be more…jolly.'

Taking a glass each they trailed after Natalie onto the terrace and sat around the table. Stuart looked at his mother with a raised eyebrow and she nodded.

'Before we talk about what just happened, Natalie, I'd like to propose a toast to Mum and Alan who have decided, in their wisdom, to get hitched. So, to Mum and Alan!' He raised his glass and the others followed suit. After sipping their wine, the women had more colour in their cheeks.

'That's wonderful news! Congratulations, both of you. I'm just sorry you had to witness what happened on such a special occasion.' Natalie smiled wanly.

'Thank you. And don't apologise, it's hardly your fault,' Alan said, gripping Tabby's hand.

'Your garden looks wonderful. We didn't have much of one when I lived here with my mother.' Tabby gazed around, looking pensive.

Stuart was impatient to know what had been going on and hurt that Natalie hadn't confided in him.

'Natalie, do you feel able to tell us what's been happening here?'

She looked at them and took a long sip of her wine.

'I think the house is haunted and…it's something to do with Tabby's parents.'

Stuart gasped and saw his mother grow pale. Oh God! Wish he hadn't asked. Before he could say anything Natalie went on to tell them of her experience. By the time she was finished Stuart felt sick.

'Why on earth didn't you tell me? You know I'd have helped in any way I could. It must have been awful being at the mercy of something so…so unreal.'

'That's why I didn't tell you. I was embarrassed and didn't want you to think I was going mad. Which, believe me, I did wonder. But now,' she faced Tabby, 'now someone else saw and heard the same thing I feel a bit better. Relieved, I suppose. Though it's not that great having a ghost in your home!' she grimaced.

Tabby patted her arm. 'I think you've been very brave, Natalie, and I can understand why you kept quiet. Personally, I do believe in ghosts – after Alan and I saw one in an old coaching inn in England when we were away for a weekend. Didn't we, darling?' Alan nodded. 'He looked like someone from the 17th century, in a frockcoat and a tricorn hat, but didn't say or do anything. Just walked through the wall without a by-your-leave.' She frowned. 'This man seems angry and obviously doesn't like us invading his space.' Looking at Natalie she asked, 'Why do you think it's to do with my parents?'

'I...I've had a sort of vision of what the kitchen looked like when your parents lived here. And I had a dream in which I think I saw your mother and a man who seemed to be her husband, in that old kitchen. He was angry with her. They were dressed in clothes from the forties.'

Tabby bit her lip. 'I see. Has anyone else seen or heard anything like what occurred today?'

'No, except the first time I heard the voice was the day I moved in and a friend was with me, but she didn't hear it. Today was the first time – and you and I were the only ones to hear it.'

'Well, it *could* be something to do with my family. No-one else has lived here since my mother – disappeared.'

Stuart, both fascinated and appalled, checked his watch. 'Sorry to interrupt, but the taxi's due shortly. Shall we talk about this later? I wanted us to have a lovely, jolly Sunday lunch, Mum.'

'And we shall! Let's agree to close the subject for now and finish this lovely bubbly Natalie's provided.' Tabby smiled and offered her glass for a refill. They managed to empty their glasses before they heard the sound of the taxi pulling up at the front. As Stuart helped Natalie into the back of the car he had to quash a sudden spurt of anger at what he saw as her lack of trust in him. Something he would find hard to forgive.

Natalie sipped her aperitif as she perused the menu, trying to avoid Stuart's eye. He was sat to her left and Alan to her right, with Tabby facing her at the circular table nestled under an old tree in the Courtyard. It was calm and peaceful there after the earlier drama in her cottage. She had sensed Stuart's annoyance at her secretiveness and knew they would need to discuss it at some point. But not now. Today was Tabby's day and

Natalie smiled at her hostess who was clearly enjoying her role. She had insisted on the best table available and ordered Kir Royales for all of them. A woman used to being in charge. Natalie remembered Stuart saying his mother was controlling and had wanted him to live near her. Tabby was now deep in conversation with Stuart and Natalie turned to Alan. A tall, thin man, with a shock of white hair, he looked totally at ease in his skin. He probably let Tabby just get on with it. He grinned at Natalie and leaning closer, whispered, 'Tabby's in high heaven. She adores that boy of hers and hasn't stopped saying how much she missed him since we met. I'm glad to finally meet him and find he isn't some sop of a mother's boy.'

Natalie chuckled. 'I believe he had to keep a distance between them but I'm pleased they get on. Not all parents and children do.' She sipped her drink. 'I understand Tabby and her mother weren't close.'

'No, so she told me. A pity, as you say. She never talks about her so I keep clear of the subject. It's best not to upset Tabby, I've found.' He quickly added, 'Don't get me wrong, she's a wonderful woman and I'm very happy to be marrying her, but I think her past has left its mark.'

'I'm sure not having a father would have been awful. Do you have any children, Alan?'

'Yes, a daughter, Rose, whose grown up now and lives in the States with her husband and two children, so I don't get to see much of them. They're all coming to the wedding which is something to look forward to.'

'Lovely–'

'What are you two talking about? You look like conspirators.' Tabby's voice cut in.

'Hardly! I was telling Natalie about Rose and saying how happy I was they're coming to the wedding.' Alan smiled at her.

Tabby's face lit up. 'Oh, yes, I'm looking forward to meeting her and the children. I'll be a step-grandma!

Fancy that!' She put her hand up to push her hair back in a 'look-at-me' kind of way and Natalie smiled to herself.

The conversation was interrupted by the waiter arriving to take their orders. Natalie found it hard to choose, settling on a terrine to start followed by duck. She wanted to leave room for dessert, fancying the Eton Mess. Once the orders and choice of wine were made, Tabby returned to her wedding.

'It's going to be a small do, naturally, as at our age friends are pretty scattered.' She sighed. 'But we'll have our family and the few friends we've made in France and it will be wonderful. Only two weeks to go!' Tabby waved her arms. She gave Natalie a speculative look. 'Why don't you come along? You could be Stuart's plus one. I'm sure he'd be happy to bring you and we'd love to have you join us, wouldn't we, Alan?' She looked from fiancé to son.

Natalie kept her head down. What on earth was Tabby thinking of? They hardly knew each other!

Alan immediately said yes and Natalie felt rather than saw the eyes swivel to Stuart. She held her breath.

'It's fine by me, Mum, but it's up to Natalie. She's only just met you both–'

'True. But it'll be fun and give us all a chance to get to know each other better. Natalie?'

She had heard the slight hesitation in Stuart's voice and wondered if he'd rather she didn't go. Not after what had happened today...She glanced towards him and his expression was blank.

'It's very kind of you, Tabby, but as Stuart says, we don't know each other yet. And there's your family and friends–'

'Nonsense! As I said, it's only a small wedding but I'd like you to be there. Please.' Tabby's voice was firm and Natalie felt trapped. It wasn't as if she and Stuart were in a relationship either...And he was clearly upset about her not telling him what had been happening...

'When is it exactly? I might not be free.'

'Saturday 17th July. The weekend after the schools break up, to accommodate Stuart and the children. He and Rose's family are staying for two weeks but you need only come for the weekend if it suited you better.'

Natalie knew she had no plans that weekend and nodded. Surely she could cope with a couple of days holed up with virtual strangers. And Stuart.

'Good. That's sorted. And here's the food and doesn't it look wonderful?'

The meal had served to lighten the earlier atmosphere and the mood in the taxi home reflected the change. Natalie sat in the back between the two men, deep in conversation with Alan, who proved to be a man with many stories to tell. Some were funny and she found herself laughing at one particular tale as the car drew up at The Old Barn. The men got out first, with Alan opening the door for Tabby and Stuart offering Natalie a hand. She moved away from the others to say, 'I'm really sorry about not telling you what's been happening, but I was scared you'd think I was mad. It wasn't because I don't trust you. I do.'

He rubbed his chin. 'If you really trusted me you would have known I wouldn't think you were mad. I...I thought we were friends.' His eyes clouded and Natalie's stomach lurched.

'Of course we're friends! But I was going through some pretty horrible experiences and didn't think I could burden you. Particularly when I suspected it might be to do with your grandparents. We hadn't long met. How could I say, "by the way, I think one of your deceased relations is haunting me"?'

'I–'

'Natalie, dear. I'm sorry to interrupt, but can I have a word, please?' Tabby caught her arm.

'Sure.' They left Stuart standing with his hands in his pockets and a pained expression on his face.

'It's about what happened this morning. I sensed something odd as soon as I walked into the cottage and then...' she shuddered. 'I was proved right and I'm so sorry for what you've had to cope with. I'd still like to see the cottage properly, if you could bear to take me round. Or I could go on my own. But it's important to me – and you, of course – that we get to the bottom of it.' She patted Natalie's hand.

'Yes, I agree. Do you want to go today or tomorrow evening?'

'Shall we say later today? Give us a chance to recover from the wonderful lunch? I could pop over about six and I promise I won't stay long.'

Natalie agreed and they hugged. She looked across towards Stuart but he had his back to her, walking with Alan to The Old Barn. Natalie sighed inwardly, hoping he would eventually see her point of view. They were only friends, after all, and she didn't have to share everything with him. She'd been reluctant to become involved with anyone and this upset with Stuart confirmed she was right to be wary. Time to stand back a bit, not let the emotions take over. Particularly if they were going to spend time together in France at his mother's wedding. Cosy wasn't the word!

An afternoon spent stretched on a lounger in the sun helped Natalie forget the problem with Stuart and her ghost. She dozed on and off and came to shortly before Tabby was due. Groaning, she headed for the kitchen to grab a glass of water. She had just downed the drink when the doorbell rang. Natalie opened the door to a smiling Tabby, alone.

'I've left the boys watching a Formula One race so it's just the two of us. Probably for the best.' Tabby pecked her cheek and Natalie led the way to the sitting room first. At least nothing volatile happened there. Tabby made appreciative comments as they went on to inspect the study before going upstairs.

'The lay-out's been changed and everything looks much bigger than I remember. I knew from the plans it would be, but seeing it myself brings it home. Oh, I love your bedroom! And what a view!' She stood by the window and Natalie joined her. For a moment they both stared out over the fields with the dotted cottages leading the way to the ever-present sea. The sun hovered in the sky, not yet ready to relinquish its role to the moon.

'When I lived here, my bedroom was a poky little room facing towards the barn, above what was the sitting room, or front parlour. My mother's room was, I suppose, a smaller version of this room. And the window was too small to offer much of a view.' Tabby sighed. 'Coming back has reminded me what a mean existence we had.' She swept her arm around. 'It was dull and dingy, a million miles away from what Andy's created. And you, of course,' she added, facing her. Tabby twisted her hands together, looking sad, Natalie thought. Not surprising...

'Shall we go downstairs? I didn't get to see the kitchen properly earlier.'

'Sure. We can have a drink.' Natalie headed for the stairs, Tabby close on her heels. As they reached the kitchen door, she stopped so suddenly that Tabby collided with her. Once more her elegant, modern kitchen was replaced by the now familiar, old and shabby one. And this time a woman, wrapped in a tattered cardigan, was bent over the range, stirring a pan.

'Mum!' gasped Tabby.

chapter twenty-one

Spring 1943

T he day had not started well for Olive. Bill was in one of his black moods – brought on by an unacknowledged hangover – and had been annoyed she hadn't got round to mending his shirts. As if she had the time amongst all her other chores! He had lashed out at her and Olive had stumbled and hit her head on the chair as she fell, leaving her dazed. Shouting, 'I'm off to catch me some rabbits,' he grabbed his cap and stormed out.

Olive pulled herself up and collapsed in the chair. His chair. She waited until her head stopped spinning before filling a glass of water at the sink. Her face smarted from his hand and she knew from experience there would soon be a bruise. How she hated him! He was getting worse by the month and Olive found it hard to admit they had only been married three years. In fact, she did a quick calculation, their wedding anniversary was that very day. Not that Bill would have remembered and she only wanted to forget. If it hadn't been for the war, she could have left him and returned to her parents, who might well have still been alive. They'd have taken her in, not wanting her to be so ill-used. Now she'd have to wait. If Bill *was* being unfaithful, she could apply for a divorce when life returned to normal and hope Ross would allow her home.

The beating he'd given her after Nell's wedding had made her determined to leave him one day, no matter how difficult it might prove. She would have to face the social stigma of being divorced, but it would be worth it. Anyway, she was convinced he *did* have another woman, spending more nights away than ever. It suited her if it meant he left her alone. Her twenty-first birthday had been the week before, but sometimes she felt fifty. Older than her poor mother was when she died.

Brushing away a tear, she pulled herself up straight and went upstairs to check the damage to her face. The old foxed mirror in the bedroom showed a vivid red mark prominent on her pale skin. She patted on a tiny amount of make-up in a futile attempt to hide it. Her long dark hair looked matted and unkempt and Olive dragged a brush through it, ashamed at letting herself go. She had always been proud of her hair, once glossy and with a natural wave envied by other girls. Olive decided she would go out sticking and get some fresh air. They were low on wood and with the nights still chilly it would be a good excuse.

Minutes later Olive was in the yard attaching a basket to her battered bike. Old it may be, but she loved her bike. It wasn't comfortable to ride now, the shops having run out of puncture repair kits; like other cyclists Olive had to use hosepipe for tyres, making it hard on her legs. Without her mother for company, Olive had paired up with friends when she wanted to go to the cinema or a show. Bill, of course, wasn't happy about her 'jaunts', as he called them, but so far hadn't tried to stop her. She guessed it gave him extra time to see his fancy woman. Olive had an idea it was a woman from Torteval, known to have been unfaithful to her much older husband for years.

The sun was warm on her back as she pedalled down the lane, heading towards her friend Elsie's place. Near her house, Olive suddenly stopped. Her face! She didn't want Elsie to see what Bill had done and reluctantly decided to go sticking alone. She and Elsie found it great fun, searching underneath the trees at Pleinmont and the surrounding fields for dead wood lying on the ground. It was one chore she was happy to undertake as they made a game of it, seeing who could collect the most. And the wood was even more vital for warmth and cooking now there being no coal on the island. The only drawback was wood burned so fast, it needed replenishing more than coal did.

Olive skirted round Elsie's cottage and headed towards The Imperial, perched on the most south-westerly point overlooking Rocquaine Bay. No longer a hotel and bar, it had been commandeered for the use of German officers and Olive dismounted and pushed her bike along the track to Pleinmont. Strictly speaking she wasn't allowed to enter the area as it contained a barrack for soldiers, but once she and Elsie had explained, with a great fluttering of eyelashes, that they were only collecting firewood, they had been allowed in by the smitten soldiers. It was now their favourite place for sticking and sometimes the bored soldiers lent a hand. Elsie was single and, with the shortage of suitable Guernsey men, enjoyed a light flirtation with the young soldiers, some not much more than boys. Olive didn't exactly flirt, but she did enjoy the attention. It was harmless, neither of them meant anything by it, not like those women they saw in Town with their German soldiers.

She had only pushed her bike a few yards into the woods when a voice shouted, 'Stop!' in English. She turned round smiling, expecting to see one of the soldiers pretending to be officious for once. Her smile faltered when she saw an officer, one she'd never seen before. His face was partly in shadow and he stood with his arms behind his back, ramrod straight. She panicked.

'Oh. I'm sorry, have I done something wrong?' She smiled, nervously.

'You should know, Fräulein, you are not permitted to enter this area. What is your purpose in coming here?'

'I was going sticking.' She saw him frown. 'I mean collecting firewood. Only the odd bits on the ground. I...I've been before and was told it was all right as long as I stayed away from the barracks.' She nodded towards the grey building a few hundred feet away. 'I...I need the wood for cooking and heating and I'm not doing any harm.' The words came out in a rush and she fluttered her eyelashes as she'd seen Elsie do and crossed her fingers.

The man came closer, allowing Olive to see his face clearly. Her eyes were drawn to his. A brilliant, almost turquoise blue, they seemed to bore into her very soul. She stood rooted to the spot.

chapter twenty-two

2010

The vision dissipated into thin air as soon as Tabby cried out, replaced by Natalie's bright modern kitchen. The women clung together for a moment before Natalie moved her leaden feet towards the kettle. They needed tea.

A white-faced Tabby slumped onto a stool, her head in her hands.

'I...I can't believe it. Did you just see the original kitchen with my...my mother standing by the range?'

'Yes, afraid so. I've seen it before, as I told you, but empty.' Natalie put mugs of tea on the breakfast bar and took a sip. 'Can you be sure it was Olive? She looked so old.'

Tabby nursed her mug, a faraway look in her eyes.

'It was Mum, for sure, but older than when I last saw her. Much older. I'd guess late sixties, about the age she was when she disappeared. She...she looked so...unkempt. I had no idea she was living in such conditions.' Tears seeped down her cheeks and Natalie patted her shoulder. She'd have put the woman as nearer eighty than sixty. Her face, half-turned towards her, was scored with lines and the turned down mouth spoke of despair. The wild hair was white and thin and uncared for. And yet Olive had been not much older than Tabby was now when she was last seen.

Natalie didn't know what to say and stared into her mug.

'Do you...have any photos of Olive? And perhaps your father?'

Tabby sniffed and pulled out a tissue to blow her nose. 'I might have a photo of my mother at home but I never saw any pictures of my father. Mum hadn't kept any, assuming she ever had some. Not even a wedding photo. I thought it was strange, but got the impression their marriage hadn't been happy. She refused to talk about him so I stopped asking questions.' After dabbing her eyes, she looked up and Natalie saw the sorrow etched on her face.

'We...weren't close and my mother was angry all the time. I wondered if it was because she hadn't wanted me. It was hard for me to ask, so I didn't. In the end I took the easy way out by cutting the link and staying in England. It was cowardly and I've felt guilty for years, and after seeing...what I saw, I feel even worse.' Her eyes were bright with tears and Natalie put down her mug and hugged her properly. Intuition told her Tabby had been looking for love all her life, feeling rejected by her mother.

'Will you tell Stuart what we've seen?' Natalie leaned back.

'I suppose so. The whole thing's come as a shock to Stuart, but I can't not tell him. He's the only family I have and I don't want to lose him by being secretive. As a boy he was forever pestering me about my parents, wanting to know more about them, and I brushed him away.' Tabby bit her lip. 'My mother never had a good word to say about Bill, my father, even though he was supposed to have been a hero for hitting a German soldier.' She took a swallow of tea and sighed. 'It cost him his life, but no-one ever mentioned him in my presence. Not that we had much to do with the neighbours, they kept us at arm's length. I never knew why, but guessed it was because Mum deliberately lived a reclusive life. Once I was old enough, she'd send me to the shops for things we needed and she barely left the farm.'

'How strange! What about you? Did you have any friends?'

Tabby grimaced. 'Not at the local primary school, for sure. Because it was thought my mother was odd, even mad, they assumed I was too so I was left out a lot. But I was bright and worked hard and the teachers encouraged me and I moved to the Girls Intermediate School in Town, the equivalent of today's grammar school. People didn't know me there and I made some friends.'

She sat quietly for a moment and Natalie was about to ask another question when Tabby went on, 'I could never take friends back home, you see. We...we lived so poorly and I was ashamed. We received a pittance from the Parish Poor Relief and our only other income was the bit Mum made by renting out a couple of fields and the sale of goat's milk, eggs and veg. She'd never have allowed me to have friends round anyway.'

'Sounds pretty grim. I had no idea.' Natalie felt a surge of sympathy for this well-groomed, attractive woman who looked as if she had been born to money.

'It was. But we weren't the only ones who struggled after the war and by the time the economy in Guernsey picked up I was at university in England. I was determined to do well and never be poor again and I did it. Well, Dan and I did it together. We wanted the best for our son and we worked hard for what we achieved.' Tears continued to seep through her eyelashes. 'I should have made sure my mother was all right, sent her money...it was mean of me to hold a grudge for so long.'

'Grudge? What grudge?'

Tabby looked her in the eye. 'She refused to let me go to university, wanted me to stay and help her on the farm. Or what was left of it!' Tabby frowned. 'It made me so angry I stormed out and went to stay with a friend in Town. When I went back home I pretended I'd given up on the idea but I hadn't. I forged Mum's signature on the forms and watched for the post. Once my application and the grant came through, I packed and left. I...I didn't come back until after Dan died.'

'Oh! I can see why you're so upset about it. With hindsight we always know what we should have done differently. But you were right to go to uni, it was your life, not your mother's. Olive sounds such a sad, bitter lady. I wonder what made her like that?' Natalie thought of Stuart. 'And Stuart doesn't know any of this?'

'No, he doesn't. I've been too ashamed to tell him, I suppose. But talking to you has made me realise I should tell him, particularly if his grandmother is haunting this place!' Tabby attempted a smile.

'I'm not sure it's Olive, even though we "saw" her. There's a man here and he's angry. Always telling me to go away. I've no idea who he is.'

Tabby shook her head. 'Neither have I, but I do sense my mother is still around.' Sighing, she stood up. 'I've taken up enough of your time, Natalie, and I must get back to the others and tell them what's happened. And have a long talk with Stuart.' She flung her arms around Natalie. 'Thanks for listening and I do hope, in spite of what's happened, you will be happy here. You've made it so beautiful it would be a shame not to enjoy it.'

Natalie smiled. 'Thanks. I'm sure there'll be a solution, don't worry.'

She could only hope.

chapter twenty-three

2010

Natalie moved from room to room, unable to settle. She picked up photos and objects in a half-hearted attempt at rearrangement, stared at the paintings on the walls and finally escaped to the garden. For the first time she felt stifled in the cottage – needed air. It was still light and Natalie wandered around the nearly finished garden, frowning at the pile of soil where the pond would eventually be dug. It seemed to be taking forever for the new liner to arrive and she vented her annoyance by stamping up and down on the earth. Something like an electric shock shot through her and she jumped back onto the grass. Shaking her head in puzzlement, Natalie wondered what could have caused it. She had experienced static electricity on touching objects in the past, but not through her *feet*. Another mystery to add to the others.

The rest of the garden glowed golden under the rays of the setting sun and Natalie allowed herself to enjoy the moment. She stood at the bottom of the garden, taking deep breaths as she gazed out to sea. She had been tested by what was happening in her home and been deeply moved by Tabby's story. Turning her head to look at the cottage, Natalie wondered what more there was to learn. It seemed it had been an unhappy home for Tabby and her mother and Natalie faced the awful possibility that the memories of the past had been stirred up by the rebuilding work – and Tabby's return.

Natalie woke on Monday morning feeling exhausted. Not only was her mind fogged from lack of sleep, but her limbs felt heavy and achy. With a groan she recalled fleeting images from her dreams. A woman and a man arguing, the woman cowering from his raised fists. The sound of loud voices and of blows being struck. And once more it appeared to take place in what had been the kitchen. The one she and Tabby had seen the previous evening. The woman was definitely Olive.

Standing under the hot shower did little to help Natalie shake off the heaviness in her mind and body. And the two mugs of double-strength coffee she downed at breakfast only resulted in a small boost of energy. As she opened the car door, Stuart ran over, an apologetic look on his face.

'Hi, Natalie, I won't keep you, but I wanted to say sorry about my behaviour yesterday.' He ran his fingers through his hair and went on, 'Can I pop round this evening for a quick chat?'

'I guess. After seven would be best.' She wasn't really in the mood for raking over things, but Stuart's eyes were pleading.

'Great, thanks. Have a good day.' He gave a quick wave and she started the engine and swung the car round. Huh! Natalie hardly expected to have a good day after the sleepless night and knew it was likely to be a tough one. She would be refuelling on caffeine all day at the office.

Stuart had listened to his mother with a sense of disbelief. What had happened to drive his grandmother into poverty? And why had his mother never admitted how bad things had been during her childhood? The word 'shame' was mentioned and he began to understand. Although his own upbringing had been comfortable, some of his pupils in Coventry hailed from poor backgrounds and the more aware ones bore a badge of shame along with their tattered uniforms. Stuart found it hard to reconcile the proud, always-in-control woman who had raised him, with the image of a poor, badly fed girl who had longed to escape the run-down farm.

Alan sat by Tabby while she recounted the sorry story of her past and Stuart saw him squeeze her hand when she became tearful. He was pleased Alan – soon to be his stepfather – didn't seem fazed by Tabby's revelations. It confirmed his opinion of him as a genuine guy.

'Did...did you tell Dad what you've just told us?'

His mother bit her lip. 'No, I was too ashamed. I only ever said Mum and I didn't get on and he seemed to accept that.' She twisted her hands together in her lap. 'I've been so wrong, Stuart, all these years I convinced myself I was right and Mum was wrong and barely gave her a second thought once I was at university. I wrote to tell her when we got married and again when you were born and she did write back. She didn't say much, your gran was a woman of few words, but she did wish me – us – well.'

Stuart barely slept that night, visions of life on the old farm swirling through his mind. And he felt guilt. Guilt for now living in the beautiful old barn and enjoying a decent standard of living whereas...he also thought of Natalie, in her equally stunning cottage, living her dream. Except her enjoyment of her home was marred by the intrusion of the past. His family's past. He owed her an apology and on Monday evening called round as agreed.

Natalie opened the door, the dark circles under her eyes telling him she hadn't slept well either.

'I was about to make a cup of tea. Want one?' she asked, leading the way to the kitchen. Stuart followed gingerly, not wanting a repeat performance of the previous day. But the kitchen was the modern version and his grandmother was nowhere in sight.

'Looks like neither of us slept well last night.' He perched on a stool while Natalie switched on the kettle and put teabags in the mugs.

She ruffled her hair, causing it to fluff up in different directions. For a moment, she looked like a vulnerable child and Stuart had to force himself to sit still and not grab her in his arms.

Natalie sighed. 'I keep experiencing these weird dreams about a man and a woman arguing here, in this kitchen. Or rather, the one it used to be. It's all a bit exhausting.' She made the tea and handed him a mug. 'Shall we sit outside?'

He was glad to agree and they went through to the terrace.

'How's your mother?' Natalie cradled her mug, her eyes not meeting his.

'Pretty upset, as you'd expect. She told us everything last night and that's why…why I came round. I owe you an apology, Natalie. I can see now why you kept quiet about, about what's been happening. And I want you to know I'll do everything I can to help. I hate to think of you coping alone with these…ghosts or whatever they are.' Stuart patted the back of her hand, feeling inadequate. What on earth could he really do about ghosts? He hadn't the faintest idea how to deal with them. He wasn't even sure he believed in them except…

She looked at him then and smiled. It didn't quite reach her eyes, but it was a smile, nevertheless.

'Thanks. For the apology and the offer of help. I guess you've had a bit of a shock, too. Family secrets, and all that. Where's Tabby and Alan? They haven't left yet, have they?'

'No, but they've gone out for a bite and a drink. I think Mum sensed I needed my own space a bit this evening and wanted to show Alan one of the local watering holes. They go back to France on Friday and Mum would like to see you before they leave. Perhaps you could come round for supper one evening? Mum's a great cook.'

'Okay, thanks. I'm free any evening.'

'Great, I'll check with Mum and get back to you.' He stood up and Natalie joined him, saying she'd walk him to the door. As they stood on the threshold Stuart again had the strong urge to grab her and kiss her. But he sensed it would be too soon and settled for a peck on her cheek.

Natalie poured a glass of wine before returning to the terrace, regretting saying yes to supper. Although not the family's fault, she was being invaded in her own home by *their* ancestors and it was stressing her out. And it was worse since Tabby's arrival. She liked the woman, but would be glad when she left on Friday. Sipping her wine, Natalie admitted to herself she was losing patience and wanted to be rid of her 'visitors'. Should she enlist the help of the Church? A part of her fought against the idea, but it was beginning to look as if she might have no choice. Either that or lose her sanity.

chapter twenty-four

Spring 1943

It was if the world around her had disappeared, blown away by unknown and unexpected forces. It was just her and the man in front of her. Olive heard and felt the pounding in her chest as she continued to gaze at him, for what seemed like hours, but was barely seconds.

The officer's face was inscrutable. The firm mouth remained closed as he returned her gaze. For a moment she thought she saw a flicker of the eyes, soon gone.

He saluted.

'I am Major Wolfgang Brecht, Fräulein, and am responsible for security in this area. But if it is true that you only wish to go "sticking" as you call it, then I see no harm in it.' Slowly, as if the muscles of his face were not used to such a thing, he smiled and his eyes brightened.

'Oh, thank you, Major! I am indebted to you. I promise I'll be quick, just long enough to fill my basket.' Olive knew she was grinning like an idiot, wanting to stay there just looking at him. This handsome man with the mesmerising eyes. He was young, perhaps a few years older than her, with the physique of an athlete. He certainly didn't look half-starved like the other soldiers. When he smiled she saw the normal man within the hated uniform of the enemy. Olive knew she wasn't meant to like him or worse, find him attractive, but...

He took off his cap and bowed.

'May I help you with your task, Fräulein? It would mean you trespassing for less time.' His eyes danced with mischief and she laughed.

'That's very kind of you, Major. I usually go over there.' She pointed further up the path towards the trees.

He replaced his cap and took hold of the handlebars and pushed her bike while she walked alongside.

'You have the advantage of me, Fräulein. You know my name, but I do not know yours.' He glanced at her and she felt her face grow hot.

'It's Olive. Olive Falla. Mrs Olive Falla.' She twisted the wedding ring on her finger, wishing it wasn't there as a symbol of her enslavement.

'Ah! My apologies, Fräu Falla. I had not seen your wedding ring.'

Olive noticed a frown cross his face and regretted not lying. But he could have found out the truth at any time and where would that have got her? She told herself it made no difference, no matter how attractive she found him, nothing could come of it. Oh, but her insides were turning to liquid and no-one had ever had that effect on her! Certainly not Bill. Even at the beginning of their relationship she hadn't been as aroused as she was now. When his hand brushed against hers on the handlebars, Olive felt a jolt shoot up her arm. She risked a glance through her eyelashes and found him studying her.

'Tell me, Fräu Falla, where on the island do you live?'

'I, rather we, live up the road in St Peters, at Beauregard Farm. Looks down towards Fort Grey, it does.'

The Major inclined his head.

'You are farmers, that is good. Part of my responsibility is to check on the farms in this part of the island, to oversee the livestock. I arrived only two days ago and have not yet visited any.'

Olive was puzzled. 'Why would a soldier be sent to check our animals?'

'I am more than a soldier, Fräu Falla, I had qualified as a veterinary surgeon before...before the start of the war. My role is to make sure your animals do not take sick as the milk they produce is so important to us all.' His expression was grave and Olive was reminded of who and what he really was. An enemy officer who could, on a whim, have her arrested on a charge of trespass and she shivered.

The Major must have noticed as he smiled and touched her arm.

'Please, let us not talk about such unpleasant things. For today, the sun it is shining and I am with a pretty girl and we are collecting wood. As friends do. We can be friends, can we not?'

His gaze was so intense Olive felt the heat flare in her face again.

'Yes, I suppose…'

chapter twenty-five

2010

The next few days passed quietly, for which Natalie was thankful. She still spent most of her free time in the garden rather than in the cottage and walked down to the bay a couple of times. Stuart phoned to confirm Thursday for supper, but that was the only contact. Natalie phoned her mother knowing she would be dying to know about Tabby. She filled her in about the wedding but didn't mention what had happened in the kitchen, worried Molly would contact the vicar. Time for that if and when she could take it no longer.

On Wednesday evening Jeanne phoned for a chat.

'Sorry I haven't called for a while, but Harry, bless him, has had a nasty chest infection and kindly passed it onto me. None of us have had much sleep and I'm only now resurfacing. How are you?'

Natalie commiserated over the bug and said she was fine. She also told her about Tabby and Alan and their wedding.

'Strange she's invited you. Do you think she's trying to pair you off with Stuart?'

'Oh, I don't think so. I assume it's because he doesn't have a partner and we are neighbours.'

Jeanne laughed.

'Well, I'm not so sure. Mothers do love matchmaking, particularly their only sons. Now, please tell me you're free this Saturday as I'd like you to come for dinner. I've invited Andy and his wife Charlotte and Louisa and Paul from Le Folie, so some new faces for you. You'll be the odd one out, but I'm happy for you to bring Stuart…!' Another laugh.

'I'd love to come, thanks, but on my own. I wouldn't want to give Stuart the wrong idea, though I'm not sure he's looking for a relationship either. He had a bad experience with his ex and seems a bit shy of women. As I am of men.'

'At least all the men at dinner are spoken for so you can relax. Everyone's lovely and I'm sure you'll get along famously.'

They talked for a few more minutes and Natalie smiled as they ended the call. A night out with normal people her own age! Just what she needed.

Tabby must have been toiling in the kitchen for hours. Natalie caught the aroma of roast beef as soon as Stuart ushered her into The Old Barn. He took charge of her umbrella, the heavens having opened at lunchtime and not stopped since. Wiping her feet on the mat, Natalie gave him a quick smile.

'Pity about the weather. Were you planning to eat outside?'

'No, Mum had wanted to cook a roast so it's worked out fine. Come along and have a drink.'

Tabby was checking on the vegetables, steam shining her face, while Alan perched on a stool alongside, a glass of wine in his hand.

'Hello, Natalie, good to see you again. Dinner won't be long,' Tabby said, pecking her cheek, before swivelling back to the pans. Alan leaned over to give her a hug and Stuart poured her a glass of wine.

'You've gone to so much trouble, Tabby, particularly in this heat.' Although it looked wintery through the rain-lashed windows, the temperature was hitting the high twenties.

'Oh, I'm used to cooking in the heat. It gets pretty warm where we live, I can tell you. When you come over next weekend do bring a bikini as we have a pool. And you'll only need the lightest of summer clothes.' Tabby wiped her brow with the back of her hand and stood back. 'Why don't you all go and sit down, you're crowding me.'

They did as they were told and settled on the sofa.

'Tell me about where you live, Alan. Are you near the sea?'

'Not really. We live between Marseille and Aix en Provence, in a small village in the hills. Neither of us can abide being among the tourists stripped out on the beaches and stay well away. It can get hot, as Tabby said, hence the pool. But we do have air-con, so don't worry, the bedrooms will be cool.'

Natalie raised her eyebrows at Stuart and he chipped in, 'Mum and Alan have invited you to stay with us in the villa rather than book a hotel, which would be difficult in July anyway. I said yes, I hope you don't mind?' He looked sheepish.

What could she say? It seemed a done deal and it did make sense, but...staying with people you barely know could be tricky.

'That's kind of you, Alan, thanks. I'd better get my flights booked–'

Stuart cleared his throat.

'Our flights will be taken care of by Mum and Alan, from here to Gatwick and then on to Marseille. Mum insists on paying and booking to save us the bother at such short notice.'

Well, she couldn't back out now, could she? Jeanne's words about mothers and their sons popped into her head. Was Tabby actually trying to pair them off? She caught Alan's eye and he grinned.

'Sorry, Tabby loves to organise everyone and everything so please don't take offence. If you're not happy with the arrangements feel free to change them. I believe you're booked on a morning flight to Gatwick, arriving in Marseille after lunch. I'll pick you up and we'll be back at the villa within forty minutes. We'll book your return flight for Sunday or Monday, whichever suits you best. Either way you'll get back to Guernsey late evening. Stuart's stopping on, as you know.'

Natalie thought she'd ask for both Friday and Monday off. Might as well make a proper break of it. She glanced from Stuart to Alan and smiled. 'That sounds wonderful, thanks. I'm looking forward to it.'

Tabby called across to say dinner was being served and they moved to the dining area the other side of the kitchen. The men helped to serve up and within minutes they were tucking into roast beef, washed down with a full-bodied Burgundy. The conversation revolved around the wedding and love shone from Tabby's face whenever she looked at Alan. Natalie smiled inwardly, thinking how lovely it was two people in their sixties could find love again.

'Where are you going for your honeymoon?' she asked, glass in hand.

'We're not going away after the wedding; it's too nice at home in the summer. Alan's never been on a cruise, so we're taking one in the Caribbean in November. It'll be something to look forward to, won't it, darling?' Tabby beamed at Alan. He nodded, his mouth full of roast beef.

'I'm envious! November's such a miserable month, all fog and rain. Can you sneak me on-board in your trunk?' Natalie suggested, to laughter all round.

'I've already asked, but the answer was no. Told I'd be *de trop* for some reason.' Stuart grinned. 'My consolation prize is being able to stay on in France after the wedding, to enjoy the gorgeous weather while getting to know Alan, Rose – my soon-to-be stepsister – and her family.'

By the end of the meal Natalie had come to terms with the planned weekend in France, deciding she had overreacted to the idea of Tabby's matchmaking. It promised to be fun.

On Saturday morning Natalie sifted through her wardrobe for an outfit suitable for a low-key wedding in the sun. She had attended a number of weddings over the years when friends from uni and work tied the knot, resulting in a wardrobe rich in designer outfits only ever worn once. Natalie frowned as she fingered the beautiful fabrics of dresses and suits. Sleeveless silk was the answer and she pulled out a pale gold, strappy short dress which enhanced her tan. And showed off her legs. Slipping it over her head she enjoyed the sensual touch of satin on her skin. Matching high-heeled gold sandals completed the understated look. Pleased with her choice, Natalie picked out more clothes for the trip and spread them on the spare bed. All she had to do now was find something for dinner at Jeanne's. Guessing at smart casual, she paired a green silk blouse with white linen Capri pants.

Natalie had just slipped into a T-shirt and shorts when Matt rang to say there was a further delay on the pond liner, something to do with the manufacturer. It meant waiting another two weeks unless she was prepared to accept a poorer quality substitute. She wasn't. Natalie brushed aside his apologies and Matt rang off. She swore softly. For a moment her mood dipped, but the sight of the pretty clothes laid ready for the evening cheered her up and brought things into perspective. It was only a pond, not the end of the world.

'Natalie! Come in. Mm, love your outfit.' Jeanne embraced her before pulling her inside. 'We're in the garden, making the most of the sun after the horrible rain the other day.'

She handed Jeanne a bottle of wine and box of dark chocolate mints before following the sound of laughter coming from outside. As ever, the sight of the garden took Natalie's breath away. Originally designed and planted by Jeanne's grandmother, it combined the best of an English country garden and the more exotic plants which flourished in the islands. Splashes of colour from red hot pokers, gladioli and roses nestled amongst palms and oleander. To the far right an old orchard held plum and apple trees. And before that stood a sturdy pergola smothered in passionflower, vine and honeysuckle, offering shade to those standing around the long weathered table. The only faces Natalie recognised were those of Nick and Andy.

Jeanne called, 'Here's Natalie, everyone. Let me introduce you all.' Turning to an obviously pregnant woman with luscious dark brown hair and creamy complexion, Jeanne said, 'This is Charlotte, Andy's wife and next to her are Louisa and Paul, the newly-weds. Andy's playing hide and seek with Harry in the orchard.'

They exchanged greetings and Natalie took in Louisa's fair-hair, freckled face and warm smile, and Paul's blond hair and piercing blue eyes. Different, but similar to Stuart's. He looked, to Natalie, to be one of those unique people totally at peace with themselves. Although uncomfortable being the only singleton, she sensed everyone's friendliness.

Nick, standing by a makeshift bar, gave her a hug and a kiss before offering her a drink. She settled for a glass of Pimm's, complete with fruit, mint and a colourful umbrella. Charlotte was nursing an orange juice and looking longingly at the jug of Pimm's.

'I know it's better not to drink when you're pregnant, but it's *so* hard when everyone else is indulging. I do think you should all sign the pledge to keep me company!' Charlotte remained straight-faced but her eyes twinkled. Everyone laughed. Natalie, hearing her plummy, non-Guernsey voice, asked how she had met Andy.

'Louisa introduced us at La Folie when I was staying there last year. It was my second visit and she and I had become friends on my first, early in 2009. I hail from London and Somerset but am pretty well settled here now. Guernsey's so beautiful isn't it?' She smiled, one hand stroking her stomach.

'Congratulations on the baby. How long until...?'

'Early October. I can't wait! I'm enormous now and heaven knows what size I'll be by then. It will be a case of a block and tackle to get me out of bed!' She pulled a face and sighed.

Jeanne squeezed her arm. 'Don't be too impatient for your mini Batiste to arrive. That's when the fun really begins. Sleepless nights, leaky boobs, no time for yourself–'

'Stop, please!' Charlotte lifted her hand. 'Don't spoil it for me. I have visions of a perfect baby who will sleep all night and most of the day, giving me oodles of time to float in a scented bath. And time to pop to La Folie for one of Lin's magical massages.'

Louisa leaned forward. 'I'm sure we can offer a babysitting service between us, can't we, Jeanne?'

Charlotte beamed. 'That's so kind of you. But I expect my husband to do his share, too. Ah, here he is, feeling a tad worn-out, are you darling?'

Andy flopped into a chair, pushing hair out of his eyes and groaning.

'That young Harry's too quick for me. I need a rest – and a drink. How do you cope with him, Nick?' He picked up a can of lager and took a slug.

Nick laughed, picking up Harry as he ran back to the group. 'You've worn out Andy, young fella. And here's Natalie to see you. Go say hello.' He set him down and Harry ran into her arms.

''Ello, Aunty 'Atalie, Mummy said you were coming. Want to play hide and seek?' His big blue eyes beseeched her.

She kissed him but refused. 'It's too hot to run around, Harry. Why don't you sit with me and have some juice? And where's Freya?'

He wriggled into her lap, accepting the proffered beaker. 'Freya's still a baby so she's in bed. I'm bigger so I can stay up late.'

Jeanne ruffled his hair. 'Not that late, darling. Just a few more minutes then it's time to get into your pyjamas and say goodnight to everyone.'

He scowled, but continued to suck the juice, his arms around Natalie. She loved the feel of his soft body against hers and looked up to see Jeanne giving her a speculative look. Natalie laughed and shook her head. A few minutes later Jeanne prized Harry from her, taking him round the table to kiss goodnight. They watched as mother and son disappeared inside.

Natalie smiled at Louisa and Paul. 'Sorry I haven't had time to talk to you before, but Jeanne's told me something about you both. Aren't you another couple who met at La Folie?'

'Yes, we've joked it must be something in the food!' Paul's smile was serene as he gazed at Louisa, who sat looking equally calm. Natalie experienced a twinge of envy. She was surrounded by loved-up couples, emphasising her decidedly single state. Admittedly it was one she professed to be happy with, but...was she? Stuart had unsettled her, against her better judgment.

Paul and Louisa told her the story behind La Folie and Natalie was enchanted. She hadn't realised Louisa had come over from London to find her father, Malcolm, the founder of the natural heath centre and spa. Nick filled up everyone's glasses.

'And you've only recently married?'

'Yes, in April. It's been quite a year! Dad's now with Gillian, the wonderful doctor who's done so much for Charlotte's mum. They plan to marry this year. And we're all excited about Charlotte and Andy's first baby, of course.' Louisa smiled at her friends.

Natalie asked Charlotte about her mother and was told she was in remission from cancer, thanks to Gillian's alternative treatments.

'My! You've all had so much going on this past year and all I've done is move back to Guernsey.'

Jeanne flopped down beside her, saying, 'A bit more than that. You had to deal with a violent ex-boyfriend who had the gall to turn up here the other week. And there's the issue of your ghosts...oh! Sorry.' Jeanne clapped her hand over her mouth as Natalie frowned. She hadn't wanted to discuss this now, even though Andy knew something of the story. Several pairs of eyes swivelled towards her.

'Yes, there seems to be some kind of...of psychic stuff going on in the cottage. Related, we think, to the family of the previous owner.' She looked at Andy. 'Tabby and her partner were over last week and wanted to see the cottage. Tabby loved what you'd done to The Old Barn, by the way, as well as my place.' She tugged at her hair, trying to decide how much to say.

'Are you telling us you're being haunted by Tabby's parents?' Andy looked shocked while Charlotte's eyes sparkled with interest. Louisa and Paul were round-eyed while Nick looked crossly at his wife. Jeanne bit her lip.

'At least one of them, her mother...' Natalie gave an edited version of events, missing out the breaking of glasses. The rest was bad enough.

No-one spoke.

'So Stuart knows everything, now?' Jeanne asked at last.

'Yes, and he's as bemused as the rest of us. But he couldn't dismiss the evidence of his own eyes. I think he feels responsible in some way, but that's ridiculous. At least now I can be honest with him.'

Jeanne stood up. 'Sorry to interrupt everyone, but the food's ready. Nick, if you could give me a hand, please.'

After they had gone Paul reached for Natalie's hand.

'It sounds as if an unhappy soul hasn't moved on. Have you spoken to a vicar?' His soothing voice and kind expression was priest-like.

'No, but I am thinking about it. If–'

'Watch out, the dishes are hot.' Nick set down a steaming casserole piled with pieces of chicken in a spicy sauce and Jeanne followed with dishes of vegetables and rice. Once plates were handed around everyone helped themselves.

'Great! Isn't it a nice change to have an Indian?' Louisa spooned rice onto her plate, grinning at Paul.

He laughed. 'She knows how much I love Indian food, since the days I spent out in the Ashrams.'

Natalie was intrigued and the conversation turned to Paul's time in India. In time the focus returned to the haunting of her cottage.

'I grew up in an awfully old house in Somerset and remember being told as a child it was haunted. An ancestor who died in mysterious circumstances, apparently, and they were supposed to appear in a particular room. Never did see anything myself, but steered clear of that area to be safe.' Charlotte laughed, a deep, throaty laugh. 'Like many children I was both fascinated and scared of the idea of ghosts. I'm not sure how I'd handle what's happening to you, Natalie. You're very brave.'

'I don't know about being brave. It's not like I can make it stop. But I do want to find out what happened to cause the…the haunting and maybe then it will go away. Find peace, as you said, Paul.' Natalie knew at that moment what she said was true. Discover the story behind the 'restless spirit' and help it to move on.

It was the only answer.

chapter twenty-six

2010

Stuart sat beside her as Natalie drove to the airport on Friday morning. His case was in the boot, alongside her weekend bag. Apart from the outfit for the wedding she hadn't needed to pack much. Low clouds heavy with rain darkened the sky and Natalie was glad to escape what promised to be a wet weekend.

'How's things in the cottage? Any more disturbances?' Stuart gave her a sideways look.

'It's been okay, apart from vivid dreams.' She gave a short laugh. 'I think I'm slowly learning more about your grandmother than even your mother knows!'

'Oh! That doesn't sound good. What kind of things?'

She slowed down as they approached a junction and glanced at him. 'Assuming the dreams are replays of what actually happened rather than my imagination, seems she and your grandfather argued an awful lot. I don't hear the words, just feel a sense of what they're saying. Or shouting. And he...he hit her. I always feel exhausted afterwards.' Natalie bit her lip. 'Should I say anything to Tabby? It doesn't seem the right time, at a wedding...'

'No, I agree, it's not. Sounds awful.' He frowned.

'You don't feel comfortable with what's happening, do you?'

'To be honest, I've never believed in ghosts or anything paranormal. I'm not religious either, so don't think we go on to an afterlife. The thought that my grandmother could be haunting your home – and your dreams – is, is anathema to me.' He shook his head.

'How do you think I feel?' Her voice was sharp. 'I've never believed in such things either, but you saw it too. I'm glad to be getting away from whatever it is for a few days. It's...it's getting to me.' Natalie gripped the steering wheel tighter, fighting back a sob. She didn't want him to see her as weak.

'I'm so, so sorry, Natalie. It must be hellish for you.' He patted her arm awkwardly, as if unsure what to do. 'Shall we make a pact not to mention anything to do with the cottage while we're away? I'll do my best to help you enjoy the weekend.'

Her throat tightened and she turned to look at him. As their eyes locked she felt herself flush. Quickly turning away, she said, 'Thanks, that's a...good idea. I'm looking forward to exploring the area. Now, can you spot a parking space?'

Natalie felt the perspiration trickle between her breasts almost as soon as Alan escorted them out of the airport. It had been hot in Guernsey that summer, but nothing like this. Must be about thirty degrees, she thought, pushing down her straw hat before scrabbling in her bag for sunglasses.

'Don't worry, it'll be cooler at the villa. Being on a hillside we get to enjoy a gentle wind.' Alan assured them as he led the way to the car park. The heat bounced off the tarmac and the parked vehicles, leaving a slight metallic taste in Natalie's mouth.

'How far's the villa?' Stuart asked, deftly avoiding a badly steered trolley piled high with luggage.

'About twenty-five kilometres. Takes about half an hour as the road winds up into the hills. Our nearest town is Allauch where the mayor will be marrying us tomorrow.' Alan aimed his key at a dusty Peugeot estate before lifting the tailgate. He loaded the luggage and offered Natalie the front passenger seat while Stuart slid into the back. She sat gingerly on the hot cloth, the heat burning through to her skin. No-one spoke until Alan had steered the car out of the parking area and on to the main road, bombarded by constant traffic from all directions. Natalie was grateful she didn't have to drive.

'How was the journey?'

Natalie smiled as she replied. 'Good, thanks. Wasn't it, Stuart?' She turned to look at him, sitting behind Alan. Stuart had proved to be the perfect companion, sharing interesting facts from the guidebook he had bought. He had also been most attentive, offering her the window seat to get the best view as they came into land. And it had been spectacular. Natalie was taken aback by the sight of the runway along the side of a lake and their approach over the hills heading towards the water. She was beginning to wish she had agreed to stay longer, but...it *was* too soon.

'Yes, it was. And thanks for paying for the tickets.'

Alan nodded. 'The least we could do after asking you to join us here for the wedding. And it cost far less than flying my family from the States!' He chuckled.

'Have they arrived yet?'

'Yesterday. And your mother's in her element playing the role of step-grandmother. Even though everyone was shattered from the long flight, she insisted on taking the kids shopping for clothes this morning. They went dressed in typical American fashion of jeans and trainers and came back in head to toe French chic, like mini models for a fashion house!' He shook his head, adding, 'Not sure what Rose thinks, but my granddaughter, Kimberley, now walks like a model, hands on hips. Looks cute on a ten-year-old.'

'Sounds like Mum won't even notice me,' Stuart said in a mock-sorrowful voice.

'Oh, she will, don't worry. Before my gang arrived she was fussing over your room, wanting everything to be perfect. Which it will. Tabby'll make sure of that.'

The villa nestled under trees on the hillside, the white walls gleaming in the sun. As the car drew to a halt in the expansive driveway, a woman who looked like a housekeeper appeared at the front door, beaming and waving her hands.

'Bonjour! Bienvenue! Bienvenue!'

'This is Adele, who looks after us beautifully and is uber excited about the wedding and meeting the family. And she has little English.' Alan performed the introductions and Adele planted exuberant kisses on their cheeks. She looked particularly taken with Stuart, pointing at his hair and eyes as she gabbled on in French. Natalie's French was rusty but she guessed Adele was commenting on Stuart's likeness to his mother. Alan nodded and replied in perfect French and gently manoeuvred them all inside out of the fierce glare of the sun. Adele insisted in carrying Natalie's luggage and Stuart carried his own into the cool, airy hallway. Natalie caught a glimpse of wooden doors leading off in different directions before a flurry of bright colours erupted into the figure of Tabby bursting through a far door.

'You're here!' She swept upon Stuart with outstretched arms and squeezed him. Natalie caught him rolling his eyes over his mother's shoulder and grinned.

Tabby turned to her and gave her an equally fulsome hug before steering them towards the far door.

'Leave the luggage, Adele will take it to your rooms. Come and join the others and we'll have lunch. Oh, I'm so excited to have everyone here, I could burst!'

Alan gave Natalie and Stuart a conspiratorial wink before taking Tabby's arm and escorting her down the hall.

Natalie and Stuart exchanged glances and, placing his hand on her elbow, he said, 'I think it's fair to say Mum's excited, don't you? Hope you don't find it all too much, meeting a load of strangers.'

She liked the touch of his hand and appreciated his calmness. Although he looked like his mother, in temperament they could not have been more different.

'It's fine, I'm sure everyone will be lovely. But if it does get too much perhaps we could sneak away for a walk.'

His eyes lit up. 'I'd like that,' he said, squeezing her arm.

Natalie wondered what was happening to her. She was flirting with Stuart! Had the alcohol on the plane gone to her head? Or was it the heat? Either way, she enjoyed the sensation of letting go of the tension which had been building up over the past weeks. She needed to relax and have fun.

Lunch, served on a covered veranda smothered in bougainvillea, was noisy and less awkward than Natalie had expected. Rose was charming and easy to talk to, wanting to know what it was like to live on such a 'teeny-weeny island' as Rose put it. Blake, her husband, said little, taking surreptitious glances at his mobile, earning frowns from Rose. Their children, Kimberley and Jed, sat between Tabby and Alan at the opposite end of the table, were noisy but seemed in awe of their soon-to-be grandma. The food, prepared and served by Adele in bright coloured dishes, consisted of mixed salads, both hot and cold choices of vegetables, meats and cheeses, all washed down with copious bottles of wine. As the wine flowed through the afternoon, the conversations grew louder with the odd outburst of laughter from shared jokes. Natalie's head swam and she had the sudden urge to splash cold water on her face.

'Sorry to interrupt, Tabby, but could you tell me where my room is? I'd like to change into something cooler and hang up my outfit for tomorrow.'

'Of course. Up the stairs and the second door on the left. You can't miss it as it's the only one painted bright blue. There's an en suite if you want a shower.' Tabby beamed.

Natalie stood and excused herself before retreating inside. For a moment she had to adjust her eyes to the dimness and as she hesitated, Stuart joined her.

'Phew! Thought I'd take the opportunity to escape as well. Do you fancy a walk round the garden after you've changed? Mum and Alan are taking a siesta shortly and the others are going out in the car.'

'Okay, give me half an hour and I'll meet you down here.'

They walked upstairs together, separating as she reached her room.

'I'm next door it seems,' Stuart said, pointing along the corridor.

Wondering if his mother had put them near each other for a reason, Natalie nodded and went in to her room. She immediately felt cooler, thankful for the air conditioning. The room was simply but elegantly furnished, a mix of old French painted furniture and a touch of modern light wood, set against soft blue walls. Muslin encased the double half-tester bed and looked inviting. Too inviting. She walked to the window and pulled back the painted shutters, releasing a contented sigh. Below her lay terraces leading down to an inviting azure pool surrounded by loungers and parasols. Beyond the pool the garden was laid out in shrubs and flower beds, bordered by olive, lemon and fig trees. Taking a deep breath she caught the scent of lavender and jasmine. Now keen to get down and explore, she unpacked quickly, hanging up her outfit for the wedding before heading into the marble-tiled shower. Huge white fluffy towels lay on a rack and a matching towelling robe hung on the back of the door. Natalie's eyes widened at the selection of L'Occitane toiletries arranged in a basket on the vanity unit. Tabby certainly knew how to pamper her guests, she thought, stepping into the shower.

Minutes later and wrapped in the robe, Natalie dried her hair with the thoughtfully provided dryer before dressing in shorts and a T-shirt. She went downstairs to find Stuart waiting for her. She noticed the gleam of admiration in his eyes as she ran down, her bronzed legs shown to their best advantage. Stuart's skin appeared pale against his cream shorts and blue T-shirt. He looked down at his own legs with a rueful grin.

'I have some catching up to do, don't I? It's so good to finally relax and enjoy the summer. I don't plan to stir much beyond the villa for the next two weeks.'

Natalie cocked her head on one side as she joined him.

'I'm not sure Tabby will let you. I bet she's drawn up a timetable of activities and sightseeing to keep you busy!' She laughed.

Stuart rubbed his face, groaning.

'I hope not! It's been an exhausting term and I need a full recharge before I face those teenage hordes again. Come on, let's go check out what promises to be a fantastic garden.'

They stepped down from the veranda, now empty of people and any remains of lunch, and headed for the pool area. Stuart placed his hand on the small of her back to guide her and Natalie sensed his hesitation, as if he wasn't sure how she would react. But she liked the sensation and moved closer to him. The wide paths allowed plenty of room to walk side by side as they admired the flowers and shrubs.

'Who's the gardener? It looks immaculate.'

'Mum's always been a keen gardener so I'm guessing it's her. Although I bet she has help. She did mention having a pool man who can turn his hand to most things. I wouldn't want to work outside in this heat, would you?' He wiped beads of sweat from his forehead.

She shook her head.

'No, for sure. This is the time to sit and admire not dig. And enjoying a tall glass of something cold. Shall we find some shade for a moment?' Natalie made for a couple of adjacent pool loungers and Stuart opened a parasol, angled to protect their heads from the sun's glare. Stretched out on the thickly padded loungers, Natalie gave a contented sigh.

'This is heaven! Doesn't the pool look inviting?' She admired the blue tesserae tiles lining the pool which made the water appear an incredibly deep blue. 'Wish I had room for one at home.'

'You wouldn't get to use it much and they take a lot of looking after. Mum and Dad had one and the cover stayed on most of the summer. I think you're better sticking with your pond,' Stuart said, crossing his arms under his head.

Natalie frowned. 'There's been a delay with the liner so heaven knows when it'll be finished. I was looking forward to sitting on the terrace being soothed by the sound of running water.'

'You could always leave the garden tap on. Similar effect.' He chuckled.

'Hey!' Natalie leaned over and aimed a mock-punch at his arm. Stuart raised the arm defensively and caught hers, knocking her off balance. She fell on top of him and he grabbed her upper arms. Somehow, they ended up in an embrace, their lips virtually touching. Natalie's heart thumped and as she stared into the tantalising blue eyes, was lost. Stuart inched forward and kissed her. At first a gentle kiss, it became harder and his tongue separated her lips. She allowed herself to let go and enjoy the sensations fizzing through her body. Stuart's hands caressed her back and Natalie arched her spine in response. Then reason prevailed.

Pulling back gently she twisted her body away from him and flopped onto her lounger. Her heart thudded, savouring the memory of the kiss.

Stuart's fingers stroked her arm and she turned towards his smiling face.

'That was some kiss, Mr Cross. You...you took me by surprise.'

'I surprised myself. I hadn't intended to, it just happened. I hope you enjoyed it as much as I did, Miss Ogier.' He continued to stroke her arm, his eyes never leaving hers.

'Mm, yes. I'm not sure where this leaves us–'

'Well, I'd say it shows we find each other attractive, don't you? Do you have a problem with that?'

Natalie swallowed. Was it a problem? It was if she were really off men like she'd told herself these past months since Liam…On the other hand Stuart was proving to be the complete opposite to Liam, a man who knew how to treat women with consideration and respect.

'Guess not. But let's not rush anything. Once you get back to Guernsey we'll have time to get to know each other…better.' Her body's irreverent response to his feather-light touch undermined her resolve to wait. Could they wait two weeks? Trying to regain control, Natalie swung her legs over the side of the lounger and fixed her sunglasses firmly in place. Best to avoid eye contact.

Before she could move, Stuart stood up and lifted her chin. His thumb traced her lips and before she could say anything he dropped a light kiss on her mouth.

'I don't want to scare you off, Natalie. Let's play it your way. In the meantime I fancy a swim and I'm going to get my things before our peace is shattered by my new sister's family. Care to join me?'

'Yes! I do need to cool off.' For more than one reason, she told herself, as they retraced their steps inside. Barely minutes later they were back downstairs, her bikini and his trunks covered by towelling robes.

The water flowed over her body like cool silk and Natalie swam a complete length before lifting her head to see Stuart power his way towards her. Exhilarated by the swim, she laughed, pushing her hair back as she trod water. Stuart's grin said it all.

'Great, isn't it? I could spend the weekend in here!'

'I think your mother would have something to say about that! You're here for her wedding, remember. Oh, and it looks like we have company.'

Trailing out of the villa were Rose and her family, looking decidedly hot and sticky.

'Mind if we join you? The children are dying for a swim.' Rose looked from one to the other, her eyebrows raised. Natalie felt herself flush. Rose was putting two and two together.

'Not at all. There's plenty of room. What have you been up to?'

Rose, stripping down to her swimsuit, slid into the pool alongside her and began chatting about their trip to the local town. The children jumped in shrieking, creating such a splash even the loungers were soaked. Blake tried half-heartedly to remonstrate, but they ignored him. Natalie watched, amused, as Stuart swam towards them and said something she couldn't hear. Whatever it was, it worked as the children began quietly swimming the length of the pool. Beside her, Rose's jaw dropped.

'You can tell Stuart's a teacher, can't you? They have a knack with kids that parents never seem to master. I must pick his brains while we're out here.' She and Natalie swam lazily up the pool, managing to stay clear of the children. Stuart and Blake trod water by the edge, deep in conversation.

Adele came out calling something in French and Rose told the others it was time to go in and change for dinner.

'We're eating early tonight as it promises to be a long day tomorrow and we don't want the kids getting overtired.' Rose chuckled. 'Mind you, the same could apply to the grown-ups, too!'

Everyone collected their things and filed back indoors, all chatting away. Natalie was pleased to have another woman to talk to and Rose seemed equally keen to chat. By the time they reached the bedrooms they were like old friends, offering to help with each other's outfits the following day. Rose moved off with her family in tow and as Natalie stood at her bedroom door, Stuart came up and gave her waist a squeeze.

'I can see you've hit it off with Rose, which is great. I like her. Though Blake's a bit heavy going. Umm,' he added, hopping from one foot to another, 'You, er, won't tell her what's been happening back home, will you? About the ghost or whatever it is.'

She shook her head. 'Of course not. It's the last thing I want to talk about – as we agreed. On top of which she might think I'm a nutter.' Although Natalie was telling the truth, she wasn't being totally honest. She was more worried about how to avoid falling into bed with Stuart. Something her traitorous body desired while her head kept saying, 'Are you sure?'

chapter twenty-seven

Summer 1943

Olive had lain awake all night debating what to do. Her conscience told her to stay away from Wolfgang, one of the enemy, following the orders of that evil man, Hitler. The man who'd ordered the invasion of her beloved island. Whose fellow countrymen were responsible for all the hardship and pain suffered by, not only the islanders, but the poor POWs forced to work as slaves. Let alone all the losses suffered by the Allied forces. She knew she should hate all Germans; her father might have lived if they hadn't arrived on Guernsey and imposed rationing and reducing medical supplies. She also knew 'Jerrybags', the women who consorted with the Germans, were considered to be the worst type of collaborators and to be avoided. Olive had seen for herself the way other women would turn their backs on a woman seen arm-in-arm with a soldier. And, apart from anything else, Olive was a married woman. Doubly scandalous. The problem was, she knew she had fallen heavily for Wolfgang and didn't want to stop seeing him. He was her escape from the awfulness of being married to Bill.

In the morning Olive got out of bed heavy-headed but with a flutter of anticipation in her stomach. Wolfgang was visiting the farm today for the first time and she had decided, though not without a pang of guilt, she wanted to continue their friendship. Which is all it was.

She took particular care over her appearance that fine June day. Not that anyone could look good in patched, drab grey trousers and a faded cotton blouse. But she washed her hair and brushed it until it shone and applied a tiny dab of blusher to her tanned cheeks. She didn't dare risk a spritz of perfume to disguise the omnipresent odour of cow, not wanting Bill to become suspicious.

Olive fought to stop herself smiling as she went downstairs to the kitchen, where her husband sat at the table mending a broken spade. He looked up as she entered and frowned.

'You done something different to yourself, girl?' he barked.

She turned away and busied herself at the sink.

'No, except washed my hair. I've been eking out the shampoo for months since supplies ran low. We'll be out of soap soon, too.'

Bill grunted.

'This blasted war! When will it ever end? Even the Jerries know they're losing. You can see it in their faces when they think we're not looking. Still as arrogant as ever, though, most of the time. And now we've got one of them officers coming round to check on our animals. Bloody cheek! As if I can't look after my own animals myself. Been doing it long enough. Longer than any fresh-faced, stuck up Jerry fresh out of veterinary college, anyways.' His face reddened and Olive panicked. Dear God, don't let him antagonise Wolfgang! She didn't want this to be both the first and last visit to the farm.

She conjured up a smile. 'No-one's saying you can't look after the animals, Bill. They just want to make sure they stay healthy and have the medicines they need if they fall sick. They've already been to old Tom's farm down along and he said the officer was very polite.'

'Huh. Well, I don't want to spend longer than I have to in the company of one of those buggers, so you can show him round. I've got work to do in the top field.'

Olive sent up a silent prayer of thanks. The last thing she wanted was for Bill to hang around when Wolfgang arrived. As she washed up the breakfast dishes she remembered the kiss Wolfgang had given her when they last met. They had seen each other a couple of times since that first meeting and Olive found him fascinating to talk to and gorgeous to look at. In fact, the complete opposite to Bill. Wolfgang was courteous and listened attentively to what she said, which, she admitted, wasn't much. There being little to discuss which wasn't fraught with difficulties. They couldn't mention the war. Nor her husband. Nor the desperate food shortage. The only safe topics of conversation were the weather, Guernsey as a place to live, and what Wolfgang did before the war. But somehow it didn't matter what they talked about. It was enough to be able to walk or sit together and hold hands. And then, then the kiss...Now Olive knew what it was like to feel your insides melt when being held and kissed so lovingly. She had wanted it to go on forever...

'Olive! Are you deaf? I said there's a jeep driving up the lane and it'll be here any minute. Get yourself ready, will you.' Bill's voice grated on her ears but the thought of spending time with Wolfgang alone, here, made her heart leap.

Grabbing a cloth she dried her soapy hands and opened the door. The jeep came to a halt feet away and Wolfgang switched off the engine and walked towards her, smiling. A movement behind her made her send a warning look to Wolfgang and the smile vanished.

'Fräu Falla I assume? Major Brecht, at your service.' He clicked his heels together and gave a small bow.

Trying not to laugh, Olive greeted him and introduced her husband, who came and stood in front of her.

'Herr Falla.' Again Wolfgang clicked his heels and bowed.

Bill did not appear won over by his politeness, saying, 'I know I can't stop you snooping around my farm, but I don't have to talk to you. My wife will show you round, I'm busy.' With that, he slung the mended spade over his shoulder and marched across to the field.

Olive shrugged. 'Sorry about Bill, but it's probably best he doesn't want to stay. We won't have to pretend we don't know each other.'

Wolfgang grinned, his blue eyes sparkling with humour.

'That is true. I am glad. I was worried it would be awkward, but now I can see we might have some fun, yes?'

'Well, if you can call it fun to check the udders of a dozen cows...' She laughed as he pulled her towards him.

'And am I allowed to examine the farmer's wife? Just to see if she is in good health.'

'There's nothing I'd like better, but it's not safe,' she said, pulling back reluctantly. Oh, to be able to lie in his arms and make love. Or even better, to spend the whole night together! But it really was far too dangerous...

chapter twenty-eight

2010

Stuart knew he was falling in love. He'd probably already passed the point of no return. Until today it had been a slow burn, the attraction acknowledged, without too much thought of where it might lead. But after that kiss in the garden...He sighed and scrubbed at his hair as if he could wash away his feelings. No way. He allowed the hot water to rinse away the exotic-smelling suds and stepped out of the shower, his head still full of thoughts of Natalie. As he combed his hair and splashed aftershave on his bristle-free face, Stuart told himself it was probably for the best that she was going home on Monday. It gave him two weeks to decide if it was *the real thing* or lust accentuated by sun and wine. And if it was *l'amour vrai*, he had a problem. Because he would want Natalie to feel the same about him and want a serious relationship. And then he'd have to share his secret. Which might spoil everything.

The first person Stuart saw downstairs was Natalie, looking fabulous in a strapless peach top and white linen trousers. Her face and arms glowed from the sun and he caught his breath when she smiled at him.

'Hi. I was on my way outside for drinks on the veranda before dinner. I think we're the first down, apart from Alan. Shall we join him?'

'Sure. I could murder a beer. You...look nice.'

'Thanks.' Natalie's face flushed and she turned away as if trying to hide it. Outside, Alan was discussing something with Adele, in French. It involved a lot of arm waving on both sides. He called them over to a makeshift bar set up in a corner.

'Glad someone's down! Tabby's faffing about, changed her mind twice about what to wear and there's no sign of Rose and co. Just had to tell Adele to put back dinner for a bit and she's not best pleased.' With that the housekeeper, muttering something under her breath, stormed off towards the kitchen.

'What'll you have? There's a superb chilled rosé from Provence, *naturellement*, for you Natalie, if you wish, and some local iced *Biere des Cigales* for us men, which I always find particularly refreshing on a hot day. Or there's home-made lemonade if you prefer.'

Natalie accepted the lemonade and Stuart was happy to try the beer. After the proverbial '*Santé*!' Stuart took a long swallow from the bottle and grinned. 'Just what I needed! And it's pretty good, too.'

Voices behind them proclaimed the arrival of Rose and her family, apologising for being late.

'Sorry, Dad, but Kimberley insisted on having her hair plaited and it took forever.' Rose ushered her daughter forward. 'She wants me to do it again for the wedding, to match the lovely dress Tabby bought her to wear. Do you think she'll make a pretty flower girl?' Stuart picked up a note of pride, mingled with exasperation, in her voice.

Alan beamed at his granddaughter, who swirled around to show off her intricately woven plait.

'Beautiful! I bet Grandma Tabby will be envious. Her hair isn't long enough for something like that. Ah! And here she is at last!'

They all turned as one to see Tabby sashay toward them, dressed in what looked like even to Stuart's inexpert eyes, a pair of designer silk trousers and matching top. He saw the gleam of admiration in Alan's eyes and smiled at his mother. She gave him a hug before kissing Alan.

'Apologies for keeping you waiting, but it is a bride's privilege, you know. I promise to be on time tomorrow as *le maire* is a stickler for punctuality.' Tabby laughed, adding, 'Who's not got a drink? Do come and get one.'

Within minutes further drinks were poured and conversations took wing. Stuart edged towards Natalie, standing to one side on her own.

'What do you think so far?'

Her eyes sparkled. 'About what; the lemonade, the villa or the company?'

Stuart laughed.

'Everything, I guess.'

'Well, the lemonade is delicious, I think the villa is stunning and the company is *très charmant*. Happy now?'

'Guess so. And it looks as if everyone's enjoying themselves, particularly Mum.' He nodded towards Tabby, who was laughing with Alan, their heads close together. Stuart, although pleased for his mother, could not help experiencing a twinge of envy. He had expected to be happily married at his age, possibly a father…Pulling himself together, he turned his attention back to Natalie, who was giving him a quizzical look.

'You all right? Seem a bit sad.'

'I'm fine, a bit maudlin, thinking about Dad,' he lied. 'All feels a bit strange, but happy.'

Natalie nodded.

'I suppose it must be. But you can tell how in love they are, so–'

'What are you two being so serious about? Come on, Adele's serving dinner.' Tabby pulled at Stuart's arm and, laughing, he followed her to the laden table, Natalie at his side. The tantalising smell of meat cooked in wine and garlic hit his nostrils.

'Mm, looks and smells great, Mum. I didn't think I'd be hungry after the spread at lunchtime, but now I'm ready to tuck in.' He sat down opposite Tabby, with Alan between them at the head of the table. Natalie sat on his left with Rose opposite and Blake and the children filling the other seats. Dishes of roast potatoes and vegetables lined the middle of the table forming a guard of honour for the huge casserole dish in the centre. Bottles of wine and jugs of fresh lemonade and water were dotted about the table.

'Please help yourselves – and enjoy!' Alan called out, waving a bottle of Burgundy.

Stuart served Natalie first before filling his own plate and pouring them both a glass of wine. He was about to take a sip when Tabby asked how he'd spent the afternoon and he happily described their time in the garden. Out of the corner of his eye Stuart was glad to see Natalie and Rose talking like long-lost sisters and smiled inwardly. Women! Didn't take them long to strike up new friendships. He had always found it difficult, but genuinely felt comfortable with Rose. A quick glance at Blake confirmed he was endeavouring to keep the children's voices down while glancing at his mobile. Stuart frowned. Blake seemed detached from his family and that wasn't good. The sound level from that part of the table rose, and Blake appeared to give up the fight.

'Are you listening, Stuart? Alan just asked you if there's anywhere special you'd like to go while you're here.' Tabby tugged his arm.

'Oh, sorry.' He smiled at Alan who appeared more amused than annoyed. 'I'd like to visit Aix-en-Provence and catch the sights...' Alan and Tabby became animated as they vied to suggest the best places to visit.

'Why don't you take Natalie there on Sunday? You can borrow my car and have a bit of time together before she leaves,' his mother whispered, giving him a wink.

'Well, I'll have to ask her, I don't know if Natalie has her own plans–'

'Did I hear my name mentioned?'

He turned to face her, wishing Tabby hadn't been so blatant with her designs.

'Yes, I happened to say I'd like to visit Aix and Mum wondered if you'd like to go with me on Sunday. You don't have to–'

Her smile was warm. 'I'd love to! I've heard what a beautiful city it is, and it would be wonderful to see where Cézanne lived.'

Tabby beamed at them both. 'There you are, that's settled. And we can recommend a fabulous restaurant for lunch. Now,' she addressed the table, 'has everyone finished? There's dessert if you have.'

Adele appeared beside Tabby, ready to clear the table. Within minutes the plates and dishes were replaced with a bowl brimming with fresh fruit salad, individual pots of panna cotta, an apricot tart and a jug of cream. Stuart felt full just looking.

'Can I have your attention, please?' Alan stood and looked around the table. 'As you may know, my lovely bride-to-be has decreed I must stay elsewhere tonight and I'm off shortly to a nearby hotel.' He attempted a hard-done-by look, but Stuart wasn't fooled. He imagined Alan would quite like to escape what was likely to be a frenzied few hours in the morning. Tabby patted Alan's hand and he continued, 'Before I go, I'd like to thank you all for coming and supporting us on what will be a very special day.' He glanced at Tabby and smiled. 'I'd like to propose a toast to you all – my family!' he cried, raising a glass.

'To family!' Glasses were clinked and Alan sat down, but not before he kissed Tabby.

Stuart found his throat tighten as he saw his mother look lovingly at Alan. Saturday promised to be a quite a day.

🌀

Natalie woke early, the sun filtering through the slats of the shutters. She stretched slowly, enjoying the silky touch of the cotton sheets. She had enjoyed a dreamless, peaceful sleep and was ready for the busy day ahead.

Swinging her legs over the side of the bed, Natalie stood and padded to the window and opened the shutters. For a moment she had to close her eyes against the glare of the sun after the dimness of the room. Taking a deep breath, she again caught the scent of jasmine and lavender and smiled. The deep blue sky was cloudless and the villas nestled on the far hills shimmered in a heat haze. Already her skin prickled with the heat while the faintest of breezes caressed her warm cheeks. For a moment she thought of her cottage with its scary secrets and 'ghosts'. Being here offered only a brief respite and she'd have to go back, alone, to face whatever else was thrown at her. Not great, she thought, frowning.

With reluctance, Natalie turned her back on the idyllic scene outside and padded into the bathroom and a cooling shower. As she soaped her body, the unbidden memory of Stuart's kiss brought heat to her cheeks. She couldn't remember the last time a kiss had stirred her as much. It had felt so *right*, stirring something inside her which had been buried so long...While drying and styling her hair, she asked herself if perhaps she was now ready for a new relationship. And Stuart was so different to Liam it might work. She bit her lip. Was Stuart looking for a relationship or a flirty romance to heal his wounded heart? Ah well, no time to ponder now, time to get dressed...

The sound of laughter from the veranda showed at least some of the family were up for the early breakfast. As Natalie stepped outside she received appraising glances of approval from Stuart and Blake, the source of the laughter, and the only ones up.

Stuart stood and pulled out a chair for her.

'Morning. You look wonderful. Love the dress.' He dropped a kiss on her cheek as she sat down.

'Thanks and you're looking rather dapper yourself this morning.' She slid into the chair, murmuring a good morning to Blake who grinned in return, waving a croissant. Natalie smoothed down the silk skirt of her dress. She knew it suited her and smiled at Stuart as he poured her a cup of coffee. He wore cream flannel trousers, a deep blue crisp cotton shirt and a silk tie which she guessed would be removed as soon as the ceremony was over. Dapper indeed.

Before Natalie could take a sip of coffee, Rose and the children joined them, dressed head to toe in their new French clothes. Hugs and kisses were shared and Adele appeared, ready to take any orders for a cooked breakfast. The only one missing was Tabby.

'Where's your mother?' Natalie asked, concerned.

'She's having a quiet breakfast in her room and will appear when the cars arrive. I think she enjoys the idea of a dramatic entrance.' Stuart chuckled, reaching for the coffee pot. 'It's going to be a bit weird, watching our parents get married, don't you think, Rose?'

She looked up from a bowl of yogurt and fruit, grinning.

'Yeh, it does seem strange, but kinda sweet. Mum's death hit Dad really hard and I was a bit worried about him for a while. Now,' she laughed, 'he's like a kid who's been given the keys to the sweet shop! And I couldn't be more happy.' Rose ate a spoonful of yogurt. 'But I don't expect to see much of him and Tabby while we're here. Just hope he doesn't overdo things,' she whispered, with a saucy wink.

Natalie noticed Stuart's look of embarrassment. No-one really liked the idea of their parents being sexually active, but if they were fit and healthy…Pushing away the unwanted vision of her own parents in bed together, she bit on her croissant.

Breakfast proceeded noisily, as if everyone wanted to let rip before the solemnity of the wedding itself. Half an hour later Adele rushed in, pointing at her watch, and they realised, with a shock, they had about twenty minutes before the cars arrived. Natalie shot upstairs to put the final touches to her make-up and pin a small, deep gold fascinator in her hair. A quick glance in the mirror and she was ready.

The wedding cars drew up outside the *Ville D'Allauch*, the ochre coloured town hall with a grand portico entrance. The French flag hung still on its pole. Natalie had shared a car with Tabby and Stuart leaving Rose's family to fill the second car. Alan was to have made his own way. The cars, festooned with real flowers had, by necessity, to be standard size rather than limos usually used on these occasions. The streets of the town were narrow and winding and Natalie loved the style of the old buildings they passed. Stuart helped his mother to alight before opening the door for Natalie. Tabby looked radiant in a lacy cream dress falling just below her knees and matched with a large brim hat. She carried a small bouquet of red calla lilies. Natalie stood back to allow the family to proceed, tucking herself in behind Rose and Blake. The heat encouraged them to move speedily inside to the coolness of the entrance hall. A smiling official escorted them to a large room presided over by *Le Maire*, who stood in front of his desk in conversation with the waiting Alan. Already seated in rows behind were the couple's local friends who turned to admire the bridal party.

At this point Natalie cursed herself for her poor French and could only guess what the mayor was saying in welcome. Tabby joined her bridegroom, resplendent in a cream linen suit displaying a red rose in his buttonhole to match his tie. Once everyone was seated the ceremony began, in French. Stuart took a seat next to Natalie and they shared a grin. Fortunately the happy couple were fluent in French and made their responses at the right moments, judging by the mayor's nods of approval. A photographer stood to one side, poised with his camera for the de rigeur photos.

Cheers and claps broke out when Alan slipped the gold band on Tabby's finger and the photographer moved in closer. The mayor shook the smiling couple's hands, and after much gesticulation from him, Alan kissed Tabby, to another outbreak of cheers. Once the formal paperwork was signed and sealed, the guests stood and the couple led the way outside.

'Ah, that was lovely! And your mum looks fab!' Natalie murmured to Stuart as they milled around in the intense heat, bereft of shade.

Stuart, running his fingers inside his collar, had beads of perspiration on his brow. He dabbed his face with a handkerchief before answering. 'Thanks, I thought it went well, as much as I could follow what was happening–'

'Gather round, please, everyone. Group photo!' called Alan, waving his hand at the guests. Obediently people shuffled into position and the photographer snapped several shots before declaring himself happy. The wedding cars pulled up and Alan and Tabby disappeared in the first, while Rose's family climbed into the second. Natalie was wondering how she and Stuart were meant to get home when a third car arrived.

'That's ours. Don't worry, we're not expected to walk.' He grabbed her hand, laughing, and followed her into the back of the mercifully cool car. Other cars arrived for the remaining guests, all heading for the villa and the celebratory party.

'Do you mind if I kiss you? We won't get any time on our own for ages and you look irresistible,' he murmured in her ear. Natalie nodded. Cupping her face in his hands, he leaned in and kissed her mouth, his tongue gently opening her lips. For a few minutes, she was oblivious of anything else. A discreet cough reminded her where they were and Stuart pulled back, grinning at the driver, who gave him the thumbs up, saying something which sounded like '*Bonne chance, monsieur!*'

Natalie settled into Stuart's arms as the car navigated the narrow streets busy with weekend shoppers and tourists. She wanted the drive to last forever.

They arrived back to find the villa transformed. The gardens were festooned with bunches of helium balloons fastened to poles, and groups of tables, shaded by a huge gazebo, covered the lawn. Vases of flowers inside and out provided extra splashes of colour.

'Wow! How on earth did all this happen so quickly?' Natalie stared, her mouth open in amazement.

Stuart chuckled. 'Alan organised it on the q.t. Mum allowed him to book the caterers and he wanted to do something special and arranged for a small army of people to set everything up once we left this morning. Looks like Mum's speechless for once.' He nodded towards Tabby, who with Alan's arm around her, gazed wide-eyed around the sumptuous settings. Waiters and waitresses circled around, bearing trays of champagne flutes and Stuart took two, handing one to Natalie.

'*Santé*! Here's to a fun party.' He kissed her lightly on the mouth before steering her towards their table.

Hours later, after a long, delicious celebratory lunch, and with all the speeches over, the guests were free to let their hair down and dance. The local band, tucked away on the veranda, and with a lead singer sounding like Elvis, had been playing tunes from the '60s in the background, and now Alan led his wife onto the terrace for their first dance, a sedate waltz to Elvis's 'Hawaiian Wedding Song', which then morphed into a jive to 'Rock-A-Hula-Baby'. The guests stood and clapped as Alan and Tabby displayed their moves.

'I think they've been practising, don't you?' Stuart asked Natalie, standing by his side.

'They're good together, for sure. Can you jive?' She glanced at him as he watched his mother dancing more like a teenager than a mature woman.

'I'm not as good as Mum, but I can make a reasonable fist of it. Mum and Dad taught me years ago. How about you?'

She found herself tapping her foot to the music and nodded. 'A bit.'

'As soon as they've finished let's give it a go.'

After taking their bows, the newlyweds opened the floor to their guests and Stuart grabbed Natalie's hand. They danced until they ran out of breath, took a break, then danced some more. The party ran on through the afternoon and the evening, by which time some of the older guests had drifted away and those remaining spent more time drinking and eating snacks from the trays brought round by the staff. By eleven even the band looked weary and were now playing slow smooches. Stuart grinned at Natalie. 'Shall we have a last dance?' Her feet were killing her but she couldn't say no and allowed him to pull her onto her now bare feet, hoping they wouldn't get trodden on.

The last dance, 'When a Man Loves a Woman', was sung with equal passion by the lead singer and Stuart drew her close as they joined the last few couples, including Tabby and Alan. Natalie closed her eyes, imagining they were the only ones dancing, aware of Stuart's heartbeat close to hers. Copious champagne had left her light-headed and willing to be seduced by her surroundings – and Stuart. As the music stopped she opened her eyes to find Stuart's unfocused gaze on her face. He tilted his head down and kissed her and she swayed in his embrace, tightening her arms around his neck.

A cough behind her broke the spell.

'Sorry to interrupt you two, but we wanted to say goodnight.' Alan's voice held a hint of laughter.

She turned round to find Alan and Tabby grinning at them.

Stuart found his voice first.

'Of course. Goodnight to you both and thanks for a wonderful time. You certainly know how to throw a great party!' He kissed Tabby and shook Alan's hand.

Natalie, somewhat sheepishly, murmured goodnight and kissed the hosts who, with a wave, disappeared indoors.

She had a sudden fit of the giggles and collapsed into Stuart's arms, who promptly burst out laughing.

'Talk about role reversal!' he spluttered, trying to regain self-control. 'Come on, I think it's time for bed.' He held her round the waist and steered her inside and up the stairs, halting outside her room. Natalie's heart beat fast. Would he ask to come in? Or should she suggest it? Stuart made the decision by saying, 'I think we've both had rather too much to drink so it's probably best if we say goodnight. It's not the right time...' His voice was husky. He kissed her cheek and pulled back, a look of uncertainty on his face.

Natalie was deflated. Was she being rejected? Or was he right and they were both drunk and might regret it? Forcing a quick smile, she said goodnight and slipped into her room, eager for the oblivion of sleep. Her last conscious thought was that Stuart might be sharing her own doubts about entering a new relationship. What a muddle!

chapter twenty-nine

2010

Bleary-eyed and stifling a yawn, Natalie headed for breakfast on the veranda on Sunday. Although past ten, she appeared to be the first one down, the table settings undisturbed. Adele bustled out, crying, 'Bonjour, Mam'selle, bonjour!' Natalie smiled a response and gratefully accepted a cup of coffee strong enough to hold a spoon upright.

'*Merci*, Adele.' She took a scalding sip before reaching for the croissants still warm from the oven. Adele must have been out to the local *boulangerie* and bought a selection of bread rolls too, all nestling under linen napkins in wicker baskets. Brightly decorated pots held a selection of jam, honey and marmalade. Natalie had taken a first bite of the croissant slathered in honey when Rose appeared with the children, quickly followed by Stuart.

Half-hearted greetings were exchanged as the grown-ups slumped into chairs. The children seemed full of beans, however, and began squabbling before they had sat down. Rose groaned, holding her head. Stuart and Natalie exchanged glances and he rolled his eyes, whispering, 'What a couple of brats! I shall do my best to avoid them the next two weeks.'

'They do rather put you off having children, don't they? Although I've always thought I'd have them one day. When the time's right.'

Stuart looked about to say something when Alan and Tabby arrived.

'Good morning, everyone! Did you all sleep well?' Alan's hearty voice cut in and Natalie looked up to see the loved-up newlyweds looking extremely perky as they sat down next to the children. She smiled inwardly, thinking what a great advert the pair of them were for mature love, her own parents being another good example. Natalie, glancing sideways at Stuart, now chatting to Tabby, wondered if she would find such a deep love herself. Ideally before she reached sixty...

Blake turned up, muttering apologies for being late, and Rose threw him a resentful glance. All was not sweetness and light with those two, she thought. The palpable happiness of Tabby and Alan seemed to diffuse any lingering tensions at the table and it wasn't long before it was smiles all round. Between sips of coffee, Tabby asked Stuart when he was setting off with Natalie to Aix. She tapped her watch. 'You need to go soon if you want to catch any of the few shops which are open. They'll be closed this afternoon.'

'Right, yes.' Stuart looked at Natalie, eyebrows raised. 'You still want to go out for the day? Not too tired?'

She searched his face, looking for signs he'd changed his mind. But no, he appeared genuine.

'I'm fine. Once I've finished breakfast I'll grab my things.' Natalie's spirits lifted, all the earlier hungover tiredness dissipated. They had a whole day, just the two of them, and she meant to enjoy it, not letting her worries about the cottage intrude. Or her doubts about the wisdom of becoming closer to Stuart. Time to think about both when she went home. Alone.

Natalie was entranced by the picturesque road to Aix-en-Provence, winding through quaint hillside villages protected by ruined castles. Vineyards nestled below them and to the north the magnificent Sainte-Victoire mountain range dominated the landscape. Neither of them spoke much; she was lost in the beauty of the countryside opening up around them and Stuart concentrated on driving an unknown car on unknown roads. The sleek Peugeot was equipped with satnav and a husky-voiced female prompted him with frequent instructions, making Natalie break out in giggles. Stuart only frowned. They pulled into the town an hour later, keen to grab a drink before any sightseeing.

Natalie spotted a pavement café with brightly coloured umbrellas shading the customers from the glaring noon sun. She ordered a coffee and Stuart a beer and while they waited he dug out his guidebook, flicking through the pages to find the right section. The air was noticeably cooler than back down towards the coast, probably no more than the low twenties, Natalie thought, both surprised and relieved. She gazed admiringly at the beauty and elegance of the baroque buildings forming the open square, the sun glinting on the ochre stone. Her eyes were drawn, as if mesmerised, to the marble fountain in the centre releasing a stream of tinkling water.

'Isn't this wonderful! It's as if time's stood still and we're back in the eighteenth century.' Natalie thanked the waiter for her coffee and smiled at Stuart, who broke off from his reading to sip his beer. He followed Natalie's gaze around the square, nodding his appreciation.

'Beautiful. And there's masses to see according to my book. Far too much for a single day so we'll need to prioritise. This is what the guide recommends...' He read out the list which included L'Atelier Cézanne in the city and his country estate, Jas de Bouffan. 'Oh, and there's even a mini-tram running around the city with an on-board audio commentary if we want to be true tourists,' he added, rolling his eyes.

'That could be fun. I don't mind looking like a prat if you don't.' Natalie grinned as he released a deep, soulful sigh.

'If we must.' He checked his watch. 'The next tram's not till 2.15 so we've time to have lunch first. Then we could...'

The next few hours passed in a blur of colour, sound and the wonderful aroma of freshly-cooked food. Natalie enjoyed every minute, soaking up the buzz of the city which reminded her a little of her old life in London. A million miles away from life in Guernsey. For a brief moment she experienced a pang of regret for her old life, but pushed it down when she remembered the beauty and peace she enjoyed on the island. And Stuart. She glanced at his profile as they drove back to the villa. In spite of appearing to enjoy himself, he had been quieter than usual that day, as if something lay heavy on his mind. Not wanting to interfere with his concentration on the driving, Natalie resisted the urge to ask if anything was wrong. If it was important, he would say something, wouldn't he?

The sound of splashing in the pool greeted them as they walked out onto the terrace to find Alan, Tabby and Rose sipping drinks on loungers while Blake and the children messed about in the water. Greetings were exchanged and Tabby asked if they had enjoyed the trip.

'It was brilliant. Isn't Aix beautiful? And there's so much to see! But it's also tiring to get everything in. Stuart wants to go back, I think.' Natalie looked at him, chatting to Alan on a nearby lounger.

Tabby sat up and leaned towards her, head on one side.

'You two seem to get on well. I've not seen Stuart as keen on anyone since Pam,' she said, sotto voce. 'Is there a chance you and…and he could become close?'

Natalie could see why Stuart needed his space from Tabby. One controlling mama!

'I don't know. It's possible, but–'

Tabby gripped her arm.

'That's wonderful. I know it's early days, but when he returns to Guernsey you'll have loads of time to get closer. And perhaps absence will make the heart grow fonder,' she added, with a wink.

Natalie felt the heat rise in her face, but was saved from replying by the appearance of Adele bearing a tray of drinks. She grabbed a glass of lemonade, took a gulp and promptly choked. Stuart came to her rescue, patting her back and in the process making her feel even more self-conscious. She managed to gasp, 'went down the wrong way' before taking deep breaths. He stood in front of her, his face puckered in concern.

'You okay? You went bright red.'

She nodded, not trusting herself to speak. Why did Tabby have to try and push them together when Stuart had seemed more distant? He hadn't even tried to kiss her during their time together in Aix! Appearing satisfied she was okay, Stuart returned to Alan's side to pick up their conversation. Natalie caught the words 'local beer' and decided not to join them, opting to chat to Rose instead. Anything to avoid talking to Tabby again.

Supper on the veranda turned out to be a much quieter affair than on the previous days, an almost tangible air of deflation hung over the table. Even the swaying party balloons had a collapsed, hang-dog appearance. Natalie forced herself to stay cheerful, joining in the desultory conversation started by Alan or Rose. A wave of extreme tiredness washed over her and she was relieved to see others yawning as the plates were finally emptied. A combination of sun, alcohol and the anti-climax after the wedding had worn them out. As Rose stood to take the children upstairs, Natalie proffered her goodnight to everyone, pleading the need for an early night. Cries of 'sleep well' and 'I'll be going to bed soon' followed her as she left the table. Stuart remained in his seat and nodded as she walked past him. As deflated as the limp balloons, Natalie climbed the stairs, wishing only for instant sleep.

After a round of goodbye hugs and kisses, Natalie slipped into the back passenger seat next to Stuart. Alan had insisted on driving when Stuart had offered, saying the roads around the airport were confusing and he didn't want them getting lost. Natalie, touched he had offered, still wondered why she was receiving such mixed messages from Stuart, but couldn't talk to him properly with Alan inches away. They resorted to small talk and what his plans were for the rest of his holiday. The drive took longer this time around and Alan explained the road to Marseille was always particularly busy in the summer as the French headed for the coast. At the airport Alan tried unsuccessfully to find a parking space in the drop-off car park, *dépose minute*, and stopped outside *Départs* on double white lines.

'We'll have to be quick, I'm afraid, or I'll get booked. It's been lovely seeing you again, Natalie, and I hope we'll meet again soon. Probably in Guernsey.' Alan gave her a hug and a kiss before moving away to let Stuart say goodbye.

Natalie looked at him expectantly.

Stuart thrust a hand through his hair before taking her in his arms.

'I know I behaved a bit odd yesterday after...well, the day before. It must have been confusing for you–'

'It was. I thought you'd gone off me–'

'No, no not at all. It's just that I'm torn. I would like a relationship with you, but I'm afraid...there's something I have to tell you first.'

Her heart thumped. 'What do you mean?'

'I–'

'Sorry to interrupt, but there's a policeman heading straight for us and he doesn't look best pleased. We have to go.' Alan waved his arm towards the uniformed man bearing down on them.

Stuart said, 'We'll talk when I get back, promise.' He gave her a quick kiss on the lips and shot into the passenger seat as Alan revved the engine and drove off. Natalie, stunned, gave a half-wave at the retreating car and turned towards the entrance. What on earth was that about? And she had to wait nearly two weeks to find out!

The flights back home seemed longer than the outward flights and Natalie put it down to being on her own. Not in the mood for small talk with anyone, she pretended to doze on the flight to Gatwick. In fact her mind wouldn't settle and she tortured herself wondering how serious Stuart's 'something' could be. Was he ill? He didn't look ill. But you couldn't always tell...Planning to leave Guernsey? No, he seemed to love the island and he couldn't leave the school without giving notice. Her mind went round and round and she felt drained by the time the plane landed at Gatwick. Natalie had a two hour wait before the flight to Guernsey and took herself off to Nando's for a decent meal in an effort to distract herself.

Natalie parked the car in front of her cottage and remained seated, breathing in the early evening air, cooled by a light sea breeze. The raucous call of seagulls provided the only sound. The cottage looked exactly as she had left it four days previously, but it *felt* different. She knew, without going in, that something had happened. Something, or someone, had invaded her space in her absence. For a brief moment Natalie considered ringing her parents and asking them to come round. That would be the sensible course to take. But, gritting her teeth, she reminded herself she was a mature woman and didn't need her hand held any more. Not totally convinced, she wheeled her case to the front door and inserted the key. She pushed it open slowly, and listened. Silence. Her heart thudding, Natalie left the case in the hall and tiptoed to the closed kitchen door. Taking a deep breath, she turned the handle and let the door swing open.

The sight brought an anguished cry to her lips.

Anything which had been on the kitchen worktops had been flung onto the floor – cookery books, fruit bowls, toaster – everything. Anything breakable lay smashed on the tiles.

chapter thirty

Autumn 1943

Ominous clouds scudded across the sky as Olive churned the butter in the chilly dairy. At least the exercise kept her warm against the draughts whistling under the door and through the badly fitting windows. She was making more than the quota required for the Controlling Committee, in charge of the islanders' rations, planning to exchange a pat of butter for some fish. Her mouth drooled at the very thought of the taste of fresh fish after so long without. Hard to get, with the restrictions on the fishermen, but not impossible if you had something as valuable as butter to offer in payment. Olive missed the taste of meat as well, another rare commodity.

As she turned the heavy wooden handle, Olive chuckled at a story she had heard the day before. An inspection was due from the *Feldkommandantur*, checking the number of pigs belonging to a farmer who had, against regulations, saved a dead animal for himself. So he hid the dead pig in his pregnant wife's bed as she was about to give birth. Needless to say, it wasn't found. She wished she could share the story with Wolfgang, and although he would have found it funny, it would have put him in a difficult situation. Olive sighed, her loyalties divided, as always. She hadn't anticipated the downside of loving an enemy. Initially, it was easy to be swept along in the aftermath of falling in love, but now she had to be *so* careful about what she said to anyone, even her oldest friends, as not only would she be a pariah, but if it got back to Bill...She shuddered. And when she did meet Wolfgang she was constantly watching to see no-one saw them together. Not at all relaxing. The islanders had always been gossipers, but now it had escalated, everyone looking over their shoulder, worried about informers.

The butter finished, Olive returned to the relative warmth of the kitchen, where she had been cooking a pot of vegetable soup in a hay-box. The lack of fuel had made it an essential way of cooking food and at least there was no shortage of hay on the farm. Earlier Olive had made a steam pudding from grated carrots, grated potatoes and oats. She was becoming good at improvisation, just like the other housewives on the starving island. As she made herself a cup of ground acorn coffee, Olive forced down the rising anger against the Germans and their invasion of her home. Bloody war! When would it ever end? Oh, to be free to eat what you liked, go where you liked...Ironically, one of the few bright spots of these blighted days was seeing Wolfgang, someone she wouldn't have met but for the Occupation. She smiled wryly at the notion and took a cautious sip of the bitter coffee. Their next meeting was arranged for later that day and her stomach flipped in anticipation. She hadn't seen him since a recent evening at the Gaumont in Town. After her mother died, Olive hadn't bothered to go to the cinema for months. But once Wolfgang had told her he went as often as he could, she made an effort to go.

For once it had been an English film, *The Great Victor Herbert*, a romantic musical and not German propaganda. Even the Germans seemed to enjoy it. All entertainment was vetted by the Germans and, with the curfew of 9pm strictly enforced, audiences had to travel home as quickly as they could after a show. This made it harder for Olive living in the outer parish of St Peters. The Germans sat on one side of the audience, locals on the other. Olive had cycled in with her friend Elsie. At the cinema she'd been able to get close enough to Wolfgang to exchange letters, without Elsie being any the wiser. They'd set up the practice weeks ago. No words were spoken, a mere nod of their heads being the only acknowledgment.

Forcing down the coffee – she needed to make some more treacle from boiled sugar beet – Olive wondered how long she could risk being out that afternoon. Her excuse, which was genuine, was the need to cycle into Town for whatever supplies she could get, including the promised fish from Henry. Long queues at the few remaining shops guaranteed a protracted trip. But she wanted – needed – to spend at least an hour with Wolfgang if she was to survive until the next meeting. He hardly had time to spare these days, being foisted with extra responsibility since fellow officers had been drafted to the Russian front. Today they were meeting on her way back from St Peter Port, at Kings Mills near a farm he had to visit.

He was waiting for her, the jeep parked in a narrow lane off Rue à L'eau. In spite of her weariness after the ride into Town and the hours-long queue, Olive fairly threw herself into his arms. Laughing, he had to steady them both.

'You are pleased to see me, yes? And I am happy to see you, *mein Liebling*. It has been too long.' So saying, Wolfgang took her face in his hands and kissed her until her head span. The familiar fuzzy, warm feeling spread through her insides and she gasped.

He released her and she saw his eyes shining with tenderness.

'Come, let us sit together. I have a blanket and a thermos of coffee and we can sit under those trees.' He nodded towards a copse on the other side of a stone wall, out of sight from anyone in the lane. Olive leaned her bike against the wall and Wolfgang helped her up and onto the other side. A large grey, army blanket lay stretched on the ground. She sat down, smoothing the old, pleated skirt over her knees. The air was warmer than earlier and she hadn't needed a coat, just her woollen hand-knitted jumper. Olive dearly wished she possessed prettier, more feminine clothes, but even if they had been available, Bill would have vetoed any purchase as unnecessary for a farmer's wife.

She sniffed at the aroma as Wolfgang poured the hot, brown liquid into two mugs.

'It's real coffee!'

He looked sheepish as he handed her a mug.

'We still have some supplies coming from France, but we have been warned they are running out. I could get you some if you wish?'

She was torn. To have real coffee! But how would she explain it to Bill? She couldn't say she had bartered for some as only the Germans had access to such luxuries. Reluctantly, she shook her head.

'Thank you, that's kind, but I'd better not. I'll make do with enjoying it while I can.' She took a slow sip and smiled at him. 'It's lovely.'

'Good. I am pleased I can offer you some little treat at least. If not for this war, I would shower you with many gifts – flowers, chocolates, jewellery–'

She laughed. 'Sounds wonderful! Is that how all Germans treat their girlfriends?' It was the first time she had referred to herself as a girlfriend and, seeing him frown, wondered if she had gone too far.

'Of course, if they want to woo her properly. Did not your husband woo you the same?' His clear gaze offered no criticism and she sighed in relief.

'Bill?! I was lucky to get a half-pint of cider at the local pub! It would never have occurred to him to buy me presents, either before our wedding or after. It's not to say all local men are like him, some of my friends were wooed with small gifts. Nothing fancy, mind. A little posy of wild flowers or a handkerchief, if you were lucky.' Olive felt a spurt of anger snake up inside her against Bill. What a fool she had been to saddle herself with a husband like him when men like Wolfgang were...she stopped before adding the word 'available'. Wolfgang was *not* available, he was an enemy soldier and she was a farmer's wife. There could be no happy ending for them.

'*Liebling*? What is the matter? You look so sad, have I said something to upset you?' He thumped his head. 'Of course, my talk of flowers and chocolates must have, how you say, twisted the knife in, yes? Please forgive me. I meant no harm.' He gave a tentative smile, his head on one side.

'It's not you, it's me being silly. There's nothing to forgive. Now, is there any more coffee?' she said brightly, wanting to lift her maudlin mood. Stupid of her to be like this when she really wanted to enjoy the precious time with him.

Wolfgang grinned and topped up her mug before pouring the last small drop into his own.

'*Prost!*' he said, touching his mug against hers. 'I know it should be wine, but we cannot be too correct, can we? Next time I will bring wine and then it will be a proper toast, yes?'

She giggled, glad the tension had lifted. While they finished their coffee, they talked about their childhoods, one of the safer subjects they could choose. Olive knew Wolfgang, one of three boys, had been born in Berlin, his father a doctor and his mother a nurse before they married. All the boys had been to university and gone into professions before the war. As she lay wrapped in his arms, Olive pictured the young Wolfgang as an earnest student, keen to work with animals, rather than humans like his father. He admitted to finding animals easier to like and she had to agree men could be pretty beastly, especially to each other. He made no secret of his contempt for the Nazis and Herr Hitler, but had been obliged to fight for his country. At least he was spared having to kill people while stationed in Guernsey. Though islanders found guilty of certain crimes could be shot, it would not be him who pulled the trigger.

She leant her head against Wolfgang's chest, listening to his steady heartbeat, drinking in the moment. She must just accept how wonderful it was to be with a man who loved her, even though he could never be hers. At least not until the end of the war and she would be free to divorce Bill. Oh, but then she would be in heaven!

chapter thirty-one

2010

Natalie swept up anything broken and replaced the rest on the worktops, brushing away the threatening tears. Opening a bottle of wine, she grabbed a glass and carried both outside. Somewhere safe. Settled in a chair, she poured a full glass and took a gulp. A rich, deep red Rioja, its warmth settled her belly, easing the knots of tension. What on earth was she to do? Call in the God squad? Perhaps it was time…Taking another gulp of wine, Natalie focused on the gorgeous view spread out before her. White vapour trails criss-crossed the soft blue sky, like a game of noughts and crosses. For a peaceful moment her eyes followed the patterns before being drawn towards the golden aura of the waning sun. It was difficult to believe anything malevolent could exist under such a sky. As if in corroboration, a mistle thrush in a nearby tree burst into song, shortly joined by a second. Natalie sat entranced, felt the tug of a smile at her lips. Was this an omen? Was the little bird telling her it would be okay to stay? She hadn't heard it here before and the sound was eminently preferable to the shriek of the seagull.

Her garden appeared lusher, greener since she had left only days before. There must have been some rain to spur on the nascent plants. A rose peeped out from amongst the green and Natalie's heart lifted some more. She *had* to stay here, she had to win against whatever, *whoever* wanted her gone. Buoyed with resolve, she phoned her parents. Not to tell them about what had happened, but to tell them about France and the wedding. She knew her mother would want all the details.

The following night Natalie returned home to find a message on her answerphone from Matt. The replacement pool liner had finally arrived and he could fit it the following week. Relieved the garden would soon be finished she returned the call and arranged for him to come on Monday. After a supper of crab salad, Natalie phoned Jeanne. After the usual greetings, she asked if they could meet for a walk and talk.

'Sounds serious! Are you okay? Has something happened?' Jeanne's concern echoed down the line.

'Yes, but I'm all right. Can you escape from your brood for an hour or two one evening? It's a lovely walk down at Rocquaine.'

'Sure. Nick can put the children to bed and I'm in dire need of a change of scene. How about tomorrow, say seven?'

Natalie agreed and replaced the phone with a sigh of relief. Jeanne would know what to do.

Jeanne and Natalie walked down the lanes, arm in arm, towards the sea. A soft breeze stirred the hedges and whispered along their bare arms. The day had been hot and Natalie, still catching up at work, was sorely in need of a stroll on the beach. On the way she told Jeanne about the weekend in France and what Stuart had said at the airport.

'Mm, the usual mixed messages men tend to give us, eh?' Jeanne said, squeezing Natalie's hand. 'I can't imagine anything he's held back could be too awful. He's an honourable guy, so I doubt he's done something terrible. The good news is, he wants to share it with you before embarking on a relationship. Which means he's pretty keen. What about you?' She cocked her head at Natalie, who tugged at her hair.

'I *am* attracted to him, for sure. But I'm still scared about getting involved with a man after what happened with Liam. Not that I think Stuart's anything like him, he isn't, but it's this business of trust. Of losing control. Letting someone else take charge–'

Jeanne stopped in her tracks and took both her arms.

'Hey, what's this about losing control? Stuart won't be your gaoler! You'd be equals, like any woman these days. Where did that idea come from?' Her eyes were wide in surprise.

Natalie was shaken.

'I…I don't know. The words just came out. I hadn't meant to say what I did. I'm as surprised as you.' She searched here mind, trying to grab at an elusive thought. A vague idea of another voice in her head…Oh, God, she really was losing it!

Jeanne hugged her. 'Don't worry. We can all say something odd at times. So, what do you really think about a relationship with Stuart?'

'I guess I'd like to give it a go, assuming he doesn't admit to being an axe murderer!' She managed a grin, in spite of feeling unnerved.

'Great! Now, what else do you want to talk about? You have that look about you…'

By now they had arrived at the main road, Route de Rocquaine, and needed to cross to the beach.

'I'll tell you once we're on the beach. It's a bit…complicated.'

The ebbing tide had left an expanse of damp, golden sand scattered with rocks. Unusually, they were the only ones on the beach as they stood facing the white tower of Fort Grey. Natalie drew in a deep breath of the ozone-rich air in an effort to clear her head. It helped. Still walking arm in arm, she told Jeanne what she had found in her kitchen on her return. Her friend's mouth fell open.

'My God! This is getting worse! You're absolutely sure it wasn't a burglar?'

She shook her head.

'Definitely. The house was securely locked and, and anyway, I had this strange feeling before I opened the door that something was wrong. To do with this...this ghost who's haunting me. Whatever it – who – is, they focus on the kitchen, for some reason. And, to be honest,' she said, feeling incipient tears gathering, 'I'm finding it hard to take.' Her voice wobbled and Jeanne threw her arms around her as the tears fell.

Jeanne didn't say a word, just stroked her back while she let it out. Fishing for a tissue in her pocket, Natalie pulled back to blow her nose and wipe her eyes.

'There's more. When Tabby was here, we both saw a vision of a woman in an old kitchen and Tabby recognised her as her mother, Olive.'

Jeanne was shocked into silence, shaking her head as if she couldn't believe what she had heard. Natalie turned to face the sea, drawing strength from the ebb and flow of the waves, the soft whoosh as they licked the sand. The idea popped into her head that Olive would probably have stood here at some time, watching the same sea, hearing the same sound. She shivered.

Jeanne rubbed her arms.

'Are you cold? We can go back–'

'No. I'm not cold, I was thinking of...of Olive. I'm sure she's trying to connect with me, to tell me something. In my dreams. And it's not her being hostile, throwing stuff around. That's a man. And he's angry about something.'

'Natalie, you can't go on like this. You need to get help. Mr Ayres, perhaps, or someone else who understands these...these hauntings.' Jeanne's voice was urgent, concerned.

'I know; it's why I needed to talk to you. I had to tell someone and didn't want to worry my parents. They'd only fuss and insist I moved in with them for a while and I don't want to do that. It would be giving in, letting *him* win. And I won't be forced out of my home!' She clenched her fists.

'Right, tell you what. I'll ring Mr Ayres and ask if he can help or at least suggest someone who can. In the meantime, please promise me you'll phone if something happens or you feel you can't cope. Agreed?'

Natalie nodded. 'Agreed. Shall we walk some more? I need the exercise, if nothing else.'

I'm busy in the field, pulling up carrots when I hear the sound of a jeep bumping down the track to the farm. My heart starts thumping against my ribcage as I guess who it is and, throwing down the carrots, I run to the farmyard where the jeep is parked. It's empty. Pushing open the kitchen door, I find Bill and Wolfgang confronting each other. Bill's eyes swivel to me as I enter.

'Here she is, the Jerrybag. I've heard rumours about you two. If I find out they're true, you're as good as dead!' He glares at Wolfgang and I feel sick. Who's spreading such stories?

Wolfgang keeps his cool.

'Herr Falla, I assure you there is no truth in such tales. I am only here to check on your animals. Would you prefer if I came another time? When perhaps it would be more...convenient?' He gave a curt bow.

I hold my breath.

Bill seems unsure how to respond. If he refuses Wolfgang access he'd be arrested.

'Tomorrow would be better,' he mutters, glaring at me and then Wolfgang.

'Tomorrow it will be, Herr Falla.' Wolfgang clicks his heels and leaves, not looking at me.

Before I can escape, Bill grabs my arm, twisting it behind my back until I yelp in pain.

'I've heard you two been seen together. You keep away from him, d'yer hear? Or you'll regret it.' He pushes me away and I stagger and hit my head. Hot, burning pain snakes up and down my arm...

Natalie woke, disorientated. Relief washed over her when she realised it was another 'real' dream and she was safe in her own bed. Squinting at the clock she groaned. Four o'clock! She shuffled, bleary-eyed, to the bathroom for a glass of water and returned to bed. How would she get back to sleep with this swirling through her brain!

Sipping the water, she tried to unravel the meaning of the dream. Firstly, was it a true replay of something which had happened during the war? Or was it her own imagination getting the better of her? The key point in favour of it being true was Olive. Tabby had confirmed the woman they both 'saw' as her mother. And she'd been an older version of the woman who appeared in her dreams. Although she hadn't seen Olive in this dream, she had seen Bill, which seemed to prove something, but what? Try as she might, Natalie couldn't accept it was all her imagination. She had seen and experienced people and events *before* anyone had told her anything. There was a pattern here. Not logical, not believable. But a pattern.

She slipped to the bathroom to refill her glass and continued her analysis. So, if it was true, what had been happening seventy years ago? An unhappily married Olive – and who could blame her, married to that brute of a man, Bill? – meets a handsome German officer and falls for him. Natalie couldn't be certain they'd been lovers but she sure got the feeling Olive had the hots for him. And there was something familiar about 'Wolfgang'...she choked on the water as realisation struck. He bore an uncanny resemblance to Stuart! Same hair, same eyes. And, of course, Tabby shared the same features!

Grabbing a piece of paper and a pen, Natalie noted down everything she could remember about the dream, including the appearance of the men. And the blasted kitchen which continued to haunt her. It began to make sense, but there were more questions left unanswered. What was Olive trying so desperately to tell her? Surely not just about an illicit affair? Fairly commonplace, she'd heard. Although Jerrybags were not condoned by their fellow locals, they weren't as maltreated as they were in France.

Natalie's tiredness fled and any thoughts of further sleep vanished. There remained a couple of mysteries. Did Wolfgang know he had fathered a child with Olive? And what had happened to Olive when the farm burned down? Was that what was she trying to tell her? And, if so, how the hell was she going to find out more than twenty years later?

chapter thirty-two

2010

Enervated from lack of sleep, but at the same time excited by what she might have deduced, Natalie waited until dawn and went for a walk. A sea mist cooled the air and helped her to wake up sufficiently for the working day ahead. That evening Natalie, as had become a habit, opened the kitchen door cautiously before entering. All was as she had left it and she hummed along to IslandFM while cooking supper. Another lovely evening to eat outside.

Half an hour later, stretched out on the terrace, Natalie rang Jeanne to tell her about her dream.

'Oh my God! To think of all that happening between those walls and no-one knowing! A bit like my gran, I guess.'

'Yes, I thought the same. Families and their secrets, eh? Obviously, it's only guesswork at the moment, but the pieces of the jigsaw are slowly fitting into place. Stuart and Tabby are in for a big surprise!'

'For sure. Will you say anything to them?'

'Not yet. I'd like to be more certain of the facts first, if possible. It's rather a biggy to tell people their father wasn't who they thought, isn't it? Even though they never met either of the men.' Natalie paused, wondering how she could broach the subject with Stuart. Tricky.

'By the way, I phoned Mr Ayres, but his housekeeper told me he's away until next week and will pass on the message to call me. Do you think you can cope with waiting?'

'I suppose so. As long as nothing else happens to spook me.' Natalie felt a stab of disappointment. Now she had finally agreed to seek help from the vicar, she had wanted his divine intervention. Now.

Friday and Saturday slid by without mishap and on Sunday Natalie set off to her parents for lunch. She stopped to pick up a bunch of scented lilies for her mother.

'Hi, Mum. You're looking well and that colour really suits you.' She kissed Molly, whose outfit of a warm peach blouse and skirt gave her a gold-like aura.

Her mother's eyes crinkled.

'Why, thank you, darling. It's sweet of you to say, your father rarely comments on my clothes. Are these for me?' She indicated the lilies.

'Sure, shall I put them in water for you? And where's Dad?' Natalie filled a vase for the flowers and peered through the window in search of her father.

'He's just popped down the road to the garage to buy some cream for the pud. He'll be back soon...oh, here he is, what good timing.'

Peter walked into the kitchen holding a pot of double cream.

'Hello, sweetheart. Can your old father have a kiss?'

Natalie sank willingly into his embrace. A real bear of a man, she always felt safe in his arms, no more so than now when she was being haunted, mentally and physically.

'Hi, Dad, good to see you both. What's on the menu today?' She sniffed the air, but couldn't smell anything cooking except potatoes.

'We're having a treat. Nick set up some lobster pots and he had a good haul yesterday and dropped off three large ones for us, ready cooked. So lobster salad and new potatoes it is.'

'Yummy! You know how I love lobster,' she said, grinning.

Her parents smiled indulgently. Even as a child she had asked for lobster whenever they went out to restaurants and had to be told, gently but firmly, it was too expensive.

Minutes later the food was on the table outside and a bottle of white wine reposed in its chilled blanket. Between mouthfuls of food, Natalie described in more detail the events of the previous weekend and Molly's ears pricked up every time Stuart was mentioned. Natalie knew there'd be further questions. And there were.

'Sounds wonderful! The setting must have been idyllic for the wedding. Did you and Stuart enjoy your time together?' her mother said, eyebrows arched.

She knew it! 'Yes, we did, thanks. But if you want to know if it's serious between us, it isn't. Not yet, anyway. We're just good friends.'

Peter rolled his eyes.

'For heaven's sake, Molly, leave the poor girl alone. I'm sure if she has anything to tell us on the romantic front she will, without being badgered by you.'

'It's all right, Dad. I know Mum's keen to see me married off, like Phil. Which reminds me, any more news on the new baby?'

Her mother, who had looked sheepish, brightened, and said all was proceeding well with the pregnancy and Phil was bringing the family over later in the summer.

'Great! I look forward to seeing them all.' Natalie hoped to impress her brother with her choice of home. Which reminded her...

'Mum, Stuart and his mother are keen to find out more about the old lady who disappeared, Olive. I think you mentioned someone in La Societé Guernesiaise knew the Fallas during the war. Could you ask them if they'd be happy to talk to Stuart?'

'Of course. I can't remember off the top of my head who it was, but I'll ask at the meeting next week and get back to you. It must be odd for Stuart to know so little about his family.' Molly sipped her wine, her forehead creased in thought.

'Have there been any more dreams or disturbances?' her father asked.

'Not really, no.' Natalie crossed her fingers against the lie. She hated being untruthful, but it was better than them gathering her up to bring home. She'd have some stick for it once the whole story came out, for sure.

The evening was warm and Natalie threw open the windows when she returned to the cottage. Trapped weary flies buzzed against the glass. As the windows opened they flew out, taking their irritating noise with them. Natalie took a glass of chilled wine outside with her and settled, contentedly into a chair. She'd enjoyed the lunch, stretched over several hours and it had been good to spend time in her old home. It held many happy memories and she smiled as she recalled some of the mischief she and Phil had got up to, particularly when joined by the tomboyish Jeanne. They'd been quite a threesome! Natalie frowned as she considered how lucky she had been compared to poor Jeanne, losing her parents so young. She couldn't imagine how awful it must have been. Her mind switched to Tabby, and her unhappy childhood, brought up in poverty in this very building. Or, rather, its original incarnation. Sipping her wine, her mind dwelt on the inequalities of life and her heart went out to Jeanne and Tabby. At least they had both since found love, happiness and success in their lives.

A fly buzzed around her head, distracting her train of thought and she flapped it away in annoyance. Her eyes were drawn to the pile of earth to the side of the garden and remembered, with a smile, that Matt would be starting work on the pond the next day. She couldn't wait for the finished result, wanting to hear the sound of water splashing over the strategically placed rocks forming a mini-waterfall. She hadn't yet decided whether or not to have a few goldfish in the larger, bottom pond, but they'd add interest and colour. Something to think about. She stretched and stood up. Time for a spot of television before bed.

Natalie hadn't been in bed long when she was startled by a noise coming from downstairs. Her heart pumped adrenaline through her body as she debated what to do. She'd stupidly left the downstairs windows open so perhaps an animal or a bird had got in. Burglaries were rare in Guernsey, she told herself, pushing her feet into slippers and wrapping a cotton dressing gown around her naked body. If only Stuart were home! She'd have phoned him, but...looking for a heavy object, she picked up the rubber torch which could perform dual duty if necessary. Her heart pumped wildly in her chest as she crept to the bedroom door and pulled it open, inch by inch. To her surprise, the landing and downstairs were flooded by moonlight. She hadn't remembered it being a full moon...she was further shocked to see the stairs were different, made of stone and not in the same place. Oh my God! What was happening? Was this a dream? Pinching herself, the pain told her it wasn't. She felt her mouth go dry. Was she about to walk into the past again?

Fear tugged at her mind and she hesitated. Then another sound came from the direction of the kitchen. Like something being dragged. Definitely not a bird, then. Taking a deep breath and willing herself on, Natalie tiptoed down the uncarpeted stairs and found herself in a strange hall. Cheap sepia prints hung on dingy painted walls and the moonlight flooded through a window she didn't recognise. Somehow she'd become part of a time-warp! Her mind reeled. How...? Licking her dry lips, she told herself she couldn't come to any harm, if it really was the past. She was only an observer. Not entirely convinced, she forced herself onwards to the kitchen as the sound of dragging grew louder. Her heart was thumping wildly as she arrived at the door and stood transfixed with horror by the scene in front of her.

chapter thirty-three

1944

Olive saw little of Wolfgang through the winter. With shorter days and the ever increasing shortages of food, she had less chance and excuse to go out for any length of time, but he did make the occasional inspection of the farm. In between these snatched moments, Olive would again agonise over whether or not to end their friendship, finding it stressful to keep such a huge secret to herself. She missed her mother – dead this past year – and would have given anything to unburden herself to her. But would she have understood? And approved? That Olive wasn't sure of and was partly glad she didn't have to endure her mother's disapproval. Depression licked at her heels and even seeing Wolfgang didn't entirely push it away.

With the arrival of spring, her spirits lifted a little. Rumours of an imminent Allied push in Europe circulated the island, encouraging thoughts of imminent salvation. Even the Germans seemed to agree it wouldn't be long.

'My superiors are warning us to be ready for an Allied invasion. It is considered if France falls, then the islands will be the next to be retaken.' Wolfgang shrugged, his face a picture of despair. Olive had gone sticking at Pleinmont and he had joined her. Her heart leapt at the thought of the rumours being true. If the Germans thought so, it must be...

'Would it be so very bad if that happened? If Hitler were to surrender, then you'd be free and we...we could be together.'

'Except, *liebling*, you have a husband.' He stroked her face before kissing her tenderly on the lips. The familiar thrill ran through her body.

'I plan to divorce Bill as soon as this war is over. I have grounds, he's being unfaithful and he's been...violent towards me. So then I'll be free as well.' She looked at him expectantly.

His eyes narrowed.

'He has been violent to you? Recently? If he dares to hurt you, I will kill him!' His normally calm face was flushed.

'Oh no, not recently. He's been better of late, spends more time with this other woman. Please don't worry about me.' Olive hesitated. 'You do want us to be together, don't you?'

'But of course. We have many obstacles to overcome first, so I do not allow myself to think too much about it. Come, we must hurry, I am due to attend a meeting shortly.'

Olive couldn't help feeling disappointed. Perhaps it had been foolish to expect an undying declaration of love, with Wolfgang promising they would be together one day. She consoled herself he was only being realistic and it didn't mean he *wasn't* in love with her. Did it?

On the evening of 6th June Olive and Bill stood in the yard and watched as hundreds of British and American planes flew over the island, heading for France. It was the sign – and sight – they'd been waiting for and they raised their arms, cheering. Excitement bubbled in her veins, knowing this was part of the Allied push to free France from the Germans. The news of the Normandy landings the previous day had been heard on illicit crystal sets and circulated throughout the island.

'Won't be long now,' Bill said, fists raised. 'We'll be the ones kicking out the German bastards next.'

Olive grunted. Her thoughts fled to Wolfgang and her stomach clenched in fear. While they continued to watch the plane-filled sky, the boom of the German guns filled the air and she prayed all the planes would escape unscathed.

By the next day life returned to normal, with news continuing to filter through about the Allied push into France. Exactly two weeks later, Olive was in St Peter Port standing in a queue to collect their rations when the noise of an aircraft engine made her and everyone else, look skywards. An RAF plane circled above the harbour before dropping a bomb. Olive screamed and threw herself on the ground, convinced she was about to die. She heard the screams of others on the ground and felt the tremors as the bomb exploded, sounds of breaking glass mixing with the screams. For a moment she lay still, too scared to move. Hesitantly, she stood up, shaking; she brushed herself down. It was like a battlefield; glass from all the windows around her covered the ground. She was lucky not to have been hurt – or worse. People walked around, looking dazed, treading warily on the shards of glass. The queue reformed and fortunately no glass had fallen into the shop. Clutching her rations, Olive collected her bike and rode home feeling scared, thinking how much she wanted, needed, to see Wolfgang.

Olive met him two days later and he was shocked to hear of her experience, holding her close to him as she talked. She started to cry, the act of telling him making her relive the terror she'd felt.

'*Mein Liebling*, I cannot bear to think I could have lost you, never expected you to be in danger. I...I have been thinking it is time for us to be truly lovers at last. Why wait? We do not know what lies ahead and must not waste the time we have. Do you not agree?'

She felt the urgent need in her body. He was right, why wait?

'Yes, I agree. But how...?'

'My fellow officers at The Imperial are on twelve-hour shifts during the day now we are on full alert. If you could get away, I will be on my own once they leave in the morning and no-one would see us. You can do some sticking in the woods, yes?' He held her tight, his eyes shadowed with desire.

She nodded. The risk would be small and if it meant she could lay in his arms at last...her heart pounded in her chest.

Wolfgang smiled and kissed her.

'I can be free tomorrow morning and will wait for you at the back entrance at nine. You will be there?'

'Yes, I'll be there.'

The next morning Olive slipped away unnoticed by Bill, who hadn't bothered coming home the night before. Part of her resented the ease with which he was virtually flaunting his infidelity, while she was forced to be furtive. It wasn't fair! But at least she hadn't had to lie to him. Olive wore a faded cotton dress over her best underwear. 'Best' only meaning the bra and knickers, in matching pink cotton, hadn't yet fallen to pieces. As she cycled down lanes edged with lush hedgerows forming arches overhead, Olive was both scared and excited. Scared Wolfgang would be disappointed in her, and excited at the thought of finally becoming lovers. By the time she arrived at The Imperial, her face was flushed from the ride and sexual desire. Looking around quickly, she saw no-one and wheeled her bike around the back. Wolfgang waited at the door, his face breaking into a huge smile as he saw her. Propping the bike against the wall, Olive threw herself into his arms and he kissed her fiercely on the mouth. Pulling back, Wolfgang grabbed her arm and steered her up the narrow back staircase, motioning her to remain quiet. His room on the first floor was spacious as befitted his rank, possessing a double bed and the type of furniture usual in a modest seaside hotel. Wolfgang wore only his shirt and trousers and without the jacket and cap looked so much younger, less commanding. An ordinary man. Olive stood in front of him, uncertain what to do. Shy. Shifting his feet, he took her hands. She dropped her eyes.

'You are sure, *liebling*? I want you so much, but–'

Olive raised her eyes to his. Those beautiful blue eyes which would forever be embedded in her mind.

'Yes, I'm sure.' And began to undress.

Olive rode home in a daze. Her whole body flooded with a warm, fuzzy glow; contented, fulfilled. Something she had never experienced before. Ever. Now she understood what people meant by the joy of making love, hugging the pleasure to herself. She hadn't known such pleasure existed and already wanted to experience it again. And again...She threw back her head and laughed, narrowly avoiding an old man crossing the coast road. Olive smiled her apology and the man's sour face broke into a smile. Her joy was infectious! Turning into the lane leading to the farm, she composed her features. Somehow she had to hide what she wanted to shout out to the world, and it wouldn't be easy. But inside she knew. She was in love. And no-one could take that away from her.

Over the next few weeks, Olive joined Wolfgang at his billet whenever possible. They were always careful to remain unseen, although he did join her in the woods for sticking once. If any soldiers saw them it would make no difference, they would turn a blind eye. Bill would occasionally give her a searching look, as if seeing something had changed within her, but said nothing. They were like ships in the night, hardly seeing each other these days, for which Olive was glad. She imagined everyone would guess she was in love, as if it was printed on her forehead. Her friend Elsie remarked on the change in her one day, asking why she looked so happy.

'No particular reason. I'm just glad it's summer and the way things are going with the Allies, looks like the war will be over soon. It's enough to make anyone happy, isn't it?'

Elsie hadn't looked convinced, but didn't press her. Perhaps she took the view better not to know. She was stepping out with a young man who'd been pronounced not fit enough to enlist, thanks to his asthma. Olive wished her friend to be happy, but felt a pang of self-pity knowing Elsie was free to marry her boyfriend, if she wished. Unlike her.

Then one terrible day in late July, Olive's world fell apart.

She was in the kitchen humming a dance tune as she peeled vegetables for dinner when Bill crashed through the door drunk, and lunged at her with his fists flying. There was no escape. She backed away, fear coursing through her.

'You slut of a Jerrybag! You've been seen sneaking into that bastard's place, you have. I'll soon knock that smirk off your face, I will.' He landed a punch on her jaw and she fell spinning to the floor. She curled up in a ball while he continued to rain blows on her head and body, all the time shouting obscenities at her. Then he stopped. For a brief moment Olive thought that was it, but he dragged her onto her feet and up the stairs, throwing her onto the marital bed. And forced himself on her. Too weak to fight back, she lay there, weeping. As he rolled off her, Olive heard the sound of a jeep pulling up outside. Wolfgang! He mustn't come in! Bill would kill him! She tried to crawl to the window and warn him, but it was too late. Bill was already buttoning his flies and heading out of the room. She followed, hoping to do she knew not what. But something.

Wolfgang knocked as Bill arrived at the open door. Olive heard Bill yell, 'You bastard!' and stumbled in to the kitchen to see Bill aim a blow at Wolfgang, who fell backwards into the yard.

She screamed. 'No! Bill, no!' and went outside, barely registering the two soldiers in the back of the jeep as she dropped to her lover's side. He lifted his head, shook it and stood up unaided. The soldiers jumped out and advanced towards Bill. Wolfgang took one look at her and his face darkened. Turning to Bill, he said, 'You will pay for this, Herr Falla.' He shouted something in German and the soldiers grabbed Bill and tied his hands before thrusting him in the back of jeep. Bill kept shouting, 'Jerry bastard! You fucked my wife! I'll make a complaint against you, I will.'

Olive could barely stand and Wolfgang half-carried her inside, setting her gently in Bill's chair. He stroked the hair out of her blackening eyes, murmuring, '*Mein liebling*! What has he done to you? And how did he find out about us? I am so sorry this has happened to you. It is all my fault.' He kissed her swollen lips and Olive knew she had to hide the worst from him.

'Someone…saw me at The Imperial and…put two and two together. I don't know who, but…they must be a friend of…Bill's.' Speaking was painful and her head and body screamed for relief from the pain.

Tears slid down his cheeks and Wolfgang brushed them away awkwardly.

'I must go. I have arrested your husband for striking an officer and he will be imprisoned. He will not hurt you again, you have my word. Are you able to manage on your own? It would not look right if I stayed.'

She forced herself to nod, saying she would be all right.

Another kiss and he was gone, shouting orders to the soldiers. Olive curled up in the chair and sobbed. What was to become of her now? If word got around, she would be doubly damned as an adulteress and a collaborator. She wanted to die.

Olive was spared public shaming, but she heard the whispers, though no-one confronted her face-to-face. The local press reported Bill's arrest for striking a German officer and he faced a military trial, no details were given, apart from the sentence; he was to be sent to prison in France for two years. Olive didn't see him again.

She struggled to cope with the milking for a couple of days, but then it became easier. Her young body recovered quickly, but her mind still suffered. Wolfgang had called the day after, alone, and told her what would happen to Bill. Olive couldn't feel sorry for her husband; he'd got what he deserved. She could only be glad she didn't have to live with him again. When he returned she would file for divorce. Her main worry was Wolfgang. He was as loving and caring as ever, but while she recovered from her beating he wouldn't make love to her. She knew it was because he didn't want to hurt her, but still felt bereft. Slowly, her life returned to its normal routine, except she no longer had to cook for Bill or do his washing. But the downside was she had to run the farm alone.

Wolfgang called in occasionally and, when her bruises had healed, made love to her again. Buoyed by this, Olive looked forward to spending more time with him. As if nothing had ever happened.

One hot August day, Olive was in the yard, scattering the food for the chickens, when Wolfgang arrived in his jeep. He hadn't said he was coming and she felt the familiar flipping of her stomach.

She smiled as he approached, but his face was sombre.

'What is it? Has Hitler surrendered?' It was something being discussed everywhere, even the Germans knew it couldn't be long coming.

He shook his head.

'No, *liebling*, I fear he has not. Better if he had, for us all. Come, let us go inside and we can talk.'

Olive felt the first ripple of foreboding as she led him to the kitchen. What could he mean? They sat down and

Wolfgang reached for her hands, a look of such sorrow on his face that she could hardly breathe.

'I have been recalled to Germany. There is to be a last attempt at fighting back the Allies and I...I have to go. With other soldiers.'

The words caused her more pain than the beating she'd suffered. Not now! Not when they could be together!

'I understand you have to obey orders, but...when...when do you leave?' She couldn't stop the tears and Wolfgang wiped them away with his fingers.

'We leave in two days...'

She gasped.

'So soon! Oh, my darling! I don't know how I'll bear it without you.' Olive took a deep breath, trying desperately to keep some dignity. 'But you will come back for me – when the war is over?'

He kissed her cheek, a sad smile hovering around his mouth.

'But of course! I do not think it can be long now. If I am spared, I will return. I promise.'

chapter thirty-four

2010

Natalie felt the blood drain from her face. A man was dragging a woman's body across the floor towards the open back door! Not her back door, the original one. The kitchen was the one she'd seen with Tabby, with an older Olive cooking at the range. The furniture was different to the wartime kitchen, a dresser now stood where there'd been a cupboard...Natalie dragged eyes back to the figures – who were they? The bright moonlight – if that was what it was, it looked too eerie for moonlight, she thought – threw everything into clear relief. The man turned his head toward where she was standing, his eyes seeming to go through her. Bill! A very much older Bill, but definitely him. But it couldn't be! He died in the war! She looked again at the woman on the floor and noticed the dark stain around her heart. Oh, God! She was dead! As Bill reached the back door, the woman's head rolled and Natalie recognised Olive. The older Olive she'd seen before...

She hesitated. If she walked into the scene, would it disappear? Her mouth increasingly dry, Natalie placed one foot cautiously on the stone floor. Nothing changed. Slowly, she followed as Bill dragged Olive through the open door towards what looked like a vegetable garden at the side of the house. The site of her new pond, she realised, with a jolt. Bill let go of the woman's legs and picked up a spade and began digging.

Suddenly it went dark and Natalie found herself facing the flickering control lights of her fridge-freezer. Switching on the torch, she found the light switch. Everything was back to normal. Except it wasn't. How could it be? It seemed she'd just witnessed the murder of Stuart's grandmother!

Shock set in and Natalie started trembling. She found a bottle of brandy and a glass and poured a large measure, gulping it down. Gasping as it seared her throat, she slumped onto a bar stool. What the hell should she do? Glancing at the clock, she saw it was nearly midnight. Far too late to ring her parents, and what could they do, anyway? Except offer a bed for the night. The police? They'd hardly rush round at this time of night to hear a garbled account of a potential murder that may or may not have happened more than twenty years ago! No, she'd have to stick it out until morning – oh, God! Matt was coming round to fit the pond! She needed to think...Deciding nothing could be achieved until the morning, Natalie swallowed some of Stuart's herbal pills and went back to bed, convinced she'd not sleep a wink. But as her head hit the pillow sleep claimed her.

The next morning Natalie awoke feeling like shit. Her head throbbed and her mouth was so dry her tongue stuck to the roof of her mouth. Reaching for the glass of water she'd brought upstairs, she took a deep drink before checking the time. Seven o'clock. As the full horror of what she'd 'seen' surfaced, she reached for her phone to call her parents. Fortunately, they were early risers and after listening for a few minutes, her father said they'd be straight round. Next she texted Matt, asking if he could delay coming round until she got back to him and she'd explain later. After a quick shower Natalie went downstairs, nervous at what she might find. But all was at it should be. It was as if last night hadn't happened.

Natalie was drinking a treble-strength coffee when her parents pulled into the drive. She opened the door and was immediately buried in her father's arms, her unshed tears flowing freely. Her mother offered soothing words as they all congregated in the kitchen.

'Right, now are you able to take us through it slowly so there's no mistaking what happened?' Her father's voice was gentle, without a hint of doubting her. She gathered her thoughts and told them exactly what she'd seen. It was a memory seared on her brain and she left nothing out.

At the end her parents exchanged glances before either spoke. Surely they believed her? Her heart thumped against her ribs.

'Don't look so upset, darling. We do believe you, I promise. It's just, it's such a horrible thing to have seen, it hardly seems possible. But it does fit what we know about Olive, about her disappearing.' Her mother paused, gazing at the floor, as if waiting to see for herself what Natalie had seen. She looked up and smiled. 'The only thing that doesn't make sense is Bill. He died in prison, didn't he? That's what Tabby was told, isn't it?'

She nodded.

'It's been puzzling me, too. But is there any proof he died abroad?' She shrugged, a tiny sliver of doubt creeping into her mind. If he *had* died, then what she 'saw' last night couldn't have happened!

Her father chipped in.

'There's one way of proving what you saw happened, and that's to dig the area you say Bill, or whoever he was, started digging. So he could bury Olive's body, poor woman.'

Mollie nodded.

'Yes, that's right. But who will do the digging?'

'I will, I'm not afraid of finding a few bones and we'd never convince the police to do it, would we? No, it's best if I do it and you two can be witnesses. Take photos.' Peter looked at the women, who nodded their heads in agreement.

Natalie was relieved. She'd had visions of Matt coming across the skeleton while digging that morning – an awful thought.

'Good. Might as well get on with it now. Where do you keep your garden tools, Natalie?' She took him to the garage where the few tools she'd bought were stored. Not that she had planned to do much digging, but...

A few minutes later she showed her father the spot she thought was the right one, though it was hard to be precise under the odd circumstances. The site earmarked for the pond. By now it was after eight and Natalie should have been on her way to work. She called the office to say something urgent had come up and she hoped to be in that afternoon.

Molly joined Natalie in the kitchen, asking if she'd eaten yet.

'No, I've only had a coffee. I'll make some toast. Have you and Dad had breakfast?' She took out the bread from the freezer and popped two slices in the toaster.

'Yes, we gobbled down some muesli, but I wouldn't mind some toast and perhaps we could all do with some coffee. I'll make it.'

Molly took a mug out to Peter and then sat down with Natalie.

'Are you sure you're all right? It must have been a dreadful shock, seeing...that.' Molly's face was creased in concern.

'Well, I do feel a bit odd. As if I've walked onto the set of a horror movie. Unreal. If we don't find a body then...' she shook her head at the alternative. Insanity.

Molly patted her hand. 'You're not going mad, I'd recognise the signs. But I do sympathise. I'm completely out of my professional comfort zone with this, so goodness knows how you're feeling!'

Concentrating on their food, they remained silent, the only sound that of a spade being thrust into the earth a matter of yards away.

'It's a bit like being in a TV crime drama, isn't it? Everyone waiting to see what or who the forensics team dig up. My favourite was *Silent Witness*, gory but clever,' Natalie said, finishing her coffee.

'Mm. I'll go and check on your father. Don't want him overdoing it and having a heart attack, do we?'

Molly rose and Natalie went with her, feeling guilty she hadn't offered to help. But there was only one spade.

Peter was leaning on the spade sipping coffee and appeared unfazed by his exertions so far. He grinned at their approach. 'Can't keep away, can you? We might be about to solve of the mystery of poor Olive. The good thing is the ground's lovely and soft after the rain we had recently.' He passed the mug to Molly and carried on digging. A hole about a foot deep yawned beneath him and it was clear to Natalie her father was an expert digger.

She and her mother fetched chairs from the terrace and sat near Peter, enjoying the early morning sun. Natalie closed her eyes, suddenly drowsy after the late night. Her mind drifted back to what she'd seen, wondering if there were any details she'd forgotten. She saw the man's face again and it still looked like an older version of Bill. If only she could have taken a photo! But as the figures were in a different time frame, she assumed it would have just captured her own kitchen. Natalie was deep in reflection when she was startled by a shout.

'Hey! I think I've found something.'

Her eyes snapped open and she saw her father kneeling down, scrabbling with his hands. She and Molly joined him and watched as he carefully moved soil from something protruding in the hole. White against the dark earth, as Peter's hands swept it clear, the faint outline of a skull emerged.

chapter thirty-five

2010

Natalie held her breath. Was it human? Or animal? After all, this had been a farm...

'Dad? What...what is it?'

He turned to face her and Molly, his expression grim.

'Looks like a human skull to me. I don't want to dig any more in case I damage it. We should call the police.' He stood up, rubbing his back.

Her mother hugged her. 'Looks like you did see a murder, darling. So don't go doubting yourself any more.' Molly turned to Peter, smiling. 'Well done. Now come in and wash your hands and I'll get you a cold drink.'

Taking a last look at the part-excavated skull, Natalie shivered. Then she followed her parents inside and picked up the phone.

'I'll call them, Dad. Sounds better coming from me. I can say we were digging for a pond, which is sort-of true.' She dialled the number and explained what had happened. The sanitised version. After ending the call she told her parents they were on their way.

'Lemonade, anyone? I could sure do with one myself.'

Her parents nodded and she pulled out three cans from the fridge. By mutual consent they took them outside to the terrace and sat down, looking towards the sea, averting their eyes from the hole in the ground.

'I suppose this'll make the local headlines.' Natalie frowned, unhappy at the unwanted publicity and invasion of her privacy.

Molly pursed her lips.

'It will, I'm afraid. Bodies don't turn up all that often over here. But it's most likely to be the proverbial seven-day wonder, and if you get pestered you can come and stay with us.' She sipped her drink, looking thoughtful. 'Assuming the body is that of a woman, and buried for about twenty years, you'll need to tell Stuart, won't you? Before the press gets wind of the connection.'

Natalie nodded. 'Yes, I've been thinking about that. I'll ring him if it looks as if it's Olive. The police will want a living relative for DNA. Bit of a shock for him and Tabby.' Where would she start? The vision? She'd have to tell him something...The sound of cars arriving interrupted her thoughts. Suggesting her parents stayed put for the moment, she went through to the front door as the bell rang.

She was faced with several uniformed policemen hovering behind two men in plain clothes, one of whom introduced himself as DI Woods and the other as Dr Vaudin. Behind a couple of police cars she spotted an ambulance.

'Right, I'll show you what we've found. It's round the side, if you'll follow me.' She noticed the excitement in the faces of the policemen. Her mother was right; investigating a buried body was a rare occurrence. The DI stood by the hole and motioned to the doctor to join him.

'Do you want my men to clear away more soil? I'll tell them to be careful.'

The doctor nodded and moved away slightly. Natalie watched as two men slipped into the type of coveralls she'd seen on television, covering their shoes and pulling on gloves. They opened a case containing small trowels and brushes and set to work.

'Right, Miss Ogier, can we go somewhere where we can talk?' The DI, a slim man in his thirties and sporting stubble on his chin, turned away from the kneeling men.

'Sure. Let's join my parents on the terrace.'

Natalie made the introductions and DI Woods took out a notepad and started asking questions. He seemed satisfied with what they told him.

'I understand you've only recently moved in, so I don't suppose you'd have any idea who the...person might be?'

This was the question she was hoping he'd ask.

'Well, I might. You see...' she told him the story of Stuart's grandmother and his interest quickened.

'That's extremely helpful, thanks. We can check the old files about the case. Is Mr...' he checked his notes, 'Cross around?'

'No, he's in France with his mother. I...I don't want to bother him until you're sure it could be his grandmother. There's been a family wedding.' She smiled at him.

'Understood. I'll go and check progress.' He stood and went back to the hole.

'Coffee, anyone? And I'll see if any of the police would like a drink.' Her parents both said yes and Natalie collected the empty cans before joining the group huddled around the now bigger hole in the ground. Police tape surrounded the site. As she drew near, Natalie felt something like an electric shock run up from her feet through her body and, swaying, felt the cans drop from her fingers. The doctor rushed to her side, asking if she was all right.

'I...I think so, thanks. Just felt a bit...dizzy.' She remembered the last time she'd felt the same thing. When she'd stamped her foot on the ground. Which now appeared to be Olive's grave.

'Sit down and I'll take a look at you.' He guided her to the chair she'd dragged round earlier and she sat down, shaking. 'It could be delayed shock. It's not a nice thing to find in your garden, is it?' Crouching down, he put a cool hand on her forehead and then checked her pulse while an officer collected the cans from the pile of soil where they'd fallen. Her parents must have seen what happened and rushed over, wide-eyed.

'What's happened? Are you okay?' her father said, eying the doctor hovering over her.

The doctor let go of her wrist and said, 'She felt dizzy. Her heart rate's fine and she doesn't have a temperature.' He turned back to Natalie. 'How are you feeling now?'

'Bit better, thanks. It's all been a bit of a shock...' Molly had gone into the kitchen and returned with a glass of water and she drank it down.

'Thanks, Mum.' She frowned as she glanced at the doctor looming above her. 'Are you here to see if the...the remains are human?'

'Yes, I'm the pathologist. DI Woods also wants me to assess how long ago they were buried.' He nodded towards the hole. 'They've uncovered a full skeleton and it's a female. I'd say she's been there for a number of years, for sure. At least twenty. But further tests will tell us more.'

Natalie glanced at her parents, who looked relieved. Beyond them, DI Woods was in deep discussion with the officers in the hole.

'How long will it take to learn the woman's age and when she died? She could be my neighbour's grandmother.'

He pursed his lips.

'Yes, I heard you mention that earlier. We'll be taking the body away shortly and I'll be as quick as I can.' He stopped to watch as a stretcher was brought from the ambulance. Turning back, he added, 'Should know by tomorrow at the latest.' He gave her a searching look. 'Sure you're okay? You're still a little pale.'

'I'm fine. Nothing a cup of coffee can't fix. Talking of which-'

'I'll make it, you sit still, darling,' Molly said and went off to ask if anyone else wanted a cup.

DI Woods, after giving orders to other policemen, joined Natalie. Satisfied she was all right, he said he'd be leaving officers to search the immediate area for anything that could be of interest and that part of her garden would remain sealed off.

'I'll phone you once we've had the pathologist's report. Are you going to stay here?' He looked as if he thought it'd be odd to stay in a crime scene.

'Yes, no reason not to. It's not as if I'm at risk from someone who killed twenty years ago, is it?' Her fighting spirit had surfaced. She saw the doubt in her father's eyes but he remained silent. Wise man.

The DI moved away and Natalie watched as the skeleton was carefully lifted into a black body bag before being placed on the stretcher. As the bearers moved past her, Natalie could have sworn she heard a faint voice cry, 'Help me, please!'

chapter thirty-six

1944–45

By September Olive knew something was wrong. Consumed by grief since Wolfgang's departure, she hadn't taken much notice of her body. One morning she had an overwhelming urge to be sick, just making it to the toilet in time. Holding her head as her stomach emptied itself, she wondered if she'd eaten something bad. A possibility considering she'd found maggots in the bread. As she splashed her face at the sink the glimmer of an idea surfaced. Surely…? She did a mental calculation. Oh, my God! Her last curse had been in July. And since then she had made love with Wolfgang and been 'raped' by Bill. If she *was* pregnant, either could be the father.

Dazed, Olive made a cup of ginger tea and curled up in what had been Bill's chair. She could be two months gone. After more than four years of trying, she might be expecting a baby! She didn't want to consider it might be Bill's. That would be too, too awful to contemplate. And she hadn't got pregnant by him before, had she? No, it seemed more likely Wolfgang was the father. She hugged the thought to herself, hoping he'd be pleased when he returned to Guernsey. Why, she could have the baby before he came back. A quick calculation – April. Roughly. She'd need to see the doctor to confirm soon. Another month and she'd go. In the meantime she hoped she wasn't going to be sick like this every day, she had the cows to milk. Sipping the tea, Olive's big regret was that her mother wasn't there. She would have been thrilled to be a grandmother and would have been a comfort during the pregnancy. As maudlin tears threatened, Olive pushed herself out of the chair. The cows needed her.

A month later the doctor confirmed her pregnancy and the expected delivery date of mid-April 1945. He would normally have prescribed iron tablets, but there were none, and he advised her to eat any meat she could get hold of, and plenty of greens. And to look after herself.

'I understand how hard it must be for you since your husband was sent away, and it's going to become harder still over the coming months. You won't be able to look after the animals on your own. Is there anyone who might help?'

'I'll ask around, Doctor. I don't want to put my baby at risk. We must pray this war will end soon and my...husband will come back to me.' Olive left the surgery grinning broadly. It was official – she was expecting a baby! Not being able to keep it to herself any longer, she cycled to Elsie's with the news.

Her friend hugged her in delight. 'Wonderful news, Olive. Your Bill will be right chuffed when he comes back, won't he? I know you've wanted a baby for years and at last something good has happened for you.' They sat outside in the afternoon sun, still warm for late September, and drank bramble tea. Elsie frowned. 'I do hope you'll cope. I've heard since the last supplies arrived in August, there'll be no more. We have to survive on what's left, and that's not enough. The Germans are shipping out loads of the slave workers to camps in Germany to save feeding them,' she said, waving her hand. 'Not that they ever fed the poor devils, anyway. It's the soldiers we want to leave; they've always had the lion share of the rations, which isn't fair.'

Olive nodded in agreement.

'You're right, but there's nothing we can do, is there? Which reminds me, do you know of anyone who could give me a hand with the animals and everything? I'm really struggling and–'

Elsie clapped her hands.

'What about my Charles? I know he don't look all that strong, but he's willing and knows about animals.'

Charles was Elsie's boyfriend, the one with asthma. Olive would take on anyone willing to work hard.

'I can't pay much, but he could have some eggs and vegetables in lieu of wages.'

'He'd be grateful for anything. I'll ask him to call round, shall I?'

Charles proved to be a godsend for Olive. Although he had to pace himself to avoid a coughing fit, he worked hard. Luckily his asthma was mild and he loved working with the animals.

By November even farmers like Olive were struggling to survive on the meagre rations. When she went into town she was shocked by the gaunt faces of people she now barely recognised. The local papers ran stories about the increase in deaths from illness and starvation, and the once jaunty soldiers crept about like shadows, no longer shouting and singing in the streets. You could see defeat in their faces. All farms were ordered to provide one head of cattle for slaughter to augment the rations. Olive sensed the despair and fear of her fellow islanders. How long could they hold out? But she *had* to keep going, for the baby's sake.

News spread that a message from the Controlling Committee had been sent to Germany, requesting help from the Red Cross. Spirits lifted immediately, but it was weeks before their prayers were answered. Olive endured a miserable Christmas, missing her parents and Wolfgang, and eking out what little food she had. It was also the coldest Christmas in living memory and without gas, electricity or coal, the islanders were frozen. Olive had some wood for a fire, but it was nearly gone. Islanders with orchards chopped down trees, desperate for the wood, bartering some for food. Finally, on 27th December, the SS *Vega* arrived in St Peter Port harbour loaded with food parcels for every household, but not for the Germans. By the 31st all parcels had been delivered and Olive opened hers, wide-eyed with delight. Not only was there a selection of food – bread, jam, tea, chocolate, corned beef, biscuits, cheese, salmon, and more – but also soap and other toiletries. She sighed with pleasure – Christmas had finally arrived.

It was while she ate the first mouthful of chocolate that Olive felt an odd flutter in her stomach. Putting her hands on the now visible swelling, she felt it again. The baby was kicking! She laughed. He or she must like chocolate too!

By the time of the third visit of SS *Vega* in March 1945, supplies were dangerously low again. There'd been no bread since February and Olive, now in her eighth month, found it more difficult to get out and about. The ship brought in tons of flour and within days the bakers were busy and when Olive collected her ration, the bread was the best she'd tasted since the Occupation began. She was upset not to be able to make clothes for her baby, but the next Red Cross parcels contained extra supplies for pregnant mothers, including donated baby clothes. Stroking tiny white matinee jackets and nighties brought a lump to her throat. One day Nell turned up with a crib and some baby blankets and clothes. She'd had a baby a year after her wedding and the little boy was now holding onto his mother's skirts.

'Oh, Nell, this is so kind of you. I didn't know how I was to manage. Thought I'd have to put baby in a drawer.' The crib was hand-carved in oak and Olive stroked it lovingly. She smiled at Nell, adding, 'I'll let you have it back as soon as it's outgrown. And anything else.'

'I'm not sure if we'll try again, certainly not till after this war is over. But the news is good, isn't it? They say the Allies are advancing on Berlin and Hitler doesn't stand a chance. The German big-nobs here are said to be planning for the end, but won't surrender. Bloody idiots! They say that the Vice-Admiral who's now in charge is a fervent Nazi and will do anything for Hitler. Huh! I just want to see my dad back here where he belongs. And I expect you can't wait for your Bill, neither.' Nell picked up her son and cuddled him, smiling as he tugged her hair. 'Enough of the war, let's talk about babies. Much more important!'

On a mild, breezy day in April, Olive felt the first contraction as she was feeding the chickens. Gasping, she walked around the yard to ease the pain. Charles came out of the barn and rushed over.

'Is it starting? Shall I fetch the midwife?'

Olive had already arranged with Mrs Sebire, who lived in the parish, to deliver the baby. Although not a qualified midwife, she had delivered dozens of babies in her time and was much respected by the mothers. Olive wasn't sure if it was too soon to fetch her, but as another, stronger contraction tugged at her body, she changed her mind.

'Please, Charles.' He grabbed his bike and rode off, leaving Olive to make her way into the kitchen and make a fire to boil water. As further pain shot through her she panicked, crying out for her mother.

'Mum, I need you! I'm scared. Why can't you be here?' She brushed away tears, trying to focus on what would be needed for the birth. The crib was ready by her bed and, although they'd already been clean, she'd washed the clothes to fit a new-born. It was her way of showing her love for the unborn child. Terry nappies, well-used but serviceable, lay piled on the dressing table. All was set.

Mrs Sebire arrived on her bike, panting. She took one look at Olive and told her to go upstairs to bed. It wouldn't be long.

Two hours later an exhausted, but exhilarated Olive held her fair-haired baby girl in her arms. It was love at first sight.

chapter thirty-seven

2010

Natalie's parents were reluctant to leave, but she assured them she'd be fine and planned to go into work. She needed distraction. Anything to take her mind off the sight of the skeleton and its grave. Back at home in the evening, she made a cup of tea and phoned Matt. After telling him about the body she asked him to keep it to himself until she gave him the okay.

'It's pretty sensitive. I don't want a load of journalists and nosy parkers snooping round.'

Matt, sounding shocked, said, 'Of course. I understand. How horrible for you! And I've just realised it could have been me finding the body. Bloody hell!'

If he only knew! 'I'm hoping to get the all clear from the police within the next few days so I'll let you know when you can come round.' After switching off the phone she took her tea outside to look at the damage to the garden. The hole was now twice as big as that morning and the piles of earth huge. A mess. Natalie stood outside the taped-off area feeling sick. Not because of the mess – that could be fixed – but by the thought of Olive lying there all those years and no-one knowing. Yards from the old farmhouse. Although she hadn't yet heard from the police, Natalie knew in her heart it was Olive, and she needed to be the one to tell the family. Not something to look forward to.

Inside the cottage the atmosphere was heavy, brooding and Natalie was glad to take her supper outside. While chewing her cheese omelette she began to wonder if it wouldn't be better to stay with her parents as they'd suggested. But she needed to be independent. She wished Stuart was home. He'd been a great support the night Liam turned up…Thinking of him now, she wondered yet again what Stuart had started to tell her in France. If it meant they were not to be a couple, could she handle him being her neighbour? So close but apart...she didn't think so. Her thoughts drifted back to the day's events and her stomach clenched with the awfulness of it all. What a bloody awful mess!

Later, she managed to lose herself in a drama on TV, drinking wine to blur the thoughts. Yawning her head off about ten, she gave in and took the glass and the half-empty bottle into the kitchen. An icy blast hit her full in the face and the angry voice cried, 'Go away! Leave us alone!' Slamming the door behind her, she shot upstairs, praying the vicar would soon be back. She needed him. Badly.

Another restless night, fuelled by images of walking skeletons and big, angry men waving their fists meant Natalie woke feeling wrung out, hardly fit for work. The sight of a heavy, grey sky did little to lift her spirits. She had only been in the office for an hour when her mobile rang.

'Morning, Miss Ogier. DI Woods. Thought you'd like to hear the results of the autopsy.' He erupted into a coughing fit.

Natalie's mouth went dry as she waited.

'Sorry about that. Should give up the fags...Right, the pathologist confirmed it's the body of a woman in her sixties and she'd been dead about twenty years. Cause of death was a combination of a blow to the head and a stab wound in the stomach. Hard to tell which was the fatal injury after all this time. So she could be the woman you mentioned. Olive Falla.'

Oh, my God! She *had* seen a murder!

'There...wasn't anything to identify her?' Poor, poor Tabby, she thought.

'A wedding ring and what was odd, there was a broken photo frame under the body. A picture of a young girl.

Blond, blue eyes. That might help. I'll need to talk to your neighbour and his mother, if you could give me their contact details?'

'May I tell them, please? I think it would be better coming from me, as a friend. Then they can ring you.'

Another cough.

'Okay. But I need to speak to them asap. We need to get this woman identified as a matter of urgency.'

Natalie agreed and once the DI had cleared the line, she made herself a coffee in the staff kitchen before returning to her office, telling her PA she wasn't to be disturbed. A few gulps of the coffee and she dialled Stuart's number.

When his phone rang, Stuart was enjoying a coffee in a bar in Allauch, one he'd visited a few times in the past few days. As much as he liked being with his family, he'd soon realised he needed his own space. At regular intervals. Glancing at the screen he was surprised – but pleased – to see Natalie's name.

'Hi, Natalie. How are you?'

'Fine, thanks. And you?'

'Good. I'm in Allauch, playing truant.' He laughed.

'Right, so you can talk? You're on your own?'

'Sure. Is something wrong?' Stuart heard the tremor in her voice and became worried.

'Yes. There's no easy way to tell you this, but it looks as if we've...found Olive's body.'

'Oh, my God! But where...how?' He listened with mounting horror as Natalie explained about the vision she'd had on the Sunday night and her father digging the garden. It was like something out of a film. Stuart signalled a waiter to bring him a brandy.

Natalie went on to describe the actions of the police and the result of the pathology report.

He took a slug of the brandy before saying anything.

'I...I don't know what to say. Completely gobsmacked! So it definitely looks as if it's my grandmother?'

'Seems like it. I know it's horrible, but at least you and your mother will know what happened to her. Or at least some of it. The DI wants to talk to one of you, and he needs DNA for confirmation. Oh, and they found a photo of a girl who could be Tabby buried with the...body.'

'How awful for you, seeing...that and...finding the body. How are you coping? I'd have been terrified if I'd seen what you did.' He felt shivers running down his spine at the mere thought of it. Natalie was one brave girl in his book. If only...

'Not too bad. Mum and Dad have been great. And I'm hoping this means I won't have any more awful dreams. I'm sure Olive wanted us to find her before she could rest easy.'

'I guess. Look, I'll have to tell Mum, but I'm she'll want to hear it from you as well. Is that okay?'

'Sure. I was expecting that. I'm at work now so not a good time. Could you ask her to ring me after six?'

'No problem. And I'd better book flights home.' He took another sip of brandy. 'I...I've missed you this week. It'll be good to see you again.' There! He'd said it. He *had* missed her. Badly.

He heard her indrawn breath over the phone.

'I've missed you too. Um, must go. We'll talk later. Bye.'

Stuart stared at the phone for a moment, still coming to terms with Natalie's bombshell. If she had actually witnessed a replay of what happened to his grandmother, then it seemed his grandfather killed her. He was a murderer. Not the hero everyone thought. But he was supposed to have died in prison. How the hell was he going to explain it to his mother?

'What? My mother was killed by my father and buried in the garden? But I was told he was dead! Oh, dear God!' Tabby's face drained of colour as Stuart told her the gist of the story. Alan, sitting beside her on the terrace, looked equally shocked.

'My poor, poor, mother! I never expected this. Thought she'd run off somewhere, perhaps met a man and started a new life.' Tabby shook her head. Alan put his arms around her shoulders as she began to cry.

Stuart felt helpless. He'd not seen her cry since his father died. And it had been a brief display of grief. Controlled. He was glad Alan was there for her. He'd know what to say.

Tabby's sobs slowed down. After blowing her nose and wiping her eyes, she looked up.

'I must go to Guernsey immediately. Poor Natalie! What my family's made her suffer! Will you come with me, Stuart? Alan needs to stay with the family.'

'Sure. I was planning to do that. I'll book the flights, shall I? We're too late for a connection today so I'll try for tomorrow.'

'Yes, do that.' She turned to Alan. 'I'm sorry to leave like this, darling, but you do see I must go, don't you?'

Alan wiped away a last tear from her eye. 'Of course you must go. And once Rose and the family leave, I'll join you.'

Stuart went inside to book their flights, pleased about seeing Natalie sooner than planned, but also anxious. He had missed her every day, and knew he wanted to be with her. But...What would she say when he told her what he dreaded telling her? And the circumstances of his sudden return were hardly auspicious.

chapter thirty-eight

2010

The discovery of the body made the local news headlines by late Wednesday morning and Natalie left work to deal with the expected fall-out of journalists and nosy parkers. She arrived home to find a lone policeman guarding the taped-off area and fending off a reporter and a pair of inquisitive locals. Oh, God, could she cope with this? It was likely to be even worse once word got out Tabby and Stuart were arriving. She told the reporter she had nothing to say and would sue anyone for trespass if they didn't respect her privacy. It seemed to do the trick and she shot inside and locked the door.

Natalie phoned DI Woods to ask if anything could be done.

'I'll get the constable to stand at the top of the lane and bar entrance to all except those on a list you provide. Hopefully, things will calm down soon. I'll issue updates to the press to keep them off your back. Mr Cross and Mrs Peters are coming to the station as soon as they arrive today and we're taking DNA samples. Should be able to confirm the woman's identity in a day or two.' He coughed. 'Sorry. If you have any more problems, ring me.'

Feeling better, Natalie went outside to offer the policeman refreshment before making herself a salad lunch and a pot of coffee. Taking his coffee, he settled himself further up the lane and she retreated to the terrace. Hazy sunshine filtered through the clouds and a wisp of a breeze stirred the miniature palms in her garden. It was as if nothing bad had ever happened there and Natalie, not for the first time, wondered if it was, in fact, all a bad dream and she'd wake up soon to find it had all been in her mind. But of course, it wasn't.

Finishing her salad, she closed her eyes and thought of the conversation she'd had with Stuart the day before. He'd sounded genuine when he said he'd missed her. A good sign. After over a week apart, perhaps he was ready to tell her what the problem was. Although the issue of a murdered grandmother was likely to take precedence in any immediate conversations they'd have. A shock for him, but he'd never met Olive. Far worse for Tabby. She'd sounded distraught when they spoke the previous evening and told Natalie she felt guilty about not staying in touch with her mother.

'If only I'd gone over while she was alive, I could have saved her from Bill. If I'd known how bad things had become on the farm I'd have taken her back to England and bought her a house. I had the money.'

Natalie had tried to assure her the fault lay equally with Olive for not keeping in touch and Tabby had calmed down a little.

'There is something else you need to know, Tabby. I...I think it's likely your mother had an affair with a German officer.'

'What! But how do you know?' Tabby's shock reverberated down the line.

Natalie told her about the dreams where she saw Bill confronting Olive and Wolfgang one day, calling her a Jerrybag. And that Wolfgang had the same blond hair and blue eyes as Tabby and Stuart.

Tabby was quiet for a moment and Natalie worried it was a shock too far. But she had to know...

'I see. It's so much to take in...My mother had a German lover and got pregnant with me! And she tried to tell you in dreams what had happened. Dear God!' A moment passed. 'If it's true, then what happened to this "Wolfgang"?' She sighed deeply. 'My head's spinning and I don't know what to say, Natalie. But we'll talk more when I get back.'

Natalie's thoughts were interrupted by her mobile ringing. Stuart.

'Hi. Just to let you know we've landed and on our way to St Peter Port for the DNA tests. Are you at work?'

She told him about the news coverage and she was at home, fending off unwanted visitors. Stuart said they'd get there as soon as they could and rang off, but not before saying how he was looking forward to seeing her. Natalie smiled. She could hardly wait.

'Natalie! My dear girl! How are you coping?' Tabby threw her arms around her and Natalie saw, over her shoulder, a smiling Stuart.

'I'm fine. Really.'

Stuart came forward and kissed her cheek, whispering, 'Shall we go for a walk, later? Just the two of us?' She nodded and he pulled back behind Tabby. Natalie ushered them into the house and made a pot of tea as they all sat in the kitchen.

Tabby stared around.

'So, this is where it happened.' She shivered. 'The detective showed me the photo they found and it was one of me, as you thought. Taken when I was eight, I think. The evidence is stacking up.' Tabby sighed deeply. 'It's horrible to think of my poor mother dying here like that. I'm sure she wanted me to know and it's why she hung around, as it were. I've heard people who die violently often can't move on.' She thanked Natalie for her tea and went on, 'Do you sense she's gone?'

'I'm not sure. Not quite. I still sense something...' She waved an arm, '...in this room. I'm waiting to hear from the vicar, he's due back now and I want him to cleanse the house, or whatever vicars do.'

Tabby sat still, as if trying to tune into something.

'You're right. It's not quite clear. Now, if you're up to it, can you describe to me everything exactly as you saw it? If you don't mind repeating it again.'

Natalie saw Stuart shift on his stool.

'Of course not...' Tabby listened intently as Natalie described in minute detail all she remembered. Would always remember.

'Thank you. Now I'd like to see where my mother was...buried.'

Natalie took them the long way round, explaining the back door was sealed off. As they approached the empty grave Tabby looked close to tears and Stuart grabbed her hand. Natalie stood back, giving them space. Even standing behind the tape, the hole was clear to see. Tabby stood with her head bent for a moment and then turned away, Stuart still holding her hand, his face solemn.

'I...I thought I heard a voice when they took the body away. A woman. She said, "Help me, please." It was so faint I wasn't sure if it was my imagination.'

'Oh, I would think it was my mother. Thank you for telling me.' Tabby's mouth was set firm.

'Have the police said anything about the man who killed her? Will they look for him?'

'I did ask, but there's not much they can do after all this time, is there? There's no evidence linking it to anyone, thanks to the fire. And we can't tell them about Bill because they'd never believe it. He was supposed to be dead. And he can't be alive now if he's haunting this place. Bastard!' Tabby spat out the word, her face flushed.

'My parents know someone who said they knew Olive and Bill during the war. An old lady. I asked them to get in touch with her so you could meet up.'

Tabby's eyes lit up.

'That would be wonderful! Even if she's got nothing good to say about my mother, I want to know everything. You know, I remember some of the older islanders would give me strange looks when they saw me and now I understand why. If I don't look a bit like Bill, but the German, Wolfgang. You said I had the same hair and blue eyes. It must have been clear to anyone who knew the family my mother was a...Jerrybag. A horizontal collaborator.' She shook her head. 'Horrible term. And I guess it's why Mum kept to herself all those years. I never understood why she wouldn't go out unless it was absolutely necessary. Must have been even worse for her once I left as I used to do the shopping.' She bit her lip and Stuart hugged her.

'Don't upset yourself, Mum. You didn't know and she wasn't a great mother to you, was she? We understand a bit more now, but that doesn't explain the way she behaved towards you. Come on,' he said, pulling her away, 'let's go to my place and you can have a rest. It's been a long day.'

Tabby agreed and Natalie showed them out. Stuart winked as he left and mouthed 'later'.

Back inside Natalie called her parents to bring them up to speed. Her mother told her they'd be seeing the old lady in a couple of days and would get back to her. Dying to know more about Olive and her lover, she hoped Tabby would let her go with them to any meeting. It would be great to have confirmation from someone who had been there. Not just in her dreams.

Half an hour later Stuart knocked on the door and they set off up the lane.

'It's hit Mum hard, but at least we know what happened to Olive. And I do hope things quieten down for you.' Stuart squeezed her hand as they walked side by side. They nodded at the policeman looking bored by the entrance. He told them he'd turned away three curious locals in the last hour.

'Were you with Tabby when I told her about Wolfgang?'

'Yes. One big shock! For both of us.' He frowned. 'I'm not keen on the idea of a German grandfather, but as it all happened years before I was born, it doesn't affect me as much as Mum. She's now wondering if this Wolfgang is still alive, and why he didn't do the honourable thing and marry Olive.'

'We'll never know. But I certainly got the strong impression Olive was very much in love with him and hated Bill. So it's odd she didn't seem to love your mother.'

He shook his head. 'Guess that's something else we'll never know. Like where had Bill been all those years and why did he come back?'

They walked along in silence for a moment, both lost in thought.

'Perhaps one day we'll all look back on this time and see it as something exciting. Something to tell the grandchildren.' Natalie smiled up at him. Stuart paled. Oh, what had she said?

'If you remember, I was trying to tell you something in France but ran out of time. I...I know this might not be the best time, but I don't want to keep putting it off.'

Natalie stared at him, a leaden weight forming in her stomach. It sounded ominous.

'What don't you want to put off? Are you trying to tell me you don't want to see me anymore?'

He pulled her round to face him and gripped her arms.

'The last thing I want is to stop seeing you! I want to have a proper relationship with you. I...love you. But...' He took a deep breath and looked her in the eye. 'When the subject of children came up in France, you said you assumed you'd have them one day, and I didn't say anything. It seemed too presumptuous at the time as we weren't actually a couple.'

She frowned. Did he not want children? Odd, for a teacher.

'I realise it's still a bit premature...but I thought you should know I can't have children. So if you do want a family, then...then it's best for us not to become involved.'

chapter thirty-nine

2010

Natalie sat on the terrace nursing a glass of chilled white wine, her body caressed by a gentle, crisp warm breeze. Of all the momentous events of the past few days, Stuart's revelation was causing her the most anguish. Possibly because it was the last thing she expected to hear. She was surrounded by friends having babies and never gave infertility a thought. She'd always assumed she could have children if and when she was ready. When she finally met The One. After Stuart had dropped his bombshell she'd been too shocked to say much, beyond needing to think about it. To be fair, he hadn't expected a decision from her. He said it was the prime reason his ex, Pam, left him for another man. A look of sadness crossed his face as he told her about the mumps he'd had as a child, making him infertile.

Sipping the wine, Natalie was glad she'd refused Stuart's invitation to join them for supper. It would have been much too awkward. Instead she'd rustled up a bowl of pasta with lashes of cheese. Always a great comfort food. Glancing at her watch, she wondered if Jeanne would have put the kids to bed. She needed to talk to her urgently and picked up the phone.

'Hi, Natalie! Glad you called, was planning to ring you this evening. Did Stuart and his mother arrive?'

She brought Jeanne up to date, ending with Stuart's news.

'Oh! What a bummer! Poor Stuart. And poor you! What are you going to do?'

'That's why I'm calling. I need to talk it over with someone out loud. It's been going round and round in my head the past couple of hours.' Natalie took a sip of wine. 'What would you do in my shoes?'

'Ah, that's not a fair question! It's too personal for anyone else to comment. You have to ask yourself if your feelings for Stuart are strong enough to sustain a relationship without having his child. Remember there's always adoption or sperm-donation. So, how much *do* you love him?'

'Well, it's early days and we haven't, you know, even done *it* yet, but I do enjoy being with him and he makes my insides melt when he kisses me, so...' Natalie remembered the last proper kiss they had in France. She so wanted him to take her to bed with him that night...now she realised why he'd held back.

Jeanne giggled.

'Sounds like there's something good going on. Why not give it a go? At the moment you've nothing to lose. He's obviously dead keen on you or he wouldn't have told you about it. The bottom line is, could you imagine life without children if it came to it? Just being with the man you love? To be honest, I've always seen you as more of a career girl.'

Natalie imagined the scenario. At thirty-six she didn't have much time left to become a mother. Jeanne was right, she'd always focused on her career. She knew her mother would like her to have children, but Phil was providing another grandchild so...how keen *was* she to be a mum? To give up her lifestyle, nice relaxing holidays, tidy house...Jeanne was a natural, but was she? Oh, God, this was so hard!

'Natalie? You still there?'

'Sure. I was thinking. You're right. I need to "go with the flow" as they say, and see how we work out. I *think* I could live without children if I was happy with the right man.'

'That's it – "the right man". If Stuart's The One, then go for it. If you miss having kids yourself, I'd be only too happy to lend you mine for as long as you like!' Jeanne laughed.

'Okay, it's a deal. Thanks, Jeanne. I'll leave you to enjoy the rest of the evening with your lovely man. Keep you posted. Bye.'

She'd no sooner clicked off the mobile when her landline rang. Natalie took her glass into the kitchen to answer it.

'Good evening, Miss Ogier. Reverend Ayres, you left a message for me. How can I help?'

Thank God! Natalie explained what had been happening over the weeks, culminating in the discovery of the body.

'My goodness! I can quite understand how distressing this must have been. Although the Church doesn't have a Deliverance Ministry here, I have helped people deal with restless spirits. I'd be happy to call round and see if I can sense anything I could help with. When would be a good time?'

They agreed on seven o'clock the following evening and Natalie gave him her address, mentioning the police presence. Relief swept through her at the thought of being 'delivered' from the angry spirit she was convinced was Bill. If it *was* him, it meant he was dead, for which she was glad. A dead haunting was bad enough, but a live one...

With the police guarding her home, Natalie felt able to go into the office on Thursday, conscious of the back-log of work on her desk. And it would take her mind off ghosts and babies.

At home that evening she ate a hurried supper before Mr Ayres arrived. Earlier that day she had phoned Tabby to see if she'd like to be there and she'd said yes immediately. Natalie hadn't spoken to Stuart and assumed Tabby would mention it to him. They needed to talk but the middle of a 'deliverance' wasn't the right time.

Tabby popped round just before seven, alone.

'Stuart wasn't keen, but said he'll catch up with you later.' She gave Natalie a quick hug. 'I don't know what to expect, do you?' Tabby's eyes were round with excitement.

'No idea! I only hope the ghost or whatever, goes quietly and doesn't smash anything else in the process.' She heard a car pull up and left Tabby in the kitchen to go and open the door. Natalie was surprised to see a white-haired man in his seventies emerge from the car. He came towards her, his hand outstretched in greeting.

'Miss Ogier, pleased to meet you. Reverend Ayres at your service.'

His eyes twinkled at her and she smiled back.

'Come in, Vicar. And please call me Natalie.'

He followed her into the hall and stood still, his head on one side. Natalie waited, not daring to say a word.

'Interesting. Shall we go into the kitchen?'

Tabby jumped off her stool as they walked in and Natalie introduced them.

'Delighted to meet you, Mrs Peters. I understand you grew up here? Although it's much changed, I imagine.'

'Yes, it's hard to recognise the old place.'

Mr Ayres moved around the room, looking thoughtful, stopping near the fridge-freezer.

'I can sense a great deal of pain here. A woman is frightened. On more than one occasion, I feel.' He closed his eyes and stood still. When he opened them his eyes were full of sorrow. 'There was – and is – a man. He's angry, enraged–'

A blast of freezing cold air whirled around the room and Natalie heard the familiar voice, shout, 'Go away! Go away, all of you!' She and Tabby gasped as a mug on the worktop crashed to the floor, as if swept by an invisible hand.

'You heard it?' She looked at them both. They nodded.

Mr Ayres kissed the heavy crucifix around his neck.

'I think we've upset him, haven't we? Which is good. Means we don't have to wait around for him. If you ladies would rather wait elsewhere, I can proceed on my own.' He looked from Tabby to Natalie. Both shook their heads.

'Could you give me the names of your parents, please?' The vicar faced Tabby.

'Olive and Bill Falla, though I don't think he was my real father.'

'No matter. I think you being here will lure him out of the shadows. Which is what we need if we're to send him away in peace.'

The air became heavy, like treacle, and Natalie found it hard to breathe. But there was no way she was leaving now. As they stood close together, their backs to a run of units, a shape began to emerge from the fug. A tall, heavy man, with grey hair and brown eyes appeared like a wraith. Natalie and Tabby cried out. He glared at them, his fists bunched by his sides.

'Bill Falla, in the name of Jesus Christ, may you be forgiven for the harm you have done to your wife, Olive. Leave now, in the name of God the Father, God the Son and God the Holy Spirit.' The vicar drew the sign of the cross in the air in front of him as his other hand gripped the crucifix.

Natalie watched transfixed as the figure seemed to swell. Then she realised another figure stood behind him. A woman. Grey-haired and thin. The woman in the kitchen.

'Mum!' Tabby cried, her eyes bright with tears.

The woman turned towards Tabby, her arms outstretched, and Tabby took a step forward.

Bill turned his head, raising his fists.

'No! No more. Leave now, in the name of God the Father, God the Son and God the Holy Spirit. Leave this house and go and rest in peace.' The vicar's voice boomed around the room and beads of sweat were visible on his forehead. Natalie was worried the strain would be too much…

The figure hesitated, and at that moment Tabby's fingers touched those of Olive, or rather went through them. Olive smiled.

The vicar repeated his exhortations and the figure of Bill faded slowly. Natalie held her breath and watched Olive, who turned her head towards her and smiled. Then she too began to fade. The air cleared and all that remained of what had happened was the smashed mug on the floor.

chapter forty

Liberation – 1945

Olive hadn't realised how exhausting a tiny scrap could be. A dozen cows were easier to care for; at least they slept at night. Thank goodness Charles was looking after the farm as she had no energy left after feeding, changing then feeding and changing through the day and night. Sitting in the kitchen one day at the end of April, Olive stroked the baby's head as she fed noisily from her breast. Her hair was pale gold and Olive knew she was Wolfgang's. The deep blue eyes were yet to take on their final colour, but she would bet they'd be the same dazzling blue as her father's. For a moment she felt at peace. She was a mother and, whatever happened, a mother she'd remain. The news from the BBC told of massive Allied air strikes against Berlin and the approach of a large Russian army encircling the city. Berlin was doomed. Olive knew there was a chance Wolfgang would be in or near Berlin where, according to the BBC, German forces were congregating in a last-ditch attempt at defence. Her heart clenched at the thought he might be killed.

'We want your daddy to come back, don't we, darling? He promised he would.' She hadn't yet given her daughter a name and needed to before registering the birth. Names passed through her head, those of family and friends. Then it popped in. Tabby, short for Tabitha, her grandmother's name. A lovely woman, Olive had adored her. She'd always been known as Tabby, a joyful name, Olive thought. It was a pity she had to have Bill's name as father, but what choice did she have? The thought of Bill coming back soon made her clutch Tabby tight, causing the baby to cry out in protest. Olive soothed her and she continued to feed happily. Bill. She would file for divorce regardless. It might be many months before Wolfgang could return, and she couldn't wait. When – if – Ross returned, she'd throw herself on his mercy and ask to move in with him. At least until he found himself a wife. And if he didn't come back, she could live in what would be her own inheritance. Satisfied she'd thought of everything, Olive moved Tabby onto the other breast.

Charles arrived for work on 2nd May waving a copy of *The Evening Press* at Olive.

'That bastard Hitler's dead! And the Russians have taken Berlin! It'll soon be our turn to kick out the Jerries.' He danced around the kitchen and Olive laughing, joined in, holding Tabby in her arms.

Over the next few days the excitement spread around the island. Not only was the Occupation about to end, but the SS *Vega* returned with more supplies on the 3rd, and Olive couldn't wait to see what treats were in store for her. Before the invasion, she had taken for granted such foods as biscuits, cake, tea and coffee, but now they seemed luxuries, foods to savour and enjoy. She smiled at Charles, going about his chores with a big grin on his face, munching on a bar of chocolate.

Peace was declared on 8th May and the islanders were informed they would be formally liberated on 9th May, the Germans finally forced to surrender. Olive travelled to St Peter Port with Nell's family in their horse and cart early that morning, anxious to be part of what was bound to be the biggest island celebration in her life so far. Tabby nestled contentedly in her arms, fast asleep after her feed. They arrived in time to see troops from HMS *Bulldog* on board a landing craft heading for White Rock. Thousands of islanders filled the streets around the harbour and a huge cheer went up when the troops arrived and marched down North Esplanade towards the Royal Hotel, used by the Germans as their HQ. Olive shouted herself hoarse, overcome by the general hysteria. She had managed to find a space at the front, with a full view of the Royal Artillery soldiers marching past. The Tommies had their hands shaken by the men and were mobbed by the women with hugs and kisses. Everyone was smiling or laughing. The soldiers handed out small gifts of chocolate and cigarettes and Olive received a bar, accompanied by a saucy wink, from a young lad. She flushed and kissed his cheek in return.

Olive watched as the Union Jack was raised at the Royal Hotel, accompanied by a monumental cheer from the locals and soldiers alike. She joined her friends as they followed the crowd to the Royal Court for more flag raising and speeches. By then they were hungry after their early start and found a space near Town Church to sit and eat the food they'd brought with them.

Nell, her eyes shining, turned to her saying, 'The Allies have released the British prisoners from the German prisons and camps, so Dad should be home soon. And your Bill. It's wonderful news, isn't it? Life'll soon be back to normal and I can't wait.'

Olive nodded, not trusting herself to say anything. The last thing she wanted at the moment was Bill to turn up. She wasn't ready...

They stayed until the afternoon, wanting to make the most of the holiday atmosphere and join together with islanders they hadn't seen for months or longer. Before they left, British planes flew over the harbour in groups of threes, circling and roaring their engines in a salute to the weary but excited islanders. Olive's mood lifted again; she'd worry about Bill later.

Over the next few days, celebrations continued around the island and Olive was invited to a couple of impromptu parties in the area after more ships arrived, bearing supplies of food and fuel. But the work had to carry on and she continued to employ Charles to help on the farm.

With a much-reduced income now that there were fewer vegetables to sell, Olive often wondered how she'd be able to buy food. She worried about Wolfgang, whether or not he'd survived the onslaught on Berlin. Sometimes she'd stay awake after feeding Tabby in the night, beset by anxiety. The worst thing was not being able to ask anyone. She could only wait.

And hope.

Summer arrived and Olive heard that those imprisoned by the Germans were due to arrive back on the island after a period of recuperation. Many had suffered serious health problems and hadn't been fit to travel. Nell called round to say she was going into Town the next day when the ship was due in, to meet her father, and asked if she'd like a lift. Olive made some excuse about Tabby not being well and would wait for Bill at home.

She hardly slept that night, panicked about seeing Bill and his reaction to Tabby. He would know the truth straight away and Olive didn't know what to do. She couldn't tell anyone and ask for help. She was on her own. If only Ross was here! Inspiration struck and in the morning, after telling Charles she had to go out for the day and he was in charge, she strapped Tabby to her back and cycled up to her family's farm. She knew it was only a brief respite and Bill would come looking for her at some point, but it was all she could think of.

The Germans had left the house in a mess, but at least the furniture hadn't been destroyed like in some of the requisitioned houses. The first thing she did was wash the bedding and hang it out to dry in the yard. The strong sun would dry it by the afternoon and she could make up a bed. Olive hoped Bill wouldn't come looking till the next day at the earliest, heading off to his fancy woman instead. He'd hardly be keen to meet the Jerrybag, would he? She bit her lip. He would want a divorce, no question. After feeding Tabby and settling her in a drawer from the dresser, Olive set about cleaning the grime the Germans had left behind. It seemed an appropriate penance under the circumstances. She was glad her mother couldn't see the state her home had been left in. Edith would turn in her grave.

She remembered her father hadn't handed in his rifle, in spite of Edith's fear he'd be found out and imprisoned, hiding it amongst some rusty junk under a disused oil tank. Praying the Germans hadn't found it while they were in residence, she waited until Tabby was asleep and took a look. The area was overgrown with weeds and it took some scrabbling about, but finally Olive pulled out something rifle-shaped wrapped in oil cloth. Unwrapping it, she saw it looked in good condition, with a box of cartridges. Good. She had a weapon to defend herself if needed.

Olive prepared a basic supper using some of the food she'd brought with her and, after locking the doors and shutting the windows, stumbled upstairs exhausted, the rifle tucked under her arm. The baby woke her twice in the night wanting her feed and by morning she was as tired as the night before. She left Tabby sleeping and picked up the gun before going downstairs, her head full of what would happen if and when Bill turned up. The rifle did at least make her feel safer, though she hadn't any idea how to use it.

She had just finished a blissful cup of real tea when someone hammered on the door. Her chest tightened in panic and she reached for the rifle. Going to the door she called out, 'Who is it?'

'The police, Madam. I'm looking for a Mrs William Falla. Is that you?'

Olive sagged with relief and opened the door to see a policeman who, on seeing the rifle, gave her an odd look.

'Oh, I wasn't planning on using it, but as I'm on my own...' She lowered the gun and ushered him in.

'Thank you, Madam. You are Mrs William Falla?'

'Yes, please sit down. Would you like some tea?'

He shook his head.

'Very kind of you, but no thanks.' He looked troubled, as if he didn't know how to proceed and Olive was puzzled. She hadn't done anything wrong, had she?

'Why are you looking for me? And how did you know I was here?'

'I'm afraid I have some bad news for you, Mrs Falla. Your husband, William, imprisoned by the Germans, has been registered as killed in a prison fire that took place three months ago. Please accept my condolences.' His eyes were full of pity, but Olive was overcome with relief. Bill's dead! Oh, thank God! Struggling to look suitably upset, she got up and walked to the sink, her back to the policeman.

'Thank you for telling me, I was...expecting him home yesterday.'

'Yes, the other prisoners were on the ship, and one of them carried a letter informing us of your husband's death. Several of the inmates were killed and the bodies couldn't be identified, but your husband was not among the ones left alive. Here's the death certificate issued by the prison.'

She turned round, her features composed in what she hoped were those of a grieving widow. She brushed away an imaginary tear and sat down, reaching for the piece of paper. In German, she couldn't understand anything other than the name and address in bold lettering – William Falla, Beauregard Farm, St Peters, Guernsey. Olive found her hands shaking. It seemed so unreal, after all this time, to be free of that bastard of a husband. And she didn't have to go through the indignity of a divorce! She looked up at the policeman, who shifted uncomfortably in the chair.

'You need to take that to the Greffe and they'll sort out the formalities for you. With regards to how I found you, I went first to your farm but found no-one there except the lad, Charles, who said you'd left early in the morning and would be gone all day. As I was leaving, your friend, Nell Bisson, arrived looking for you. Apparently she'd heard about your husband and wanted to tell you herself. She wondered if you'd come here and gave me the address.' He coughed. 'I'm sorry not to have come before, but it was getting late by this time and I was needed urgently back in Town. I came as soon as I could today.'

Olive nodded.

'I'm grateful to you, officer, you did your best. I...needed to make sure everything was all right here, not having visited since the Germans left. They'd left it in a bit of a mess so I stayed longer than planned. I did leave a note for my husband to tell him.'

He shook his head.

'I didn't see no note, but that's not important, now.' He stood up as Tabby let out a yell from upstairs. 'I heard you'd had a baby, Mrs Falla. Such a pity she'll not know her father,' he said, sorrowfully.

'Yes, it is. Thank you again for going to so much trouble, officer.' She led him to the door and they exchanged goodbyes. She watched him mount his bike and ride down the farm track before closing the door, a huge grin on her face. She was free! All she had to do now was wait for Wolfgang to come back and they'd become a proper family.

June slid into July and Olive settled into widowhood, accepting the condolences of her friends and neighbours, offering an appropriately sad face to most of them. But one day she broke down and confessed to Elsie what Bill had been really like and how she hated him.

'I'm glad you've finally admitted it. We all saw what a horrible man he was and he treated you so badly. I know you tried to hide them, but there were times when I saw the bruises, Olive. I know we're not supposed to talk ill of the dead, but I say good riddance.' Elsie patted her arm and smiled.

Olive was taken aback.

'I should have had the guts to tell you, but I was so ashamed. I...I was planning to ask for a divorce when he returned.' She brushed away a tear, relief mixed with sorrow for all the beatings she'd endured. Perhaps if she'd told someone it would have been different...

Elsie nodded.

'I'm not surprised. And we all knew about his woman on the side. But what about Tabby? Bill wasn't her father, was he? She's blond and with those unusual blue eyes...' She tilted her head at Olive, who felt the heat rise to her cheeks. 'You thought I didn't notice you and that officer exchanging notes, didn't you?'

Olive gasped.

'Oh, don't worry, I shan't tell anyone, though there were a few whispers. I could tell he was a good man, for all he wore that hated uniform, and he made you happy, didn't he? Knowing what your Bill was like, I thought you deserved someone better.'

She flung her arms around Elsie and sobbed. Elsie stroked her back, soothing her.

'I...I'm waiting for him to come back. He said he would, but I don't know if he's still alive, he was sent to Berlin before...'

'He wouldn't have known about the baby, would he? Nor Bill I suppose. At least you've been spared facing him with the news. He'd have guessed right away, he would.' Elsie continued to rub her back as Olive tried to calm herself.

'No, neither of them knew. But if you've guessed Tabby's not Bill's then everyone will and I'll be vilified instead of condoled.' Olive blew her nose and took a sip of the tea she and Elsie were sharing in the kitchen while her baby slept.

'Some of the older ones might be a bit snooty with you, but it'll be just one of the many recriminations flying around. People are more concerned about those who made money they shouldn't during the Occupation. There's talk of bringing some to trial, but I don't know if it'll come to that. Anyways, I suggest you keep your head down and continue to act the grieving widow.' Elsie finished her tea and stood up. 'Best be off as Charles is taking me to a dance this evening and I want to wash my hair.'

Olive saw her to the door and just as she was leaving, Elsie turned and asked if she'd heard from Ross.

'No, but it shouldn't be long now, unless he was sent to Burma. It'll be a relief when the Japs admit defeat and our lads can come home.' She paused, leaning against the door frame. 'You know, it's funny, me and Ross didn't get on all that well, but I miss him. He's all I've got now, except for Tabby.'

Giving her a hug, Elsie said she was sure she'd hear soon and set off on her bike.

Three weeks later Olive answered a knock on the door to find a post-boy she knew holding a telegram.

'It's addressed to your father, Olive, but as both your parents have gone, I thought…' He thrust it at her, looking awkward.

'Thanks. It's probably from Ross.' Dear God, please let Ross be all right!

He tipped his hat and jumped on his bike and Olive went in to the kitchen and sat down, her heart thudding, and ripped open the envelope. She pulled out the thin sheet of paper bearing the typed words: *I regret to inform you of the death in action of your son, Ross*… and burst into tears.

The legalities seemed to stretch on forever and Olive fretted about what she should do. She had inherited

Beauregard Farm on Bill's death but there was no money, the only assets were the land and livestock. With her brother's death, she now stood to inherit her parents' farm and she would struggle to run one, let alone two farms. After seeking legal advice, it looked better to sell the family farm and live in Beauregard, it having the livestock and more land. Olive would then have some capital behind her to invest in livestock as needed and provide income for her and Tabby. But she hated the thought of selling her old home, it held some good memories whereas Beauregard...well, not so good. Except it was where Tabby was born – her birthright. Olive, with Tabby tucked in her arms, walked to the edge of the field overlooking Rocquaine Bay.

'Mummy has a big decision to make, darling. Would you like to grow up here? We've more room and it's in better condition than...than your grandparents' farm. Can we be happy here, do you think? I'd need to block out some...memories, but perhaps that won't be too difficult, particularly when your father – your real father – comes back. He loved the animals, you know. Was so gentle with them, he'd make a wonderful farmer.' Olive felt the ache in her insides as the image of Wolfgang filled her mind. His smile, the tenderness of his touch, his kiss...she shook her head, telling herself not to be maudlin, he'd be back one day. She just had to be patient. Tabby let out a gurgle of delight and waved her arms as a cow came into view.

'I think that means you want us to stay. So be it.' Olive smiled and lifted Tabby above her head, making her scream with delight.

The following months dragged by for Olive, her only consolation was seeing Tabby grow stronger, crawling around the house after her and always smiling. At last her parents' farm was sold and she had some money in the bank. Enough to tide her over for a few years, but no more. She was able to keep Charles on, increasing his wage so he could support his new wife, Elsie. Seeing them together, so obviously in love, was like a dagger in her own heart. She knew it was wrong of her to feel jealous, but as time went by, her hopes dwindled.

The letter came on a blustery November day, when Olive was sweeping the kitchen floor. Tabby was in her high chair, waving a rattle given to her by Elsie. The postmark was blurred but she made out the word *Deutschland*. Taking a deep breath, excitement coursing through her, she tore open the envelope and pulled out the single sheet of paper.

Dear Olive,

Forgive me please for not writing before, but much has happened since I last saw you. I am also aware your husband is now likely to have returned and did not want to cause you any more problems with him.

I survived the onslaught on Berlin without injury, but sadly, my brothers were both killed in other battles. My parents were much saddened by this and have turned to me for financial and moral support. I regret to say I was not entirely honest with you when I said I was single. Although unmarried, I did have a fiancée who has waited patiently for my return and, to please my parents, we were married last month...

At this point Olive cried out in pain and shock. Gasping for breath, she bent over, the words hammering in her head. Tabby, startled, began to cry, her cries becoming louder as Olive sobbed. Leaving her daughter alone, she crawled upstairs and threw herself on the bed. Anger, grief and hate swept through her as she faced the awful truth that Wolfgang – the man she'd loved so, so much, even bearing his child – would never come back. He'd loved another woman the whole time he was with her. She hated him! Hated him! And knew she could no longer love his child. The little girl who looked so like him.

chapter forty-one

2010

Tabby collapsed on a stool and Natalie put her arms around her. Tears glistened on her cheeks and Natalie passed her a tissue, before turning her attention to the vicar. Eyes closed, he was mouthing what she took to be a prayer and his face was grey with what looked like exhaustion. She waited until his eyes flicked open.

'Are you all right, Mr Ayres? Would you like a drink?'

'A cup of tea would be most welcome, thank you. I must sit down, I've quite tired myself out.' He managed a smile as he perched on a stool.

Natalie put the kettle on and made tea for all.

'I can't thank you enough, vicar, for what you've done. To see my...my mother was so moving and...and healing. We didn't get on, you see, and I've felt so guilty about it.' Tabby dabbed at her eyes.

'I'm delighted to have helped. Angry souls do not make for peaceful houseguests and your mother needed to pass on too. A terrible business,' he said, shaking his head.

Natalie handed round the tea, suggesting they sit outside. The warm, salty air was refreshing after the earlier oppressiveness in the kitchen and Natalie felt the tension in her shoulders ease at last. Seeing that monster Bill so clearly had been frightening. She hadn't expected that. And poor Olive! She'd looked so thin and unkempt.

'I will say a prayer by the grave, before I go. To make sure Olive has moved on. I would hope you will no longer be troubled by dreams or visions, Natalie, but if you are, you only need to call me.' The vicar's colour had returned and he looked more rested as he drank his tea.

'Thanks. You've been wonderful, just as Jeanne said you'd be. I...I had my doubts about calling you, as I'm not a big fan of religion, but I'm glad I did.'

Tabby, smiling, nodded.

Mr Ayres finished his tea and stood up. Natalie and Tabby walked with him to the grave and stood back while he prayed. Natalie closed her eyes and heard a voice say 'Thank you'.

Opening her eyes, she saw Olive, smiling, standing next to Tabby.

She blinked. Olive was gone.

෬

Stuart saw the vicar drive off and, impatient to know what had happened, walked across to Natalie's.

'Hi, come on in. Tabby was about to fetch you. Would you like a drink? I've opened a bottle of wine but you can have lager if you prefer?' Natalie ushered him in, and headed for the kitchen.

'Lager, please. How did it go?' He looked around, half-expecting to see the aftermath of a battle between good and evil. Instead, all looked normal as Natalie took a can from the fridge.

'Fine, we think. Tabby's outside, she'll tell you all about it.'

He followed her to the terrace and his mother stood up and hugged him. She looked a lot happier than she'd done earlier, which was good.

Stuart listened with a growing sense of unreality as Tabby described what had happened. Perhaps he should have been there, but...the sceptic in him had won out. He looked from his mother to Natalie, and again saw a change. Natalie had appeared nervy and tense earlier, and now she looked at ease, as if she'd let go of some heavy load. He smiled. Whatever had happened, no matter how bizarre it sounded, at least some good had come of it.

'I'm glad for you, Mum. If it's set your mind at rest and you've stopped feeling so guilty about Olive, that's good.' He turned to Natalie. 'Do you feel he's gone? The angry ghost?'

She nodded.

'Yes, I do. There's a change in the atmosphere already. The vicar blessed the house before he left, so...' she shrugged, 'I can look forward to enjoying my home at last. All I want now is the police to say we can fill in the...the grave so Matt can finish the garden, and I'll be happy.'

Stuart sipped his drink, wondering if she'd had time to consider what he'd told her. And if so, what was her answer? If it was no, he didn't think he could go on living next door. It would be too painful.

A few minutes later, Tabby stood, saying she wanted to get back to phone Alan, and would see them later. Natalie offered him another drink and he accepted gladly. Good, she might want to talk.

On her return, she handed him the can and filled up her glass. She twirled the wine around before looking up at him. His stomach clenched. She was going to turn him down! He knew it.

'I've been thinking about what you said, and if I'm honest, I was upset about you not being able to have children.' She took a sip and he waited for the punchline. 'But it wouldn't necessarily mean we couldn't have a family one day, if...if we were together. And again, being honest, I'm not entirely sure if I *do* want children.' His heart skipped a beat. Was she...? 'So why don't we see how it goes between us? If we do decide we love each other enough and want to be together, then great. If not, well...' She smiled. Her beautiful smile.

'May I kiss you?'

She nodded.

He stood and pulled her up and into his arms. Then, taking her face in his hands, he kissed her. A long, lingering kiss.

❁

Natalie woke the next morning after the best sleep she'd had for weeks. And she knew why. The kiss with Stuart had led to some pretty amazing love-making in her bed, and she uncurled with pleasure at the memory. It was only a shame he'd had to go home instead of spending the night with her. But it didn't seem fair to leave Tabby on her own after such a momentous evening. And they had all the time in the world...

Before leaving for work Natalie rang her parents to tell them about the vicar's visit and the successful outcome. They listened in on speakerphone and Natalie heard her mother gasp a couple of times. Before she could end the call, Molly chipped in.

'I was going to ring you today as we saw Mrs Le Prevost last night at our meeting. She's the lady who remembers Olive. In fact, so does her husband Charles, who worked for her at one time. She said they'd be happy to talk to Tabby and suggested tomorrow morning. They live nearby in Rocquaine. I'll give you her number...'

Natalie wrote it down and said she'd talk later. Brilliant! She nipped across to Stuart's house to tell them and Tabby was delighted, insisting that Natalie go with them. As Natalie left, a grinning Stuart followed her to snatch a kiss.

'Mum's going out with some old school friends tonight, so would you like to go out for dinner? Or I could cook?' He held her so tight she had to break free, giggling.

'Let's go out. Crabby's should be fun on a Friday night and it's not far. My treat.' She kissed him and dashed for her car as he tried to pull her back.

Laughing, she drove off, willing the hours to fly by.

Just before Natalie nipped out for lunch, her mobile rang.

'Good morning, Miss Ogier. DI Woods. We've received the DNA analysis from the lab and it confirms the deceased was related to Mrs Peters and her son. So, we'll inform the coroner and arrange the inquest. Just a formality, you understand.'

'That's great. Does this mean I can reclaim my garden?'

'Yes, we're not likely to find any evidence to identify the killer, so I'll get my men to come and remove the tape and fill in the hole. I can't let you keep the constable, I'm afraid.'

'That's okay, we'll manage. And don't worry about the hole, I'm having a pond installed.'

As she walked round the corner to Waitrose, Natalie phoned Tabby. She'd also heard from the police about the DNA, and Tabby said she'd agreed to visit the Le Prevosts at eleven on Saturday. Next call was to Matt, arranging for him to come round on Monday. Relieved there was progress at last, she joined the queue in the café for her usual sandwich and large cappuccino.

'Good morning, sleepyhead.'

Natalie opened her eyes and smiled. Stuart stroked her face before kissing her gently on the lips. She flung her arm across his chest, moving closer.

'Good morning to you, too. And what a lovely day it looks.' She'd not bothered to draw the curtains and the sun poured through the open windows, a breeze carrying a hint of the sea.

'Sure does. And we need to get up soon, it's nearly nine. I think we, er, wore ourselves out last night, didn't we?' He grinned, his blue eyes hooded from sleep.

She giggled, remembering the passionate love-making, freed from the constraint of time. How wonderful it was to have the night together. With many more ahead...

'Do we have time before...?'

'Oh I think so, don't you?' he said, his hands stroking her breasts.

As they ate breakfast on the terrace, Natalie felt happier than she'd done for years. She could hardly believe how her life had changed in a matter of weeks, and gazed wonderingly at the man who'd wrought the change. Stuart looked equally happy, a permanent smile on his face as he sat opposite, his fingers stroking hers when he wasn't eating. They probably looked like a couple of besotted idiots, she thought, sipping her coffee. But who cared? She was in love and it felt good. More than good.

'Thought we all could go out for lunch after we've seen the Le Prevosts. I don't want Mum to feel neglected.'

'Good idea. She may be a bit emotional, too. They do good grub at The Imperial which is within walking distance.' She bit into her toast and chewed for a moment, wondering if they would learn something it was best not to know. 'Is Alan coming over soon?'

'Yep, on Monday. Rose and co are leaving tomorrow, and from what Mum said, he's relieved. He found the tension between Rose and Blake hard to handle without Mum there to keep the peace.' Stuart sighed. 'It reminded me of my relationship with Pam before she left.' He gripped her fingers, saying, 'I hope we can do better.'

She smiled.

'I'm sure we can.'

The walk to the Le Prevosts' cottage took ten minutes. Tabby, walking alongside Stuart, had winked at Natalie when they set off, making her blush. Thank goodness Tabby would be staying in a hotel with Alan when he arrived. It would be so embarrassing having her next door...

The door was opened by a short, tubby lady in her eighties, who smiled in delight when she saw Tabby.

'I'd know you anywhere, Tabby. Those eyes and that hair!' Her sharp eyes turned to Stuart. 'And you must be

Stuart, the image of your...mother. Come in, all of you. Charles is in the garden.'

They trouped through the small granite cottage and into a surprisingly large garden at the back. An enormous parasol shaded a table and chairs set on the lawn, on one of which sat a thin, bald-headed man of similar age to his wife. He nodded as they approached.

'Please excuse me not getting up, but it's me legs. Takes me an age to move, it does.' They all shook hands and again, Tabby was under scrutiny. 'I recognise you, Tabby. Not that we've seen you for many a year, have we, Elsie?'

'No, we haven't, but that's no matter. I've made a pot of tea, if you'd like to be mother, Tabby, please.' A huge pot sat on the table with cups and saucers. Elsie seemed to notice Natalie for the first time. 'I'm sorry, where's my manners? You must be the young lady as bought the cottage that was Beauregard Farmhouse. Natalie, isn't it?'

'Yes, you know my parents. And we do appreciate you agreeing to talk to us. Especially Tabby.'

'Well, it's a pleasure, I'm sure. I did hear about what's been happening up at Beauregard, Tabby, and I'm sorry to hear about Olive. She didn't deserve to die like that, she didn't.' She shook her head, a sadness falling across her face.

'No, she didn't, Mrs Le Prevost–'

'Please, call me Elsie. That's what you knew me by when you was little.' Elsie waved her hand.

'Right, Elsie. Had you been in touch with Mum before she...disappeared?'

The old lady bit her lip.

'No, I'm sorry to say we'd had a falling out a few years before, hadn't we. Charles?' Her husband nodded. 'It was over you, Tabby. I'd been telling her she ought to get in touch with you and let you know she was struggling. But her pride wouldn't let her.' She shook her head. 'Silly woman! Olive always was so stubborn. She'd told me you was married, that you'd contacted her, and you'd had a baby. But I don't think she heard again and she said it wasn't her place to get in touch.'

Tabby looked upset.

'I...I should have phoned, she was right. But, but I didn't. And I bitterly regret it now. How long had you known each other?'

'Oh, since we was at school together. I was at her wedding to Bill, which, to be honest, was a poor affair. He was a skinflint and no mistake. Among other things.' She pursed her lips.

Natalie was bursting to ask questions, but bit her tongue.

'Is it true Bill was violent to Mum?'

Elsie and Charles shared a look. He nodded.

'Yes, he was. And he had a bit on the side, but Olive didn't mind about that. Meant he left her alone. They didn't get on, but I expect you knew that.'

'Mum never said anything about him at all, but I guessed. And I...know about the German officer.'

Elsie's eyebrows shot up.

'How did you find out? Olive swore me to secrecy, so I thought I'd be the one to tell you now.'

'It's complicated. But I look like him, don't I?'

'You do, for sure. Bill would have known if he'd seen you. But he never did, of course. Although he knew about Olive and Wolfgang, that's why he hit him and got arrested. He deserved it, after what he did to Olive.'

Elsie took a sip of tea.

'Before Wolfgang turned up at the farm, Bill beat your mother badly, so badly she needed my help after. He'd...also forced himself on her, he was that angry about Wolfgang. A bit rich considering he'd been carrying on for years himself!' She shook her head, her eyes unfocused, as if looking back to the past.

'Oh!' Tabby's hand came up to her mouth. Stuart patted her shoulder, his face set.

Tabby asked more questions and Elsie told her what she knew about Wolfgang and Olive, saying she knew he had promised to return after the war. Instead, she'd received a letter telling her of his marriage to a previously unmentioned fiancée.

'Olive was beside herself, she'd loved him so deeply. And you. But when he betrayed her, as she saw it, she lost heart and found it hard to love you. I did try to tell her, it wasn't your fault, but she didn't listen. I'm so sorry, Tabby. You were a lovely little girl, too.' Elsie pulled out a hankie to blow her nose.

Tabby's eyes glinted with tears and Stuart put his arm around her. Natalie watched, a lump in her throat as the sorry story unfolded.

'Did...did anyone see someone near Beauregard on the day of the fire? We know now my grandmother was killed before the fire was started. And it's likely to have been a man,' Stuart said, looking from Charles to Elsie.

'We heard tell a stranger had been asking questions about Olive, but we didn't see him, did we, Elsie?'

'No, and we didn't think anything of it at the time. If we'd known poor Olive was killed...' She patted her eyes.

'I don't suppose you have a photo of Olive and Bill's wedding, do you? I don't even know what he looked like,' Tabby said.

Elsie's brow was furrowed.

'I might do. My father took some photos, they had no professional photographer. Let me think...' She sat lost in concentration for a minute and Natalie and Tabby exchanged glances.

'The only place it could be is shoved in the back of my old album of family photos. It's in a box at the bottom of my wardrobe, if you'd like to fetch it, Tabby. It's a wooden box, oak, that Charles made for me. You can't miss it. Upstairs, first door on the right.'

Tabby left and Natalie offered to pour more tea. After topping up the cups, she sat down, her heart beating with anticipation.

Tabby returned moments later, bearing the wooden box, and placed it on the table. Elsie opened it and pulled out a faded leather photo album. Natalie moved the tea things to the side and Elsie spread it out, turning towards the back. A few loose photographs fell out. Tabby picked them up, handing them to Elsie, who flicked through them.

'Here it is! Thought I might still have it. I nearly threw it away after Bill was arrested, but Olive looked so pretty then, I couldn't. Here,' she passed it to Tabby, who studied it for a long moment before handing it to Natalie.

She saw a young woman in a traditional white wedding dress holding a small bouquet of wild flowers, staring at the camera, a nervous smile hovering around her mouth. Her hair was long and dark and she did indeed look pretty, Natalie thought. Her arm was hooked through that of her groom, a tall dark haired man with the look and build of a boxer. A thug. And the man she'd seen in her dreams.

Bill.

chapter forty-two

2010

They stayed a little longer, Tabby wanting to hear more about the Occupation as well as anything they could tell her about Wolfgang. When Elsie mentioned he had been billeted with other officers at The Imperial, Tabby gasped.

'How strange! We're having lunch there.'

'I think someone saw them together there and told Bill. And they first met at Pleinmont when Olive was collecting firewood, she told me.'

Before they left, Tabby asked them if they'd join them for lunch, but they declined, saying they'd have some soup before their afternoon nap. Both Elsie and Charles did look tired and Tabby didn't press them. Promising to stay in touch, they left.

Natalie again let Stuart take his mother's arm as they walked the short distance to the pub. She was glad of the time to think. Her head buzzed with what the couple had told them, the jigsaw nearly complete. She was upset on Olive's behalf about Wolfgang's perfidy, having convinced herself he had been an honourable man killed in action. Although Elsie had said his letter mentioned family reasons for his marriage, in her mind he had behaved badly.

The pub was busy, with customers spilling onto the lawn outside overlooking the bay. Inside Natalie pushed her way through the crowd to ask if they could have a table in the restaurant, appropriately called The Water's Edge. The waitress said they were lucky, a table in the window had just been vacated and would be ready in a minute. Stuart ordered drinks as they perused the menu.

'I recommend the seafood as it's caught in the bay. Can't get fresher than that!'

The waitress called them to their table, Rocquaine Bay laid out before them.

'Wow! You can see across to Fort Grey. I don't know why I haven't been before. Did you come here, Mum?' Stuart pulled out chairs for Tabby and Natalie and all eyes turned towards the vista of golden sands leading up to the striking white top of Fort Grey, now a maritime museum, and once used by the Germans.

'Yes, with friends after swimming on the beach down there.' She pointed to the small beach with a jetty below. 'Of course, it's changed now and we only ever had crisps with our drinks. Couldn't afford to eat out in those days.' Her face clouded. 'And it's strange to find out my mother and…and Wolfgang met here, in a room upstairs.' She lifted her eyes to the ceiling. 'A bit surreal, isn't it?' Tabby looked at them, an air of sadness about her.

Stuart cleared his throat.

'It is. Would you rather we went somewhere else? If it upsets you–'

'No, I'm fine. I'm glad we came here, all part of laying the ghosts, don't you think?' She smiled at Natalie. 'Thank you for suggesting it, and for all you've done to help me clear up the family mystery. I think this calls for a celebration, don't you? Let's have champagne! And I, for one, will have the Moules and Frites. Perfect!'

By Monday Natalie felt as if she'd put on pounds. Tabby had insisted on taking her and Stuart out for dinner on Saturday night and her parents invited them all for lunch on Sunday. Natalie had phoned her mother on Saturday afternoon to tell her about the meeting with the Le Prevosts. She knew her mother was dying to meet Stuart and only hoped she wouldn't come on too pushy, like Tabby, who continued to make it plain she was delighted they were a couple. There was one fly in the ointment.

'Does Tabby know you can't father children?' she asked Stuart when they were alone, finally, on Saturday.

'Not exactly. She knew the mumps could result in infertility, but we never discussed it when I was older. She's not the sort of mother you can talk to like that.'

'Well, perhaps now would be a good time to tell her. If she sees we're serious, then she'll start dropping hints about babies, it's what mothers do. And I don't want that. Did she not say anything when you were with Pam?'

'A bit, but I didn't know I was infertile for years. Then Pam insisted we got checked out and found it was me with the problem. A few months later she left.' He stroked her face as they sat on the sofa in her sitting room listening to music. 'You're right, I should tell her and I will. What about your mother?'

'I'll tell her. At least Phil's made her a grandmother; it reduces the pressure on me.'

If Molly had been disappointed, she'd hidden it well, offering a warm welcome to Stuart and Tabby on Sunday. Natalie relaxed, letting the conversations flow around her. Stuart and her father were soon deep into discussions about the Grammar, where her father had taught for years, and Tabby and her mother talked about Natalie's cottage and the now resolved mystery. As they left later that afternoon, Molly whispered in her ear, 'Stuart's lovely, darling. I hope you'll be happy together.'

Knowing Matt was due early on Monday, Stuart had left her to get ready and returned home for breakfast. Natalie was in the kitchen when she heard his pickup and grinned. So much had happened since Matt's last visit. She found him staring at the hole in the ground.

'Morning. I see the police have saved me some digging. Is everything all right now? Must have been awful for you.' He scratched his head.

'Wasn't great, but it's all sorted now. So, remind me what we'd agreed for the pond?'

She left for work knowing that in a couple of days her pond and waterfall would be installed and working, complete with aquatic plants. She only needed to buy the fish. Simple.

As Natalie pulled into her drive, Stuart nipped out of The Old Barn. She smiled at him.

'Missed me that much, did you?' she said as he wrapped his arms around her.

'You bet. It's going to be hard with you going off to work and me having nothing to do all day except chilling out on the beach or going to the pub–' She stopped him with a kiss.

'Don't rub it in! Did Alan arrive safely?'

He walked with her into the cottage, saying Alan and Tabby were now ensconced in a suite at La Grande Mare at Vazon. 'Mum's been given the go-ahead to bury Olive and she's arranged the funeral for Saturday at St Peters Church. She thought you might want to attend.'

'Of course. I feel as if I know Olive intimately. What about the inquest?' she said, reaching for the kettle.

'Next Monday, but you won't need to be there. We'll go with Mum. It's just a formality and the DI said he expects the verdict to be "unlawful killing by person or persons unknown". Once that's over Mum and Alan will return to France and, hopefully, life can return to normal.' He tried to kiss her, but laughing, she pulled away to make the tea.

'Time for that later! Let's take the tea outside and see how Matt got on today.'

No longer out of bounds, they used the back door and walked the few feet to what had been a big hole and a pile of earth. Matt must have worked hard; the top and bottom pond liners were in place, separated by rocks to form the waterfall. As yet the ponds were empty. A small weeping willow and a castor oil bush formed a backdrop, with space for further planting and a seat.

'Looking good. So your garden will soon be completed. Are you pleased with it?'

She smiled. 'Very. And it seems right, somehow, doesn't it? The renovation of the cottage, giving it a fresh start after all the drama of the past. Laying your grandmother to rest, finally. Us. New beginnings.'

'We do have one problem, though.'

'What's that?'

'Assuming we make a go of it, where shall we live?' He waved his hand in the direction of The Old Barn. 'We hardly need two houses.'

Natalie chewed her lip.

'Good point. I do love my cottage…'

'I know. And it's got a bigger and better garden, complete with pond.' He hesitated. 'I do have a suggestion. But it's only a suggestion, you can say no.'

She tilted her head and grinned.

'Uh huh. Tell me.'

'Seems Mum's falling in love with Guernsey and I thought perhaps she and Alan could use my place as a holiday home. Better than selling it to a stranger, yes?'

'I think that's a perfect idea. As long as they're keen. Have you said anything to them?'

'Of course not. Far too soon. In the meantime we can keep both our homes and spend time together or apart, as we like.' He put his arms around her, and kissed her. A long, lingering kiss.

Coming up for air, she murmured, 'I think together sounds better, don't you?'

COMING NEXT

The Betrayal

The Guernsey Novels Book 6

Theft and betrayal lead to death – and love.

1942. Betrayed by his friend Ernest, Leo, of Jewish descent, is sent to a concentration camp by the Germans occupying Guernsey. Ernest steals Leo's valuable paintings, including a Renoir. Leo's family escape to England, but Leo never returns.

2011. During a refurbishment, Nigel finds a hidden stash of paintings in the antique shop bought from Ernest's widow. He and his sister Fiona believe one may be a missing Renoir. Shortly afterwards, Nigel is found dead, an apparent suicide. Refusing to accept the verdict, Fiona employs a detective to find out the truth.

Leo's grandson, Michael Collins, is tracked down. He arrives in Guernsey to stake his claim to the painting, but his attraction to Fiona makes him want to help.

Who knew about the stolen Renoir? And are they prepared to kill – again?

Anne Allen

Printed in Germany
by Amazon Distribution
GmbH, Leipzig